MURDER MERINGUE PIE

MURDER MERINGUE PIE

AUNTIE CLEM'S BAKERY
BOOK TWENTY-ONE

P.D. WORKMAN

 PD WORKMAN

ISBN: 9781774685020 (KDP Paperback)
ISBN: 9781774685051 (KDP Hardcover)
ISBN: 9781774685068 (Large Print)
ISBN: 9781774685075 (Lulu Paperback)
ISBN: 9781774685044 (ePub)
ISBN: 9781774686225 (Accessible Audio)

ALSO BY P.D. WORKMAN

Auntie Clem's Bakery — Culinary & Pet Cozy Mysteries

Gluten-Free Murder

Dairy-Free Death

Allergen-Free Assignation

Witch-Free Halloween (Halloween Short)

Dog-Free Dinner (Christmas Short)

Stirring Up Murder

Brewing Death

Coup de Glace

Sour Cherry Turnover

Apple-achian Treasure

Vegan Baked Alaska

Muffins Masks Murder

Tai Chi and Chai Tea

Santa Shortbread

Cold as Ice Cream

Changing Fortune Cookies

Hot on the Trail Mix

Fateful Plateful

Cut Out Cookie

On the Slab Pie

Wedding Cake Crush

A Waffle Death

Murder Meringue Pie (Coming Soon)

A Fowl Play on Christmas Day (Christmas crossover story)

Recipes from Auntie Clem's Bakery

Reg Rawlins, Psychic Detective — Paranormal Mystery & Adventure

What the Cat Knew

A Psychic with Catitude

A Catastrophic Theft

Night of Nine Tails

Telepathy of Gardens

Delusions of the Past

Fairy Blade Unmade

Web of Nightmares

A Whisker's Breadth

Skunk Man Swamp

Magic Ain't A Game

Without Foresight

Careful of Thy Wishes

Time to Your Elf

Undiscovered Tomb

Missing Powers

Thrice Spared

Cloaked Campaign

Sleepwalker's Sanctuary (Coming Soon)

Cat Tales in the Swamp (Short Story)

Tainted Truffle Treachery (Coming Soon)

A Fowl Play on Christmas Day (Christmas crossover story)

Lunar Lies (Coming Soon)

AND MORE AT PDWORKMAN.COM

*For the protectors
and those on the outside*

CHAPTER 1

It was Sunday morning, so Erin was having a relaxed breakfast with Terry rather than having to be at the bakery in the wee hours of the morning to bake bread and get everything ready for the day.

When she had first moved to Bald Eagle Falls, she had been surprised and taken aback by the insistence of the women in the community that the bakery could not be open on Sunday, because that would be breaking the Sabbath. It didn't matter that Erin was an atheist—that was a whole other problem—she was still expected to comply with the unofficial town by-law on the matter.

But that wasn't the most confusing part. They had been excited when she inherited the storefront from her Aunt Clementine, who had run it as a tea shop until her health began to fail. They hoped Erin would reinstate the ladies' tea after church services. She couldn't open the bakery to sell her gluten-free goods that day, but she was expected to open for a couple of hours and supply tea and treats for the church ladies.

She'd been not only confused, but a little resentful of the idea to begin with. But now, a couple of years in, she enjoyed the tradition. It meant that she did not have to get up early on Sunday, even on the days she took the Sunday shift, and she enjoyed meeting with the ladies of the community in something other than a baker/customer relationship.

Today, Bella was taking the shift for the ladies' tea, so Erin and Vic did not have to be there. And it was one of those rare days when Erin and Terry were both home all day—or could go out and spend the whole day together.

"Do you want to go into the city?" Terry asked. "We could go to a movie, dinner, run some errands...?"

Erin was trying to run her errands during the week so that she could have Sunday to relax instead of chasing after bakery supplies and getting caught up on grocery shopping and anything else she needed to do, ending up more exhausted by the end of her "day of rest" than if she had gone to work.

But a movie and dinner with her "Officer Handsome" sounded nice.

"Maybe," she agreed. "But no shopping."

"That's fine with me," Terry agreed with a smile that brought out the dimple on his stubbly cheek. He washed his toast down with a sip of coffee. "I'm quite happy to avoid malls and line-ups."

Erin and Terry heard a bang from the backyard and, looking out the kitchen window, saw Willie storming down the steps from Vic's loft apartment over the garage. Without another word, he hopped into his truck, slammed the door shut, and drove away with his tires spinning in the gravel. Erin watched with concern as he left.

"Uh-oh. That doesn't look good," Terry observed.

Erin looked away from the window, embarrassed. She didn't want to pry into Vic's private life. She didn't want to be that nosy neighbor who was always craning her neck to see what was happening.

"None of our business."

Terry gave a nod of agreement. As a law enforcement officer in Bald Eagle Falls, he knew which relationships were most likely to be volatile. He'd never been called to Vic's or Willie's residences to deal with a domestic dispute. They might shout, argue, or slam doors, but it had never escalated to violence as far as Erin knew. She'd never seen any indication of physical abuse in the relationship. They were just two very passionate people who didn't hold anything back.

The door to Vic's apartment opened again, and this time it was Vic's tall, willowy figure. She let Nilla out and locked the door behind her, then came down the stairs at a more sedate pace than Willie had. She let Nilla into the dog run to do his business, and then joined Erin and Terry in the kitchen.

"Mornin' ya'll."

"Good morning." Erin scratched Nilla's ears and chin when the fluffy white dog ran over to her. K9, Terry's partner, heard the little dog running around the kitchen and came to investigate. The shepherd and the small dog sniffed each other and ran to the back door to be let out. Vic let them out to play. She sighed and sat down at the table. She ran a hand through her long blond hair, hanging loose instead of in a bun like she wore it when baking at Auntie Clem's. It was the opposite of Erin's short, dark hair that never stayed in place like it was supposed to. Erin poured hot water from the teapot into Vic's cup and Vic chose a teabag from the selection on the table.

"That man." She shook her head. "I love him dearly, but he does have a temper."

"Mmm." Erin didn't ask for the details of their argument.

"What's going on?" Terry apparently didn't have the same compunctions. And Erin supposed that if Vic didn't want to talk about it, she wouldn't have brought it up or would just tell Terry it was none of his business.

"I don't rightly know. He's been on edge all weekend. But it isn't anything to do with us. It's just… probably work, I guess. The mines would be my best guess. But he hasn't said. He doesn't want to talk about it, but then he gets a call or text and just goes off like that." She motioned toward the backyard.

So it wasn't an argument. It was something different, an outside irritant. "Well, I hope he doesn't take it out on you. I always feel like slamming doors are aimed at me, even if they aren't. It's hard not to take your partner's anger personally."

Vic nodded. "It gets my back up," she admitted. "I get it; I know he's mad at something else, but I'm the only one there to hear him complaining or slamming doors. So I can't help feeling like he's aiming the gun in the wrong direction."

"You don't know what's going on with work that's bothering him?"

"He doesn't share that stuff. Never has. The closest I get to his mining operations is when we go spelunking together."

Erin's transgender employee was far more adventurous than Erin was. Caves and tunnels underground were *not* Erin's thing. She wouldn't have expected Vic to still be interested in spelunking after being caught in a tunnel collapse, but Vic and Willie had been right back at it as soon as they had their casts off. It wasn't like it had been a natural collapse. But the fact that there were people out there who would intentionally set explosives to trap or kill someone else did not reassure Erin. That was just one more good reason to stay away from caves. It had been a long time before she could even look into a cave, let alone walk a few steps into one. And a tunnel or shaft where she would have to crawl… no way. No, thank you.

"Well, whatever bee Willie has got in his bonnet, I hope he deals with it soon," she told Vic.

"Me too, sister." Vic sipped her tea. "Me too."

$\mathcal{M}$onday afternoon, Vic and Charley, Erin's half-sister, helped Erin carefully pack several pies for a catering order.

"Lemon meringue does not travel well," Vic worried. "All you need to do is go over one bump, and the tops will all be sticking to the boxes."

"I'll go slowly," Charley promised. "No potholes."

Erin had seen Charley drive before. She wasn't sure the woman knew the meaning of "slowly" or "carefully." She could just see Charley unloading the boxes at their destination and finding that all of the meringues were pasted to the tops of the boxes.

"I really don't want these to be wrecked when you get there," she fussed. "I should have told them no. Made them go with apple pie or something with a top crust that would travel better."

"I'll get them there in one piece," Charley assured her. "You don't have to worry about it. Clive William Fontainebleau III shall have his pies."

"If he's happy with the results, he could be a profitable client. I don't know how many of these fancy parties he holds, but if we can supply him with desserts regularly, it could be lucrative."

"Don't pin your hopes on it," Charley warned. "I know guys

like this. They're not loyal to one supplier. He'll go wherever he can get the best deal. And he'll keep asking for a lower price until you're not making anything."

Erin frowned. She hoped it wasn't true. But she hadn't heard many good things about Mr. Fontainebleau, so she couldn't argue with Charley's assessment.

"So you don't think it will be worth it?"

"I'll tell you what you do," Charley said. "You raise your prices next time. Tell him that they are *artisanal* pies. That he won't get quality product like that from anyone else. Especially not gluten-free. If he wants high-quality, gluten-free pies, you are the only game in town. Anywhere in the state, in fact."

Erin's cheeks warmed. "I couldn't do that."

"That's what you've got to do. Make him respect you. Make him want pies from Auntie Clem's Bakery and nowhere else, because no one else even compares. Why do you think guys like him buy Rolexes and Cartier's? It isn't because they tell the time better than any department store wristwatch. He wants people to see that he is willing to pay for the very best."

"I don't know." Erin slowly boxed another pie. "I'll think about it."

"Whatever you do, *don't* lower your prices. No matter where he says he is going to go instead."

Erin pressed her lips together, thinking about it. Charley was probably right. Charley was the one who had experience in dealing with big shots like Fontainebleau. She should take Charley's advice.

"You do your part and get them there in one piece. Then… maybe I'll get you to help with any negotiations too. I'm not sure I can stand up to a guy like that. Or his office manager, since I never talked to Mr. Fontainebleau directly."

"I'll take care of it," Charley agreed. "You can count on me."

Peter Foster showed up at Auntie Clem's Bakery after school had let out, without his mother and siblings. Erin had rarely seen him by himself, though she knew that he had sometimes been allowed to go to the store to pick up something his mother needed when she had been pregnant and on bed rest. The young boy looked at the cookies in the display case, standing tall and looking important.

"Hi, Peter. How's it going?"

He smiled, showing off the gaps in his teeth. "Good."

"Are you here for a Kid's Club cookie, or are you buying something? I have something in the back for you if you need it…"

The Foster family didn't normally take advantage of Erin's offer of free day-old bread. But they'd been struggling lately, and Erin hoped they would take what they needed.

"I'm just looking," Peter told her archly. "I'm going to visit my dad at the bookstore."

"Oh, I see. How is he enjoying working there?"

"He says that Mrs. Naomi is a good boss. And mom is glad that he *finally* has something stable since they cut back his hours at the other job."

"I'm sure it's a big relief for her. Especially since she wanted to be able to stay home with the little ones."

Peter nodded his agreement. "It's a good thing that you told Mrs. Naomi that Dad was looking for something. You're a good friend."

"Thank you. I'm glad I could help. Are you sure you don't want your Kid's Club cookie?"

"No. I'll get mine one day when I bring the girls."

"Oh, okay. That sounds good, then. Can I walk with you over to The Book Nook?"

"I don't need you to. I know where it is."

"I know, but I need to talk to Naomi about the book club."

Peter shrugged. "Okay. You can come over with me."

Erin trailed Peter down the street to The Book Nook and followed him in. The bells over the door jingled to announce their arrival. Both Naomi and Mr. Foster looked up from shelving books to greet them.

"Well, there's my son," Mr. Foster said, smiling. "School's out already?"

"Yes. You know I wouldn't skip!"

"That's what they all say. And Miss Erin. How are you?"

"Good. Peter just stopped to say hello to me at Auntie Clem's, and I needed to talk to Naomi about the book club, so we came over together."

Mr. Foster nodded, looking calm and relaxed about this. Erin was glad she hadn't gotten Peter into trouble, but she wanted to ensure that his parents knew where he was and were okay with it. They were strict about some things and lenient about others, and Erin hadn't quite figured out where the line was. She didn't want to be accused of encouraging Peter to do anything he wasn't supposed to.

Erin felt her phone vibrating, so the next time she went into the kitchen to take a tray of cookies out of the oven, she pulled her phone out and looked at it. Charley had texted her. Opening the text, Erin saw the pies that she had sent over for the party all laid out on a black granite counter, with Charley's comment that they had gotten there safe and sound, with no breakage or meringue stuck to the top of the boxes they had transported them in. The golden peaks on the white meringue looked picture-perfect.

Mr. Fontainebleau can eat pie to his heart's content

Erin was relieved. She texted Charley a heartfelt thank you and returned to the front of the shop to let Vic know they had arrived safely.

"See?" Vic said. "All that worry for nothing. Everything went smoothly. He's sure to call you back for another job."

CHAPTER 3

*E*rin had already turned the sign on the front door over to
Closed and locked the door, so she was annoyed to hear
someone rapping on the glass a few minutes later. Once the bakery
was closed, it was closed. She couldn't keep serving people who
showed up after closing or she would be there all night. There had
to be a hard cut-off.

But the man standing on the other side of the door did not
appear to be a customer. Not someone she had served before. Erin
stood there looking at him for a moment, trying to figure out what
to do. He could see her through the glass and indicated a package
in his hands. A delivery? Bakery deliveries normally came to the
back door, and she wasn't expecting anything. Especially not a
small, light package like the delivery man had.

"Vic?"

Vic came out of the kitchen, wiping her hands on a towel.
"What's up, boss?"

"You weren't expecting a delivery, were you?"

Vic shook her head. "No. I haven't ordered anything. Maybe it's
a wrong address."

"Can you just stay here for a minute to make sure…?"

It hadn't been that long ago that she'd opened the door to the wrong person, and she didn't want to take any chances. Someone with nefarious purposes would not be as likely to try anything with Vic standing there. And Vic was armed if he did. Though Erin wouldn't want any gunplay under any circumstances.

With Vic stationed there watching, Erin unlocked the door and opened it just a crack.

"Yes? I'm not expecting anything."

"Are you Erin Price?"

"Yes," Erin admitted, her anxiety growing. Should she call Terry or the emergency dispatcher?

"This is for you."

Erin reluctantly opened the door far enough to take the small package from him. It was lightweight. He didn't try to grab her wrist or push his way into the bakery. He just nodded, gave her a pleasant smile and walked away.

Erin locked the door again, blowing out a breath of relief. Nothing to worry about unless it was a bomb, and she assumed by how light it was that it wasn't a bomb.

"What is it?" Vic asked curiously, leaning against the doorframe.

Erin unwrapped the brown paper and found a small bouquet of flowers.

"Oh, how sweet," Vic gushed. "Is it an anniversary?"

Erin shook her head. "No… nothing that I can think of."

They had already passed the anniversary of Erin's arrival in Bald Eagle Falls. Could it be the anniversary of when she and Terry had started dating? Another significant event along the path?

"Is there a card?"

Erin extended two fingers to grasp it and pull it from the bouquet. It wasn't in Terry's hand, but it had probably been written by the florist on Terry's instructions.

For the sweetest lady in town

Being a baker, Erin supposed it was apt. But not something Terry had ever said to her. Wouldn't he put something on the card that was meaningful to them both? Something they had shared?

He had also never thought to send her flowers before, even on Valentine's Day.

She read it to Vic, who seemed to think it was swoon-worthy, but Erin was increasingly uncomfortable with the delivery. She looked through the flowers to ensure there was no other message or something she hadn't seen. It seemed to be just what it was at first glance—a small bouquet of flowers. No threat. No bomb. No hidden meaning.

Erin put it down on one of the small tables at the front of the bakery and pulled out her phone to call Terry. Vic watched, looking perplexed that Erin wasn't over the moon about getting flowers from her guy.

The phone rang a few times before Terry answered.

"Piper. Oh, hi Erin."

"I just got a special delivery."

There was a second of silence. "Okay… what was it?"

Erin's heart sank. She had been hoping he would confirm that he had sent her the flowers. "You didn't send me something?"

"No. What are you talking about? What did you get?"

"I got… flowers."

"Flowers." Terry sounded taken aback. "No, I didn't send you any flowers."

Erin didn't say anything, considering.

"Do they have my name on them?" Terry asked.

"No. No name."

"Maybe they were for Vic. Or a wrong address."

"No. He said they were for Erin Price."

"Well… I guess you have a secret admirer." Terry gave a laugh that sounded forced. "Is this the first time you've gotten something like that?"

Did he think she regularly got gifts from anonymous senders that she didn't bother to tell him about? Then why start now?

"No. This is the first time."

"Huh. Well, I'm sure it's nothing to worry about, but do you want me to pick you up? Make sure you get home safely?"

"I've got my car here. You don't need to come."

"I can if you want. I can drop you off in the morning and you can pick up your car tomorrow."

What would make her any safer tomorrow than today? If the secret admirer had malicious thoughts toward her, he would just wait for his opportunity. She couldn't have a bodyguard with her all the time. Sooner or later, she would be by herself, an open target.

"No. We'll just take my car home tonight. It will be fine."

"If you're worried…"

"I'm not worried. It's just a sweet gesture. Someone who didn't stop to think about whether I already had someone else in my life. Or an appreciative customer."

She thought about Fontainebleau, but was sure that he would never extend a gesture like that. He dealt with her on a business basis and wouldn't be sending her flowers no matter how impressed he was with the lemon meringue pies. But maybe someone else? Someone she had done something nice for recently?

Maybe even Peter Foster or his father. Something to say thank you for helping find Mr. Foster a job.

That was probably it. It was the kind of thing she could see Peter doing. He was very thoughtful and mature for his years. He could have suggested to his mother that they should get something for Erin, and they decided to make it anonymous to keep her guessing and give her a little thrill. Make her look at all her customers differently, wondering which of them had done such a nice thing. Maybe that was why he had stopped by the bakery earlier. Not to visit with her on the way to seeing his father, but to see if the flowers had been delivered yet.

"Okay," Terry said, a note of relief in his voice. "As long as you're not upset by it."

"No. It's very sweet of whoever sent them. I'll take them home and put them on the table."

"Maybe you should keep them at the bakery. You wouldn't want Orange Blossom to get into them. He still jumps up on the table sometimes and, if you put something that smells so interesting up there, he'll be knocking them over before the night is out."

"You're probably right. Do we have a little vase here?" Erin asked Vic. "Just a glass would work."

Vic disappeared into the kitchen to get her one. She could put the flowers out in the customer area to brighten everyone's day tomorrow.

Of course, she would have to explain where they came from, but she didn't think there was anything wrong with getting flowers from a secret admirer. It wasn't like she was cheating on Terry or had any thought of doing so. It was just an appreciative customer or friend. Maybe even a thank you from Melissa for doing the catering for her wedding, though she had already received a formal thank you for that.

She arranged the flowers in the glass Vic brought out to her and put them on one of the tables.

"There. That will brighten things up tomorrow."

Vic nodded. They both returned to the kitchen to continue cleaning up and prep for the next day.

CHAPTER 4

Terry got home not long after Erin. She watched him enter through the front door and re-arm the burglar alarm immediately. Then he turned to her and gave her a firm hug.

"So what's this about someone else sending my girl flowers?"

Erin raised one brow. "Looks like you're going to have to up your game."

He chuckled. "I guess so. Can't have someone else showing me up."

"That's right."

Orange Blossom was immediately underfoot, meowing urgently. He knew that Terry getting home meant that it was time for supper, and he wanted his right away.

"You know, I'm not going to forget to feed you," Erin told him sternly. "Have I ever forgotten to feed you even once?"

He rubbed against her leg, yowling still louder. Erin laughed and led the way into the kitchen, with the animals following her like the Pied Piper. Orange Blossom, and then K9, and then Marshmallow, the rabbit. Blossom was the only one who made any noise. He was the only one who ever made any noise. But he made up for the others.

Erin got them each their dinners, and soon they had peace.

Erin transferred the casserole she had left to cook in the slow cooker to the table.

"Mmm, smells great," Terry approved, sitting down at the table.

They dished up and began to eat, asking each other about their days.

"Any more drama over there?" Terry asked, nodding toward Vic's loft across the backyard.

"No. Haven't seen or heard anything from them. Willie's truck is here, so I guess he is too, but I haven't seen him."

Terry nodded. "Glad there are no ongoing problems."

"Yeah, me too. I know I might be oversensitive, but I hate it when other people are fighting."

"You are sensitive, but I don't think *over*sensitive. You just care about other people."

Terry's phone buzzed. He pulled it out of his pocket and laid it on the table. "No phones at the table" might be a good rule for most couples but, because Terry was one of the few law enforcement officers in Bald Eagle Falls, he couldn't just ignore any calls or messages that he got. She saw his eyes skim over the message on his screen, and his brows bunched together in a frown. He took a couple more bites of the dinner, then pushed his plate away, sighing.

"You have to go?"

He nodded. "There's been a suspicious death."

"Oh, dear. Who is it?"

His eyes flicked over to her for an instant, then away. He knew there was no point in keeping it from her. In a few minutes, the gossip would be spreading around Bald Eagle Falls, and Erin would find out.

"A mining magnate with a big property and house out in the bush."

Erin blinked several times as she processed this. "Mr. Fontainebleau?"

Terry's head jerked back toward her. "What?" he demanded sharply.

"Was it Clive Fontainebleau? The Third?"

"How do you know him?"

"I sent some pies out there for his party."

"Really." Terry scowled, shaking his head. "How did you get involved with that?"

"His assistant called me. They were looking for someone who could cater the desserts, and I'm the closest one unless they want to go into the city, so…"

She took in Terry's disapproval. "What happened to him?"

Terry sighed. "They think he was poisoned."

CHAPTER 5

*E*rin's stomach plummeted. "What?"

"He died after the party. And there are suspicions it could be poisoning."

"I didn't poison him!" Erin immediately protested.

That was what everyone was going to think. Once again, Erin's baking was going to be called into question. The lemon meringue pies had been perfectly good. Some people worried about salmonella in meringue because it wasn't cooked for long enough to kill the bacteria, but Erin had never heard of an actual case of food poisoning from meringue. And salmonella would not kill that fast, she was sure.

"There was nothing wrong with those pies," she insisted.

"I'm sure there was not, Erin," Terry soothed. "I don't think that you had anything to do with it. What reason would you have to kill someone like Fontainebleau? You've never even met him— have you?"

Erin shook her head.

"You haven't, right?" Terry persisted. "If you did know him or have some beef with him, now is the time to tell me, not later when we figure it out on our own."

"No. I don't know the guy. Never met him. Never had anything to do with him until his assistant called me about the dessert."

He stared at her for a moment longer, trying to discern the truth. Then he nodded. Which Erin hoped meant that he believed her. She had kind of messed things up before by implying she didn't know a victim when she actually did. Terry wasn't going to forget that any time soon.

"All the food he ate will probably have to be tested," Terry told her. "Now, *I* know that you didn't have anything to do with this, but we'll need to make sure that we act in an unbiased way. So I'm going to ask you not to use any of the ingredients you put into those pies. Anything that is left over, just put to the side. Open up new bags. So that we can test all of the ingredients that came out of the bakery if we have to."

Erin supposed she was lucky that he wasn't shutting down Auntie Clem's Bakery altogether until they'd had a chance to do their testing. "Fine. I'll make sure that all of those ingredients get put to the side."

"Thanks. I appreciate that. I'll get back to you when I know something. Maybe they didn't even get to the dessert course."

"Okay. Thanks."

Erin walked him to the door and didn't know what else to say. Terry paused with his hand on the doorknob.

"This is going to be a big deal," he warned. "Fontainebleau was a very important person in these parts. He employed a lot of people in his mines and factories. He was not well-liked, but he was well-known."

"So it's going to blow up. It's going to be in all of the news outlets."

He nodded. "Newspaper, TV, internet. We're not going to be able to keep it quiet, and there will be a lot of scrutiny. A lot of people watching to make sure that we don't make a misstep."

"You don't think reporters will come here, do you?"

"It's possible. Since I'm going out there as law enforcement, and you catered the dessert for the event, I think it's actually quite likely. Sorry."

He kissed her goodbye, let K9 out ahead of him, and left to deal with the investigation.

~

Erin looked at the clock. How long did she have before people started to call to ask her about the murder?

With someone as influential as Fontainebleau, it wouldn't be long before word leaked out. Bald Eagle Falls had a very efficient grapevine. And there had been a lot of people at the party. Erin had provided eight pies, which, if cut into six slices each, would mean forty-eight guests. And each one of them a potential leak. Not to mention however many servers or domestic staff Fontainebleau had in his employ to make sure that the evening ran smoothly. There was no way to keep the sixty or so people who were on the Fontainebleau Homestead quiet. And with the call going out to the police in Bald Eagle Falls, each of the law enforcement officers and administrative staff knew about it too, and one of them in particular...

The phone rang.

Erin sighed and pulled it out of her pocket. Was there any chance it was just a call from Vic or a friend wanting to come over for a visit or to place a special order at Auntie Clem's?

She immediately put that thought to rest. The caller ID said Melissa Lee.

Melissa worked part-time for the police department and was the fount of all knowledge, eager to spread whatever news she picked up while filing or doing administrative duties at the police department offices in the town hall. Erin would not expect her to have been there when the call went out on Fontainebleau's suspicious death. But maybe Melissa had gotten herself onto the message distribution list when bulletins went out to all of the Bald Eagle Falls law enforcement officers.

Erin took a deep breath before answering the call. "Hi, Melissa."

"Erin! I just wanted to call and see how you are doing. It's been a while since we talked."

"Yes, it has." Erin sat back down at the table and had another bite of the casserole. "I'm actually just sitting down to eat."

"I don't know how you could eat at a time like this! I would be at my wit's end if I were you. Terry told you what happened, didn't he?"

"I know he got a call out," Erin told her, feigning ignorance. "I don't know what that has to do with me."

"Didn't he tell you who it was for? Clive Fontainebleau? You just filled a catering order for him, didn't you? And now he's dead under suspicious circumstances. I would be in a panic. What if there was something in your pies? What if… rat poison got mixed in with the flour or something like that?"

"It wasn't the pies. There was nothing wrong with them. Nobody knows what happened yet, so don't spread that around. We don't know what he ate or if it even was something he ate. They might not have even eaten the dessert; it is still early in the evening. People like him usually eat late."

Melissa *tsked*. "I don't know. I certainly wouldn't be so calm if I were in your shoes!"

Erin took another deep breath and let it out slowly. Melissa liked drama. She liked to stir things up and was probably disappointed that Erin wasn't panicking like Melissa thought she should. Erin took a few bites of her dinner. She'd already told Melissa that she was sitting down for dinner, so if Melissa heard her eating, she would assume that was why she wasn't responding to Melissa's prodding.

"Right now, we don't know anything," Erin told her. "So there is no point in getting all worked up over it. I doubt it was anything to do with my pies or anything he had at dinner tonight. Most poisons don't work that fast."

Though she remembered how quickly she had been affected when she'd been poisoned with belladonna. She had been lucky to get to the hospital in time for them to counteract the poison. If something like *that* had been administered to Fontainebleau without him or someone close to him figuring out what was wrong, it could have been very quick.

"Well, you're taking it all very well," Melissa said, disapproving.

"Maybe it just hasn't hit me yet."

"That's probably it," Melissa agreed.

CHAPTER 6

*E*rin was able to get off of the call with Melissa—she never seemed to be able to talk to the woman for less than an hour when she called—put away the leftovers, and put the dishes into the dishwasher, when there was a tap at the back door, and Vic stuck her head in.

"Yoo-hoo. You up for visitors?"

Erin shrugged. "Sure. Let's take some tea in the living room."

Vic entered, and Willie behind her. Erin looked him over. As always, his skin was stained dark by the processing he did of whatever minerals he got out of his mines. So he looked dirty, even though she knew he was not. Whatever mood had taken him the day before when he had been slamming doors and racing off in the truck seemed long gone. If anything, he seemed cheerful.

"Terry got called out?" Vic asked.

Erin suspected that she knew very well what had happened. Melissa's gossip was burning up the lines in Bald Eagle Falls.

"Yes. Something to do with Mr. Fontainebleau," she said vaguely.

"That's what I heard." Vic helped to get the tea things ready and took a tray out to the living room.

"It wasn't the pies," Erin told her firmly.

"Of course not!" Vic agreed. "That's what I told M—that's what I said. There was nothing wrong with those pies. They were a work of art. And it isn't like there is any poison in the kitchen at Auntie Clem's. Nothing got accidentally spilled into the flour."

"No," Erin agreed. They both knew that the suggestion was ridiculous. And Melissa undoubtedly knew that too. It wasn't the dark ages. Erin kept a very clean kitchen and was scrupulously careful of cross-contamination, cooking for people with allergies and other health issues as she did. They followed very strict protocols and, even if there had been poison in the kitchen to deal with vermin, it would never have been on the counter at the same time as baking ingredients.

"Terry doesn't think it was anything to do with you, does he?" Vic asked.

"He knows I didn't have anything to do with it."

Not that his supposed faith in her had ever stopped him from investigating her before.

They all sat down in the living room.

"I don't even know anything about this guy," Erin said. "I hadn't really heard of him until I got the call that he wanted the desserts at his party catered. But I gather he's quite a bigwig around here."

Willie nodded. "Yeah, he thought he was a pretty big cheese in these parts. And it's true he had a lot of money and employed a lot of people. But I wouldn't go as far as to say that he was well-liked or respected."

"You didn't like him," Erin stated the obvious.

"I won't be mourning him, that's for sure. Having someone like him around here, trying to scoop up all of the old mining claims and compete with the independent miners... we don't need that kind of help."

"He was your competition?"

Willie shrugged. "A little guy like me can't compete with the likes of Fontainebleau the Third. But yes, we were competitors."

Erin poured hot water into each of the cups and let everyone select their favorite teas.

"And he's been around here for a long time? I don't recognize the family name from any of the genealogy Clementine was doing."

"Not an old Tennessean family," Willie agreed. "Relative upstarts. Probably came from up north. New York types. His father, Fontainebleau the Second, he did live here. But I don't think the first Fontainebleau ever set foot in the state. It was probably the second who established the Homestead."

"That's what he calls the place where he lives," Erin acknowledged. "Is it really a homestead? Like a farm or ranch?"

"No. Never been a working homestead of any kind. It's just posturing. Pretending that he came from a gritty, hardworking background, I guess. Instead of being born with a silver spoon in his mouth."

She sipped her tea. "Have you ever been out there?"

Willie raised his brows. "Out where?"

"On the Homestead. Have you ever seen it?"

"I've seen pictures. It's quite the place. Huge mansion. I don't know how many people live there. Certainly much bigger than you need for one family, or even half a dozen. All the amenities. Staff to keep the place running and the grounds looking pristine. Even though he doesn't actually use them for anything."

"And he throws parties."

"And he throws parties," Willie agreed. He slurped his tea and put the cup down. "I wouldn't be surprised to hear that the governor was one of his guests. Wine and dine all the people who had anything to do with the mining industry or regulation. Make sure that he had everyone on his side and could pull all the political strings that he needed to."

Erin could hear the bitterness in his voice. There was no way for a small miner like Willie to have any influence on the governor or other people high up in the government. He was just a little fish, trying to stay away from predators like Fontainebleau, who would gobble him up, given half a chance.

"Do you know if he has any family?" Erin wondered if there were a wife out there, grieving for her suddenly deceased husband. Or a son or daughter grieving for a parent. Willie might enjoy seeing his competition cut down in his prime, but other people were affected. Family and friends and all of the people that he had employed.

"I don't know." Willie looked at Vic. "You've been around here long enough to know the big names. Did he have any kids? They would probably go to some big boarding school rather than public school out here, but you might still have heard of them."

"I think there is an ex-wife and a current wife. He was definitely on at least his second marriage. And some kids… yes, I think so. Maybe a son and a daughter. Maybe more. Like you say, they probably never went to school here."

Erin nodded. There would definitely be mourners. Maybe the ex-wife wouldn't be sorry to see him go, but his kids and the current wife would, she assumed.

"You think one of them killed him?" Vic suggested, leaning forward.

Erin hadn't even been thinking along those lines. "Uh… I don't know. I don't know anything about them. I guess… it's possible. When there's a lot of money involved like this, sometimes people are impatient to inherit. Or to prevent him from doing something they didn't want him to do with 'their' money."

Vic nodded eagerly. "Makes a lot more sense than some random baker who had it in for him."

"I don't imagine they will be lacking for people with motive to kill him," Willie said. "He didn't exactly endear himself to the public. Or his employees."

"Well, it's nothing to do with us." Erin sat back. She didn't want to speculate about someone else's untimely death. There was no reason for her to have anything to do with the investigation.

No one she knew was involved in it, and she was sure the police would quickly prove that her pies had nothing to do with it.

CHAPTER 7

$\mathcal{T}$hings were always busiest at Auntie Clem's after a murder. The townspeople came out to gossip about it and to hear the latest news. To speculate on who might have been involved. Of course they were most interested when they thought that Erin herself might have had something to do with it. She didn't want the reputation of someone who was always in the middle of crimes in and around Bald Eagle Falls. It was just because it was a small town, and she happened to be connected with a lot of people. It was just coincidences and perception.

"Is it true you made the pies for the party last night?" Cindy Prost demanded, sounding properly shocked and horrified. She was a heavyset woman and, unlike her daughter Bella, had a habitually dour expression and a sharp tongue.

Bella was on shift, so Erin knew that Cindy wouldn't dare go too far in her accusations, or Bella would jump in to set her straight.

"Yes, I did," Erin agreed calmly. "But that did not have anything to do with Mr. Fontainebleau's death. Nothing at all."

"Is that what Officer Piper said? Was that an official conclusion from the police investigation?"

Erin hadn't actually been able to talk to Terry about his investigation. He wouldn't tell her very much anyway, only what he thought was or would shortly be public knowledge. But Erin had to go to bed early to be able to get up to bake before Auntie Clem's opened in the morning, and he hadn't been back yet. He hadn't awakened her when he had returned and, when she had left that morning, he had been asleep, snoring on the couch.

"No. I'm just telling you that they had nothing to do with it."

Cindy opened her mouth to argue, then Bella came through the door from the kitchen, and she clamped her mouth shut again.

"We were shocked to hear about Mr. Fontainebleau," Bella told Erin, having overheard them talking about him. "I can't believe that he died like that."

"What did you hear?" Erin asked. "I mean… I heard that it was suspected poisoning, but…"

Of course, anything Bella had heard was probably third-hand gossip and about as far from the truth as possible. Terry was the one who had told Erin that it was suspected poisoning, so she knew that to be true.

"Yes. I heard that he was raving. Had a fit and keeled over. Of course, they're far from any hospital or medical services out there. As soon as anyone got to him, it was too late anyway; he was dead."

"He had a seizure?"

Bella shrugged. "Some kind of fit. I don't know. He wasn't right. Everyone could see he wasn't right. And then he toppled over and was just gone."

"Did this come from someone who was out there?"

Bella became suddenly reticent. "Oh. Just a rumor. You know, what's going around Bald Eagle Falls about it."

"Someone must have seen. There were a lot of people out there. The people he'd invited to the party and whoever else he'd hired to work it."

"None of the people out there were from Bald Eagle Falls," Cindy said with certainty, a snap in her tone.

Willie had said that it would be bigwigs. The governor and others in high-ranking positions, so maybe Cindy was right. Perhaps no one from town was on the guest list. But Erin was sure that he would still need some local help to run the party and keep everything going smoothly.

"I just wondered who you'd heard it from. If it was from someone who was actually there when it happened."

Bella shrugged. "Everyone is talking about it. I guess someone must have been out there to see."

The bells over the door jingled, and a couple more customers walked in. They were starting to get a bit of a crowd. "What can I get for you, Cindy?" Erin asked, hoping to move things along.

"Well, I don't think it's going to be a lemon meringue pie," Cindy said. "I'm probably going to be avoiding those for a while."

Erin rolled her eyes as a couple of the other women giggled. "I don't have any lemon meringue pies today," she pointed out, indicating the display case. "So, what *would* you like?"

Cindy picked out a loaf of bread and some chocolate caramel bars. She looked at her watch. "And then I'd better be getting on my way," she said, in a tone that suggested that Erin had been keeping her there.

Bella rang up her mother's order on the till. "Do you think maybe we should get a little more than that?" she suggested. "We might have company..." She pushed back a lock of wavy blond hair that had escaped her hat and looked at her mother.

Cindy scowled at this suggestion. "I don't suppose I have any say in the matter."

Bella just raised her brows and blinked, waiting for Cindy to make a decision.

"Yes, you'd better make it... three loaves. And... maybe a dozen cookies." She looked at Bella. "Will that be enough, do you think?"

"Maybe some rolls too? Or some pizza shells? I bet they'd like pizza."

Cindy sighed loudly at this. She indicated the pizza crusts. "Two of the large. And... I think that had better be it. We can't have them eating us out of house and home."

Bella rang up the additional items and made change for her mother. "Okay, see you later. Let me know... if anything happens."

Erin helped the next customer, again having to answer several questions about the lemon meringue pies and Mr. Fontainebleau. Erin couldn't figure out how the news of his death and the details associated with it could get around town so fast, and yet people still had to ask her over and over again if it might have been something to do with her pies or if she was worried that the police would consider her a suspect. Why didn't the news of her innocence—or at least her protestations of innocence—spread just as quickly as the news that she had made the pies for the party?

They served the rest of the customers as efficiently as possible, going over the grim news as often as necessary. As much as Erin would have preferred to discuss other things, she couldn't deny that the news of Fontainebleau's death had brought many people to the bakery, so she'd better do the best she could to satisfy their curiosity or thirst for scandal.

"So…" Erin wiped her forehead with the back of her hand as she took a deep breath, the bakery empty of customers for a few minutes. "You have company coming?"

Bella looked surprised by this question, then apparently remembered that she had been talking about it with her mother in front of Erin. "Oh. Yeah. Possibly. We've been helping out a friend. Don't know. Might have her and her kids for a little bit."

"Oh, that's great." Erin had been out to the Prost place a couple of times. They were goat farmers. "It's a nice place to let kids run around and play in."

Bella nodded. "It's good for kids to have lots of sunshine and physical activity. Much better than them having to sit at desks all day."

It was still summer break, but the kids would return to school before long. Unless they were homeschooled.

The bells jingled and Erin straightened and looked to see who it was. Another of the ladies there to ask her if she'd poisoned Mr. Fontainebleau with her lemon meringue pies, she supposed.

But it wasn't. It was a man she didn't know.

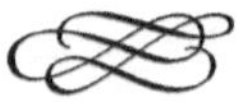

Erin smiled. "Hi there. I don't think we've met before. Welcome to Auntie Clem's Bakery."

The man's eyes traveled around the bakery, taking it all in. The bakery display case, the small tables with chairs at the front of the bakery, the cold case to the side that housed their various frozen treats. His eyes returned to Erin and Bella.

He was tall and lean. His age was difficult to pin, maybe forty or fifty. His dark hair was dusted with gray specks, and his eyes crinkled with smiling wrinkles. "Is one of you Erin Price?"

Erin nodded. "That's me."

She half expected the man to hand her a long envelope and tell her she'd been served. Her mind jumped to all kinds of scenarios that might have to do with Fontainebleau's death. They couldn't file a wrongful death suit the very next day after he'd been killed, could they? That wasn't the way it was done. The police needed to investigate and find out what had happened before any charges were laid, and it wouldn't be until after a criminal trial was finished that a wrongful death suit would be filed. That was the way it worked.

But it could be something else. Could it be something to do with Brandon's death? She hoped he hadn't left her anything. She didn't want anything from his estate. She didn't want anything to do with him. If he'd left her something, she could refuse it, couldn't she?

The handsome man was reaching toward her, but he didn't have legal papers in his hand. It was something else—a small package. Erin reached out to take it from him, frowning slightly.

"What's this?"

He shrugged. "Delivery for you."

"I wasn't expecting anything."

It looked like a wrapped box of chocolates. Had Terry decided to send her something after the flower delivery? Just to show that he could match any anonymous suitor? She smiled at the thought. Having a secret admirer might not be half bad if it spiced things up a bit at home. She and Terry were not exactly in the honeymoon phase anymore, and a subtle nudge for him to do something romantic now and then wouldn't hurt.

"Well, thank you." Erin nodded and smiled at the deliveryman.

He gave a brief nod and left the bakery again. Bella raised her brows at Erin.

"What's this? Another special delivery?"

Erin shrugged, her face warming. "Must be from Terry." She shook it, but it didn't rattle like chocolates.

"Well, open it. Do I get to see?"

Erin looked at the door. There was no one else in the bakery, but she would prefer not to be in the middle of opening a gift when a customer came in.

"I'll open it in the kitchen," she decided.

Bella stayed in the front, but stood at the doorway looking into the kitchen to watch Erin unwrap the delivery.

Deciding to unwrap it methodically instead of just ripping the paper off, Erin unstuck the tape at each end of the oblong, unfolded the paper, and then slid the box out from the wrapping paper sleeve. She was right. It was not a box of chocolates. A quick peek inside the box verified what the logo stamped in foil on the outside suggested. Not chocolates, but a lacy, filmy negligee.

"What is it?" Bella prompted.

"Not for your eyes," Erin told her. Her cheeks were hot, and she was pretty sure she was turning a brilliant red.

"Oh-ho!" Bella laughed. "Officer Piper!"

Erin looked down at the wrapping paper and box. There was no card or tag. The only way she knew it was for her was that the deliveryman had asked her name. There was no address or name on the package. What delivery service didn't put some kind of label or waybill on their deliveries? She opened the box again to see if there was a card under the negligee, but there was not.

Erin felt another wave of heat, but this time it was not embarrassment. She looked around to see if there was anyone else watching her, but there was only Bella.

"Bella, did you know that deliveryman?"

"Hmm?" Bella looked back toward the door as if he might still be standing there. "No, I didn't know him. Why?"

"There's no card or label anywhere."

"Well, he said it was for you."

"Yes. Exactly. How did he know that?"

"He must have a list."

"But this is a package without any markings. How does he know this one was mine?"

"Maybe yours was the only one he had. It isn't like the big city. They don't do a lot of deliveries here."

Erin supposed that was probably true. The deliveryman might simply remember which package was which. It was distinctive, even if it wasn't labeled.

"Officer Handsome didn't write you a steamy note to go with it?" Bella teased.

"No. There isn't anything with it. I guess I'll have to ask him about it when I get home."

"Ask him what?"

Bells jingled. Bella turned around to deal with the new customer. Erin put the package into her small office next to her purse. She wouldn't be leaving *this* gift at Auntie Clem's.

~

Erin's mind was on the package for the rest of the workday. She tried to stay focused on her baking and her customers but couldn't help her mind going back to the lacy white and blue negligee over and over again as she sleepwalked through her day at Auntie Clem's. Everyone wanted to know about Fontainebleau and the pies, but Erin's mind was focused on this new mystery.

She wanted nothing more than to go home and talk with Terry and ensure everything was right with the world. She didn't have anything to worry about. He had just decided to counter the secret admirer's gift with one of his own. One that was blatantly more personal and intimate, showing his ownership of her. Not just flowers like anyone might give her, even little Peter Foster, with some help from his parents.

Eventually, it was time to close up shop and head home. Bella had her car there and Erin had hers, so they parted ways in the parking lot.

Terry's scheduled shifts had been amended due to the Fontainebleau investigation. He had been out late the night before, and she imagined that after he had woken up, he had probably spent most of the day at the police department offices assisting with the investigation into Fontainebleau's death. It would be "all hands on deck," and they would want the public to see that they were earnestly engaged in solving the crime. It wouldn't do to fall short on this one.

Not that they had ever been any less than diligent in solving any of the crimes that she had known of while she'd been in Bald Eagle Falls. However, she had been able to unravel some of them faster than the police department. That was just luck.

And she wasn't going to get close to the Fontainebleau murder, if that was what it was. Hopefully, it wasn't even a murder. He'd just slipped in the shower and hit his head, and a slow brain bleed had eventually overwhelmed him later in the day. It could be something as simple and innocuous as that.

She could see by the lights on in the house that Terry was home ahead of her. This probably meant that he had come home for supper, but would be returning to work after the meal for more work on the Fontainebleau case or for night patrol. Either way, she was glad he was home for a few minutes.

He was watching TV when she stepped into the house. It would have been nice if he had thought to start on supper, but she supposed he was just as tired after work as she was. Maybe more so, since he'd also been up half the night.

"Hi, hon." She bent down to kiss him briefly. She tossed the small box on the coffee table. "I got your special delivery."

He looked at the box and then at her. "What?"

"Didn't you send that?"

He stared at it. "This isn't the flowers that you said you got. What's going on?"

Erin swallowed. "I got another delivery today. Not flowers this time. I thought maybe it was from you. Trying to outdo my secret admirer."

"Well, that would have been a romantic gesture," he admitted, scratching the back of his head. "But that's been about the furthest thing from my mind today. Is that…" He stared at the box.

"You can have a look." Erin went into the kitchen to begin warming something up for them to eat. She didn't want to watch Terry open the box and examine the contents.

He was behind her almost immediately. It took only an instant to grab the box and flip the hinged top open.

"Who sent this?" he demanded.

"I don't know."

"Where's the card?"

"There wasn't one this time. No message. Just… whatever message you want to call *that*."

"Who delivered it?"

"A man. I don't know what company he was with. I'm sorry, I wasn't paying much attention and it was so quick. He gave it to me, and I thought it must be from you, and he was gone. He wasn't wearing a uniform and there wasn't any identification on the package. No name, no number, nothing."

"How was it packaged? Just like this?"

"Wrapping paper."

"What did you do with it?"

"I… threw it in the garbage at Auntie Clem's."

"We need to get it back."

"Um… okay. I think I just threw it in my office wastepaper basket. That doesn't get emptied every day."

"There might be fingerprints."

"Can you do that?"

He shook his head, brows drawing down. "Can I do what?"

"Just run random fingerprints through the system? Doesn't there have to be… a crime?"

"There is. Stalking."

"Is it?" Erin was glad to have him put a name on it. She wasn't sure how she was supposed to feel about someone sending her anonymous gifts. The flowers had been one thing; that was sweet and something anyone might do to make another person feel good. But the negligee felt very personal and intrusive if it had not come from Terry. Still, it wasn't a threat, and she wasn't sure who it had come from. Was she supposed to feel threatened? Complimented?

"Yes. This is stalking. Someone is trying to scare you. And I am going to put a stop to it. We'll find out who it is and put him behind bars."

Erin breathed out a pent-up breath. "Okay."

He looked at her, head cocked slightly. "Did you think I wouldn't?"

"I didn't know what to think. I didn't know how I should feel about it."

"You thought maybe this was just someone's idea of being… friendly?"

"Well, when it was the flowers, yes. I just thought it was a nice gesture. Something sweet. And there was nothing threatening about the note. When this came today, I was hoping it was just you…"

"Rest assured, I will not send you lingerie at work. Or send you anything anonymously. We live together. I will give you anything… *personal* here. In person. Maybe someday I'll send you flowers at work; that is kind of a nice idea and something someone who is more romantic than me might have thought to do. But I won't send you anything anonymously or anything that I think might embarrass you."

"And you don't think that this was just someone... misguided. Someone who intended to do something nice and it just came out wrong."

"If they have something wrong with them that prevents them from understanding social cues, maybe. But a normal guy would not send a woman lingerie anonymously and think it would make her feel safe and happy about herself."

"Yeah, I guess you're right."

"What did Vic say?"

"Vic wasn't on today. It was Bella. And I left her thinking... that it was from you."

"So now *she* thinks I'm the type of guy to send you lingerie at work." Terry flushed red around the collar.

"She thought it was very sweet. She's a teenager. Everything is romantic at that age. I just didn't want to tell her that it was anonymous."

"Okay... but I think you should let your employees know what is going on so they can be on the lookout for anyone or anything that is out of place. The more people there are who are aware and alert, the better."

Erin nodded. "I suppose. I'll tell them."

CHAPTER 9

It was a while before they sat down to dinner. Erin couldn't seem to keep her mind on task for long enough to get everything done and even simple, routine tasks took longer than usual as she kept stopping to figure out what she was supposed to be doing. Erin was beginning to regret that she hadn't just put out bread and jam and called it a day. Eventually, they sat down to a simple repast.

"So tell me about your case," she told Terry. "I haven't heard anything from you, but I've been hearing from the rest of Bald Eagle Falls all day."

"I suspect you have. Nothing like the possible murder of a mining mogul to get a small town buzzing."

Erin nodded, smiling. "They *have* been buzzing!"

"Of course, there has not been an autopsy yet. That will happen pretty quickly. They'll want to push it through because of how important Fontainebleau was. Maybe we'll have preliminary results tomorrow. But the victim did exhibit some outward signs that suggested he had been exposed to a toxin."

Erin nodded, waiting for more. Terry didn't fill her in on the details.

"Like he was foaming at the mouth, or what?"

"No. His skin. He had an unusual rash. And his behavior before he died was quite erratic. The ME's office suggested it might be mercury poisoning."

"Mercury poisoning. You mean like from fish?"

"You can get it from fish, yes. I would think that someone like Fontainebleau would know not to eat swordfish every day, and to try to source his fish from uncontaminated waters, or at least that his chef would know that. But there are other ways to get mercury poisoning too."

"You don't think someone intentionally poisoned him, do you?"

"We have to investigate that possibility. Until we know where the mercury came from, it could have come from anywhere, and intentional poisoning remains a possibility. But I'm inclined to think… maybe it was something to do with his mining operations."

"Do they mine for mercury? I don't even know where it comes from."

"Not here. But I gather it is used in processing minerals that they do mine here."

"So he might have been exposed at work? You hear about companies like that dumping toxic waste."

"I wouldn't jump right to that. In fact, that would be a good way to get my hands slapped. I'm not suggesting that Fontainebleau or his company was responsible for his death."

"No, I guess that wouldn't be a good idea."

"I'd get slapped with a slander lawsuit before I even finished talking."

Erin nodded, laughing. "Yes, you probably would. But it could be because of something that they were doing in his mines or factories? A mistake that exposed him to toxins?"

Terry shrugged. "No comment. We are investigating. You know I can't share anything about an active investigation."

He wouldn't share anything with her that wasn't already public knowledge or soon would be. Unless she managed to worm it out of him without his noticing.

"If he was exposed to mercury, then what about other people in his company? People who are working in those mines or factories every day? Aren't they at risk too?"

"There have not been any reports of other deaths or problems. If there were a leak or exposure at one of his industrial sites, you would expect some other reports. We'll have to dig down deeper, of course, but he didn't have employees dropping like flies."

That was something, at least. The police investigation would help to protect those workers if it turned out there was a contamination problem. As long as there wasn't a cover-up. With how wealthy and influential Fontainebleau had been, Erin wondered whether his family or estate would be able to hide anything they were able to discover in their investigation. It seemed like the wealthy always managed to suppress anything that showed them in a bad light.

"So you know for sure that it wasn't the pies," Erin teased.

"They're still testing all of the food, but chances are he was poisoned over a longer period of time; it wasn't something he ate for dinner that night."

"Oh." Erin had been anxious to hear that. Of course she knew that the pies had been perfectly safe, but she still had a lump in her stomach when he talked about having to test them. People would think that the police were still suspicious of the pies. Or that there was something they weren't saying. They wouldn't find anything in their testing. They couldn't. But she still didn't like it. "Of course."

"I have it on good authority that the pie was excellent," Terry told her with an encouraging smile. "Certainly no funny taste or smell."

"They were beautiful pies." Erin sighed. She thought about the perfectly peaked meringue tops, golden brown, with little dots of melted sugar. She loved making all kinds of pies, but the extra attention required to cook a meringue pie and the care it took to get them just right made them all the more special.

"I have no doubt. Don't worry about the testing. It is just routine."

"I know. And it isn't going to find anything. It's just that people will keep talking and speculating that it was something in the pies until you prove that it wasn't. And even then, maybe they'll still talk about it. Like they talk about the chocolate muffin killing Angela, even though they know that wasn't what killed her."

"Do they still say that?" Terry's brows went up.

"In a joking way. They still buy them, so they obviously don't think I'm trying to poison my customers, but they still talk about them being murder muffins." Erin rolled her eyes. "People say the silliest things."

"Yes, they do. Don't worry about the things they say or about jokes. They're at Auntie Clem's buying the 'murder muffins.' Maybe you should label them like that and see if more people will buy them with inventive names. You could come up with murderous names for all of your baked goods."

"I don't think so!"

Erin was *not* going to sell murder muffins.

CHAPTER 10

$\mathcal{A}$s Erin had expected, Terry returned to the office when he finished eating dinner. Erin defrosted a bag of cookies from the freezer and sent them back with Terry so that the rest of the law enforcement officers in Bald Eagle Falls could enjoy a treat while they put in long overtime hours. They needed something to boost their energy while putting in double shifts. Sheriff Wilmot always protested that he was trying to lose weight and that his wife had warned him off eating sweets—but he always took some anyway.

After Terry had returned to work, Erin heard a tap on the back door and was not surprised to see Vic. She joined Erin in the living room as Erin worked on her planner, checking her task list and seeing what else she needed to do to stay on top of her week. It was good to have her lists in front of her when her mind was so scattered by all that had happened. Everything was there in black and white—or color-coded—so she didn't have to remember it but could work through it a little at a time.

"So... how are things going with Terry?" Vic asked. "I guess he's probably too busy with the murder investigation right now to pursue many extra-curricular activities."

Erin looked up from her planner, puzzled. She followed Vic's eyes to the small lingerie box on the coffee table. Her face heated.

"Oh! Uh… actually, that is evidence—another delivery from my secret admirer. I need to remember to grab the paper it was wrapped in when I get back to the bakery tomorrow. If you can remind me? In case there are any fingerprints."

"Oh." Vic nodded. "Sure. So can I see…?" She reached for the box.

"You'd better not get your fingerprints on that. Terry hasn't dusted it yet. I guess he forgot to take it with him today."

Or did he know that there weren't any prints on it?

Was it possible that Terry *was* the secret admirer? Testing to see whether Erin would be faithful to him or be distracted by another suitor? Seeing whether she would tell him everything right away or keep it from him? She thought that he had gotten over any doubts that he'd had about their relationship after finding out about Brandon, but maybe he'd just been waiting, biding his time and figuring out a way to test her.

"Erin?"

She looked at Vic, blinked, and shook her head. "Sorry, I was off somewhere else. What?"

"How did Terry react? Did he freak out?"

"No." Erin thought back. He'd been pretty calm about the whole thing. Especially if he thought this was someone trying to scare or threaten her. Shouldn't he have reacted with more emotion, even rage, if he thought someone was threatening her?

And shouldn't he have reminded her to set the burglar alarm and not open the door to anyone?

"He was pretty good about it. He already knew about the flowers, so I guess it wasn't a surprise that the guy would send something else. He wants to test the wrapping paper for prints and then run a database search to see if the sender is in the system somewhere. And then… charge him with stalking, I guess. That's what he said it was."

"There are no threats," Vic pointed out, looking down at the box. "Unless there's something inside or there was a card that came with it?"

"No. No threats. But Terry said that it could be considered stalking anyway. I don't know. I'm sure he knows all of the ins and outs of what qualifies. But you always hear about how women are told that there's nothing the police can do about actual stalkers… the ones who make threats or break into the person's house… so, I didn't think this would qualify."

"Or maybe because of all that bad press, they decided to tighten up the laws," Vic suggested. "Make it so that it was a crime they could prosecute."

"Oh. Maybe. Hadn't thought about that. Maybe they are improving the laws. There are so many ways you can stalk someone now. With all of the social media and information online, it's a lot easier to find out things about the person you want to target. So more stalkers… better laws to deal with them…"

"That's probably it," Vic agreed.

Erin nodded. She wasn't sure whether she was satisfied with the explanation or not.

"Anyway… I guess that's how things are with Terry and I right now. I mean, it isn't anything to do with our relationship, but that's what he's concerned about right now. That and the murder."

Except how concerned was he with the stalker if he hadn't remembered to take the evidence with him to work?

"Yeah, I guess that's a lot to deal with right now."

Erin shrugged. She looked toward the back of the house but, of course, could not see the parking pad from where she sat in the living room.

"And Willie's not home tonight?"

"I guess he has stuff to look after too. Seems like he's been pretty busy with business lately. I hope that whatever has been bugging him, he gets through it pretty soon. I like to be the focus when he's around."

Since he didn't live there, that made sense to Erin. Willie chose whether to be at Vic's or home or dealing with business. If he chose to be with Vic, then it would make sense for her to be his focus, for him to be able to put work aside and be with her.

Though, being undistracted when other things were going on in life was hard. She could see how it was a problem too.

"Vicky..." she said tentatively, "Have you noticed anything strange about Willie's behavior lately? I mean... anything different? Not just him being private about his own affairs, but... mood swings, confusion, irritability, anything like that?"

"You've met the man, right?" Vic asked with a laugh. "Yeah, he's been irritable lately. Like I said. Something going on with work. Distracting him. I don't know what because he doesn't share."

"And that big blow-up the other day."

"Well, it wasn't really a big blow-up, but... yeah. He did go storming out of here because of whatever was going on in his business. But that's just Willie; we're both—"

"Passionate people," Erin finished. She'd heard that line a few times before. A good excuse for their arguments and generally rocky relationship. They loved each other, but they certainly made a lot of noise about it.

Vic nodded. She shrugged with one shoulder. "Why? You're not worried about domestic abuse, are you? Because I can tell you, he's never raised a hand to me. Or me to him. We may shout and slam doors, but we're not mean and we don't hit. I had enough of that growing up. There's nothing wrong with a good air-clearing discussion, but I wouldn't let him abuse me."

Erin smiled, grateful for that. "That's good. But I wasn't really thinking about that. I was thinking about... his skin."

"His skin?" Vic blinked several times and stared at Erin, trying to understand the segue. "You're worried about the way he looks? I don't care; why should you?"

"No. I know it's from his mining and processing. And that's actually what has me worried. Terry was saying that Fontainebleau might have died from mercury poisoning, maybe from some environmental contaminant at his factories or mines. So... if Willie is doing his own processing, and he's obviously not in a lab with protective gear to keep his skin from being contaminated in the process…"

Vic nodded her understanding slowly. "Then what if he's poisoning himself, absorbing all kinds of bad stuff through his skin."

Erin nodded. "He could be, you know."

"And what does that have to do with whether he's irritable?"

Erin indicated her phone, where she had done a couple of internet searches before Vic's arrival. "I was looking at some of the common symptoms of mercury poisoning. Or other heavy metals. And mood swings and irritability are high on the list. Terry said that Fontainebleau had been behaving erratically before he died. Heavy metals affect the brain."

"He's not stupid. Stuff like lead poisoning, it causes brain damage that lowers the IQ, right? But Willie's smarter than anyone you've ever met. He might not say a lot, but he picks things up really fast. Sees things that no one else does. Understands a lot of really complex stuff that I could only hope to get someday."

"I know. And maybe that means that he's just fine and moody is just moody, not a symptom of anything else. I just think… one of us should ask the question."

"Me, you mean."

"I don't know. Someone should suggest that it's not the healthiest way for him to be living and he should maybe get tested to make sure that all of his exposure to whatever he works with hasn't affected him physically. Other than dyeing his skin."

"Huh. Well, maybe when he's in a good mood, *you* can ask him that."

Erin didn't particularly like the idea. She had a suspicion that Willie was not going to react in a positive way to such a suggestion. She would rather not be the target of his anger or get the cold shoulder. But she supposed she couldn't ask Vic to either.

"Yeah… well, we'll see if the subject comes up. Maybe we could get Terry to talk to him about it."

Vic laughed. "Yeah, that sounds like a good idea."

CHAPTER 11

$\mathscr{E}$rin had scheduled Vic and Charley for the afternoon shift, which meant that she was free to run some errands for herself and Auntie Clem's without it eating into her evenings or weekend. She was getting better at making use of her employees and not insisting that she herself had to work every shift. They had even managed without her when she had been away with Vic or dealing with Melissa's wedding arrangements. That meant that she could put more on to them and not worry about doing it all herself.

She was just coming back from the grocery store when she saw a small group of children playing on the climbers in the school playground, and she thought that she recognized the older girl as she got closer. She pulled up to the curb and watched them play for a moment, listening to their happy shrieks and enjoying the smell of the freshly cut grass. Then she got out and approached the little family. She did not want people thinking she was some predator watching the children from a distance.

Erin nodded to the thin woman watching from the park bench beside the playground with a baby in her arms.

"Hello, Adrienne."

Adrienne stared at her for a minute before finally giving her a small smile and nod. She looked away from Erin again, down at her baby, as if to make sure that she wasn't fussing and was comfortable. Erin joined her on the bench, sitting far enough away not to crowd her, but close enough that it wouldn't be awkward to visit. The baby had grown a lot over the intervening months since she had seen it last, but it still had the big eyes and thin face that Erin remembered. Not pudgy and round like a healthy baby should be. But maybe Adrienne naturally had skinnier babies. She was a thin woman. Maybe it was genetic, and not because they weren't getting as many calories as they should.

"Out enjoying the sunshine?"

The thin woman nodded. "Yes. Kids need plenty of fresh air and sunshine. But they still get bored sometimes, like to come into the playground to play somewhere new." She hesitated. "It's good for them to use their imaginations and to find things to do wherever they are. But nice if they can go somewhere designed for kids now and then."

"Sure," Erin agreed. She remembered using her imagination to turn junk into toys, a bare backyard into a more interesting setting, and long hours of unstructured time into engaging games or pastimes. She had not grown up babysat by screens and technology. Neither were Adrienne's children. "It's a nice change of pace."

Adrienne nodded, looking down to comfort the baby who was not complaining.

One of the children ran over from the climbers and stood by her mother. She put an arm around Adrienne, cuddling in close to her.

"Mama?"

"It's just Miss Erin," Adrienne told her. "You know the baker lady."

The girl was about eight, Erin thought. Her name was Hope, if she remembered correctly, but she wasn't certain enough to use it without making sure first.

"Hi," she greeted. "We've met before."

The girl nodded and buried her face into Adrienne's neck for a moment. Erin didn't remember her being so shy before. But kids went through phases.

Adrienne patted her on the back for a moment, then gave her a little nudge away. "There, now. You're a big girl. You can play with the others. Everything is fine here."

Hope didn't go back to the other children, even though they called for her to. She stayed close to her mother, holding on to her. Adrienne didn't try to shake her off, but was clearly hampered by Hope's clinginess.

"It's nice that you can come and play here," Erin tried.

"Uh-huh."

"What do you like to play best?"

Hope's shoulders raised and fell in a shrug.

"I used to like to play pirates," Erin told her.

Hope looked at her for a moment, then at Adrienne as if to ask for permission to talk. Adrienne nodded encouragingly.

"Pirate *tag* or *being* pirates?" Hope inquired.

Erin laughed. "Both, I guess. We played pirate tag while pretending to be pirates."

Hope sniffled and wiped her nose with the back of her hand. "Did you walk the plank?"

"Yes," Erin chuckled. "You can't play pirates without walking the plank, can you?"

Hope shook her head. Then, seeming to realize that Erin was intentionally drawing her out, she turned away from her and again buried her face in Adrienne's side.

"Can we go home, Mama? I want to go home."

"You and the others wanted to come to the playground. The others still need more time to play. You go play too, enjoy yourself."

Hope shook her head and didn't rejoin them.

Erin met Adrienne's eyes and saw that it was time for her to leave. Adrienne didn't like her making Hope nervous. "I'll… head back out. I'll see you later, okay? We'll talk another time."

Adrienne nodded. Erin returned to her car. Once she was gone, the girl would hopefully return to playing with her siblings.

On the seat beside Erin lay the wrapping paper from the gift from the secret admirer. Erin parked in the lot behind the town hall. She walked through the main part of the town hall to the police department offices.

Clara Jones was sitting at her desk in the reception area. Her eyes went over Erin quickly and Erin thought she detected slight disappointment in Clara's features when she saw that Erin had not brought any baked goods with her. Erin usually bribed her way in with something sweet. Or at least paved the way; it wasn't exactly a bribe.

"Miss Price?"

"Is Terry in?"

"He is… Is this regarding a case?"

Clara didn't really have any right to ask. She knew that Terry would see Erin if he were able to, and Erin didn't have to be bringing evidence on an active case for Clara to let her in. Clara was just snooping into what it was that Erin had come by to see Terry for. If it wasn't an active case, then what was so important that it could not wait until Terry was home?

Maybe Erin should have brought Terry some soup for dinner to show that she was performing a valuable service, rather than just wanting to talk to a law enforcement officer who needed to be focused on the cases at hand. Especially with such a big case on the books. Mr. Fontainebleau's people would not be happy with any reason for delays.

Not that they could see what was going on in the Bald Eagles Falls police department, to see whether they were talking to their wives or partners instead of keeping their noses to the grindstone.

"I have something he asked me to bring by."

Clara waited for more information, and when it was not forthcoming, relented and called Terry's line to advise him that Miss Price was there to see him.

There was a response from Terry. Clara clearly didn't like it. "Are you sure? I can ask her to just leave whatever it is here for you."

She knew very well that Erin could hear what she was saying.

Clara hung up the phone. "He'll see you in his office," she conceded.

"Thank you, Clara."

Erin walked down the hall to the office that was now somewhat cramped since Terry shared it with Stayner. He stood up from his chair to greet her and give her a quick hug and kiss. He stretched and rolled his shoulders before sitting down again. It was probably the first time he had gotten up in several hours.

"What can I do for you?" Terry asked, when it was clear that Erin did not have a box of cookies or thermos of soup for him.

She produced the wrapping paper, which she had slid into a plastic zip-top bag to prevent it from being contaminated by anything else.

"You wanted me to get you the wrapping paper from that second gift," she reminded him.

"That completely slipped my mind. I've been so focused on this Fontainebleau case. Thanks for bringing it by. I guess… we should start the paperwork on an official complaint. Do you mind filling in a couple of forms?"

Erin wrinkled her nose. That wasn't exactly what she'd had in mind when she had decided to bring him the wrapping paper, but she supposed that if he was going to run any fingerprints found on the paper through their database, he needed a file to record it under. They needed to do everything by the book. Random searches of fingerprints were not something that they were supposed to be doing.

"I suppose so."

"Sorry. I know it isn't any fun."

"I'm not sure it's worth it. I mean… this guy hasn't made any threats." Erin thought back to receiving the lingerie. Even if it wasn't accompanied by any kind of written warning or threat, there was a certain creep factor involved in getting such an intimate thing from a stranger or anonymous source. It was inappropriate and the sender surely knew that such an anonymous gift would not be welcomed by most women.

"Do you want to wait until he escalates?" Terry held up his

hands to halt any protest. "It is extremely unlikely that this will turn into anything. Most stranger stalkers are not dangerous and never do anything to harm their target. It's the ones who are former intimate partners that are the problem, and as far as you know…"

"I don't think this is anyone I know," Erin agreed. But of course she couldn't be sure. She hadn't expected Brandon to ever show up in her life again either. She hadn't expected that anyone in Bald Eagle Falls was paying her anything more than a normal amount of attention. But she'd been wrong about that. Was there any chance that some interest from the past had shown up in Bald Eagle Falls to harass her? It didn't seem possible.

"So, chances are this will never turn into anything," Terry reassured her. "If something pops on the fingerprints, then we can give this guy a warning to knock it off, and he probably will. If nothing pops, then we know that he at least doesn't have a criminal record, and probably he'll just give up after a while. There's no reason to think that he will escalate. But we should still do what we can."

It was the opposite reaction to what women usually received when reporting a stalker. So she should be happy that her boyfriend was in the police department and wanted to take it seriously.

"Okay."

Terry took her through the forms required to be filled out to file her complaint, asking her questions and adding details as needed. When they got to the end of it, Terry produced a mobile fingerprint scanner to take her prints.

Erin stared at the scanner and shook her head. "Why? You don't need my prints."

"You touched the wrapping paper, right? We need to be able to eliminate your prints and just focus on the rest."

A lot of people were caught by "elimination prints" if Erin was to believe what she saw on crime shows on TV. The cops always said that the fingerprints were to rule someone out, just so they could get the prints that would put them at the scene of a crime. Though Erin had not committed any crime, she was still reluctant to cooperate. This was the point at which she would be telling a person of interest on TV to assert their right to remain silent or request a lawyer. They didn't have to give their fingerprints to anyone.

Terry waited for her to agree. He pointed at the wrapping paper. "Your prints are on that, right?"

"Yes."

"Then we have your prints. We can feed them all into the computer and run them against the database."

That was true.

"You're not giving me anything new by giving me your fingerprints. You are just giving me another copy of the same thing, with your name attached. So we *don't* have to run them through the database."

"You won't run my prints through the system?"

"What are you afraid we're going to find if we do?"

Erin shrugged uncomfortably. "I don't know. I haven't done anything. But... I don't know if they could be in there from somewhere else."

"Like what?"

"Like somewhere I was where a crime occurred. It does happen, you know."

"Well, yes, I do. Especially to you."

It was probably surprising that they hadn't run into this problem on any of the previous cases. But the fact was, he'd never asked for her fingerprints before.

"I think you're just going to have to trust me. I am not going to run your prints through the system. Just to compare them to what we find on the wrapping paper, so we know which ones not to put through."

But would he be left wondering where else her fingerprints might lead after that? Would he run them anyway, because he was curious about her past and what she might be trying to cover up?

"It's just that I've never had to give my prints for anything before," Erin explained. "I've never been arrested or had to give elimination prints before. It's kind of scary."

He nodded as if this were perfectly reasonable.

"Okay..." Erin looked at the scanner. "How does this work?"

CHAPTER 12

*D*espite officially having the afternoon off, Erin was tired when evening rolled around. More exhausted than she thought she should be, she wondered if she could be coming down with something. She would have to be careful to get enough sleep and eat properly. Maybe take some vitamin C. She didn't want to get sick. That could prevent her from going to Auntie Clem's for a week or more, even if it were only a twenty-four-hour bug. People didn't want someone who had been sick near their food.

Terry was sleeping, resting up for a night shift. She didn't think he should still have been working in the afternoon if he was taking a night shift. It didn't give him a full eight hours to sleep between shifts. But he said he didn't need to; he would have a nap and then sleep after the night shift. But she wasn't sure he would. Since the initial call-out, he'd been putting most of his time into helping out with the Fontainebleau case.

Erin moved through her tai chi forms in the backyard, alone at first and then joined by Willie as he pulled the garden hose across the yard to wash off his truck while she exercised.

"I hear you think I'm going crazy." He directed a stream of water at his truck, rinsing off a layer of dust from gravel or dirt roads.

"What?" Erin frowned and looked at him, losing her place in the tai chi flow for a moment, trying to figure out what he was talking about.

"That I'm becoming unbalanced like Fontainebleau because of my exposure to toxic chemicals."

"Oh. That. Well, I didn't mean that…" She looked away from him, grimacing. "I didn't mean that you're going crazy. I was just worried when we started talking about how Fontainebleau might have been exposed to mercury or other heavy metals at his mines or plants. Because… I know your skin is exposed to whatever you do to process your minerals."

"You don't think that I'm careful? That I'm aware of the dangers?"

"Well… I just know that your skin is exposed, and you can absorb mercury through your skin. That's what I'm worried about."

"I follow traditional processing methods. There's nothing wrong with that. It's the same way that people have been processing metals for hundreds of years. People like Fontainebleau might be afraid to get their hands dirty, but I'm not. I don't care how people look at me; I know I've earned this from good, honest work."

He paused for a moment to look at the skin on the back of his hand, then shrugged. He was proud of the stained skin he had earned. Proud that he had done all of the work himself and not had some lab or plant somewhere do it for him.

"And you don't think that there's any danger to how you've been doing it? There must be all kinds of safety standards you have to follow, environmental stuff and precautions to keep from poisoning yourself…"

He continued to spray the truck, working down the length of it. "I know what I'm doing. Like I said, people have been doing this for hundreds of years. I didn't just come up with my own process. Though I've tweaked it in places, learned from experience."

"But traditional ways aren't always the best or the safest. I mean… there's a reason for the expression 'mad as a hatter.' "

"So you *do* think I'm crazy."

"No. I don't. I don't think there's anything wrong with you. Not that we can see yet. But it could poison you over time. Like with the guys who made those old felt hats. They used mercury for that, and it poisoned them over time. Not all at once. If you have been accumulating mercury, you could get treated, to reverse the process. So that you don't end up like Fontainebleau."

He shook his head. "I'll take it under advisement."

Erin didn't look at him, focusing on her tai chi forms and keeping her gaze steady on a point in the distance. "Fine."

"I'm not going to change my business practices. It's the guys like Fontainebleau who are the big polluters putting mercury into the environment. If he died from his own soil or groundwater contamination, then he got what was coming to him. The EPA should be inspecting all of his operations and finding out where the contaminants came from."

"Terry said that they are. They know the mercury could have come from one of his plants, so they're looking for it. It could be harming wildlife or his workers."

"He's probably dumping massive amounts of the stuff. I work in a very controlled environment and don't use many of these chemicals. It's just a drop in the bucket compared to an operation like Fontainebleau's empire."

"I wasn't really concerned about you contaminating all of Bald Eagle Falls's groundwater. Just about your own health."

He didn't say anything for a while, apparently focused on the complex job of washing off his truck.

"Well, I appreciate your concern," he eventually said gruffly. "But it is misplaced. There's nothing wrong with my health."

"Okay. That's great. I'm glad."

Willie finished washing off his truck in silence, rolled the hose back up to put it away neatly, and grunted an indistinct goodbye to Erin before going up to the loft to join Vic.

Erin decided to do her routine one more time, tense from her discussion with Willie rather than relaxed like she had hoped to be.

There was a movement in the woods beyond her fence, and Erin turned her head slightly to try to identify it. With a stalker on the loose, she should be aware of her environment. Terry didn't think the guy would escalate into doing something violent, but sometimes cops were wrong. Sometimes those people who were "unlikely" to escalate were the very ones who did. He wanted her to remember to set the burglar alarm when she was inside, but when she was outside, she was exposed. She had been approached in the yard before and couldn't forget that.

But the shape that she was able to make out in the trees was not a stranger to her. No stalker. It was the tall, slim redhead who lived in the summer cottage and acted as groundskeeper in Erin's woods. Running off kids who would leave behind campfires and beer cans, squatters who could end up injuring themselves and then suing Erin because it happened on her property, or anyone else who might conceivably cause Erin problems, including a secret admirer lurking around, trying to catch a peek at her while she did her tai chi at the end of a long day.

"Hi, Adele."

Adele moved closer to where she could talk to Erin without either of them having to raise their voices and be overheard or attract attention.

"Evening, Erin."

"How's everything today? All quiet?"

Adele's shotgun pointed down, gripped casually. "Well, quiet for now," Adele conceded.

Erin wasn't sure she liked the sound of that. "Has someone been hanging around? Anyone giving you problems?"

"There have been some reporters around. Think that they can set up a nest and get some telephoto shots. You or Officer Piper; I'm not sure what they think they're going to get that's interesting enough to publish, but you never know what these guys will make up."

"Reporters?" Erin repeated with dismay. She remembered Terry warning her that they might show up. Everything had been quiet, so Erin had thought that he had just been overly cautious. But maybe she just hadn't been paying close enough attention. She had expected them to jump out, bar her way, and drill her with questions. Not to lurk in the trees and see if they could get candid shots of her. "I didn't think we'd really see any. Did they leave when you asked them to?"

"So far, so good. Even those who think they have the right to be on what they think is public property are usually convinced by my arguments." Adele lifted the shotgun slightly. "They realize that they might have been mistaken."

"Well... that's good," Erin couldn't help snickering at the thought of the reporters being chased off by Adele and her shotgun. Adele could be very convincing, though as far as Erin knew, she had never fired even a warning shot. The reporters would not know enough about her to realize that she would never voluntarily hurt another creature.

Erin realized that it had been longer than usual since Adele had picked up any baked goods from her. While she herself did not eat a lot, Adele did collect baked goods from Erin's free day-old bread program regularly, which she then distributed to a family or families who remained unknown to Erin.

"How is everything else? Everyone... okay?" Erin asked tentatively. She had a stated "no questions asked" policy for the day-old bread program, in place so that anyone could pick up baked goods from Auntie Clem's without fear of being judged for taking advantage of the offering. Erin didn't need to know anyone's circumstances or even who was the eventual recipient of the baked goods. Just that they were going to feed hungry mouths somewhere that wouldn't be filled if it weren't for her generosity.

Though Erin didn't consider it generosity to give away what would have gone in the garbage otherwise.

"Yes," Adele said neutrally. "Everything is fine."

"Good. I just... want to make sure that people are taken care of."

"Circumstances change. Fluctuate."

That could mean that one of the families Adele had been helping out was now in better circumstances, able to buy goods on their own rather than taking the day-old bread. If so, Erin was happy to hear it. She nodded.

"Good... I hope that's good news." Erin stretched and let her arms fall to her side. "As far as these reporters go…" she shook her head. "No one has approached me directly yet. It isn't like I know anything about the investigation or Terry would reveal anything to the public. I don't know how long this thing is going to go on. I guess since you don't come from here, you didn't know this Fontainebleau guy?"

Adele shook her head. "I've known men like him. But I haven't had the privilege of knowing your Mr. Fontainebleau, thankfully."

"He's not *my* Mr. Fontainebleau."

"He's your client, isn't he? Or *wasn't* he?"

"One time. And I don't even know if he ate the pie before he died. And it was his assistant who contacted me, not he himself."

"Of course not. A man like that wouldn't be making his own phone calls about catering a dinner. That would be…" Adele shook her head, rolling her eyes and searching for a word.

"Ridiculous? Beneath him? Unthinkable?"

"Any of those would do," Adele agreed. "Anyway, the sentiment is the same. It's best to stay far away from anyone like that. They will use and abuse anyone in their sphere."

CHAPTER 13

Returning home after a long day at the bakery, Erin was bone tired. She picked up the mail from the floor beneath the mail slot and tossed it onto the coffee table to look at later. The house was quiet. She hadn't seen Terry's truck out front, so he was probably back at work again, working hard on the Fontainebleau case. Were they making any headway on it? She hadn't had much chance to talk to Terry about it, but was interested in hearing whether they had made any progress. Did they know the contamination had come from one of his work sites? It seemed like justice if he had ended up poisoning himself. As Willie had said, he got what he deserved if he had been dumping that stuff into the environment against the strict regulations meant to keep him from doing just that.

The mail hit the coffee table with a soft slap and spread out like a deck of cards being displayed by a dealer. There was a large, thick envelope that seemed out of place. It wasn't a bill or advertising flyer, which was about all she got in the mail these days. She bent over and picked it up.

It was stiff. Cardboard inside an envelope to keep it from being folded. Her name and address were on it written in an unfamiliar hand, but there was no return address, either in the corner or on the reverse side. Erin used her finger to slit the flap and pried apart two thin pieces of cardboard to see what was in between.

They were old newspaper articles. Not printed on copy paper. Not microfiche copies like she'd gotten when she was doing research at the library on pre-digitized copies of the Bald Eagles Falls weekly. But actual cut-out-of-the-paper newsprint copies.

Erin held the envelope open and tipped the articles out onto the coffee table.

She was still leaning over the articles when Terry got home twenty minutes later. He entered, K9 at his side as usual, and looked surprised at the papers spread out over the table.

"What's all this? More of Clementine's genealogy?"

"No. Another delivery by the… whatever he is. Secret admirer. Stalker. Whatever."

"Threats?" Terry asked sharply, stepping closer.

But they weren't single words cut out of a newspaper or magazine to form a message for her. They were actual articles.

"No. They're about Fontainebleau."

"Fontainebleau." Terry sat down on the couch beside Erin and looked at them. "These are old. Someone's been following his career for a long time."

Erin nodded. "They go back thirty years. Unless they were stolen from the library or historical society, whoever sent them to me must have collected them in some file or scrapbook."

"And why give them to you?"

"I don't know." Erin smoothed one of the articles out. "What am I supposed to do with these? How exactly is this the normal progression after flowers and lingerie? I would have thought… chocolates? But not old newspaper articles about someone I didn't even know."

"Maybe they were meant for me rather than you."

"They were addressed to me."

"But they could have been sent to you on the assumption that you would pass them on to me. Someone who was paranoid about sending them to the police department's address."

"I suppose. Whoever it is must know that I don't live alone here. If it's someone who lives in town or knows my address, they must know that, right?"

"I would expect so."

"So… if you think this was meant for you, then… why? Is this information that you don't have?"

Terry picked up one of the articles to read it. "Well, I admit that we don't know a lot about his early life. About his father and how he got his start in this business. Which it looks like is what these articles are about. The early observations on a promising career. A rising star."

Erin nodded. She had already read through each one. Nothing had jumped out at her as being out of place. "But most of it is… it's canned publicity. Stuff that came out of company press releases, not investigative journalism. It isn't a tell-all that suggests he was dishonest or got his fortune through ill-gotten gains. There's nothing… startling here."

Terry's eyes went from one yellowing article to the next, skimming over them. "No, not at a first look. It's just like you say. The story that the company would want to tell. Get some favorable press. Let people know who your new guy is. Make it all sound good."

"Why would anyone send it to us, then? It isn't anything that is going to help with the investigation."

"Maybe that's not the reason it was sent." Terry sat up, dropping the article back onto the table.

"Why else would it be sent?"

"To show you… how he got here. Maybe… humanize him, make him look like someone you could like instead of as remote as he was before he died. Rich and famous. Someone who just ordered everyone else around. The mining mogul who knew he was better than anyone else."

"That isn't what I thought about him," Erin protested. Though, truth be told, it wasn't that far from the truth. He hadn't been real to her. Just a name and a big order sheet. The money that the job would add to Auntie Clem's bank account. "I'm sure he was a good guy. I never talked to him, but just because someone is rich, that doesn't automatically make them snobby or corrupt."

She had learned from more than one source that he was corrupt or at least suspected of it. He could pay for what he wanted and do whatever he wanted without getting in hot water. Because he was who he was, a man with millions of dollars and almost as many "friends" willing to help things along.

"If you're 'sure he's a good guy,' then maybe these articles have done their job. Because that's certainly not what I have learned from my investigation." Terry looked around as if someone might have overheard them. Someone who would report to Fontainebleau's company or estate that Terry had been slandering him.

"Well… that isn't what I've heard either," Erin admitted. "But he must have had some good qualities. And maybe he was trying to change. He'd never used Auntie Clem's Bakery before. Why start now? Did he have guests that follow a gluten-free diet and he wanted to accommodate them? Or had he decided to buy local, even if it was a little more expensive than it would be to go with a big catering company further away."

Erin looked from one picture to another, showing Fontainebleau the Third as a young man, just starting out in the business. Learning the ropes by working as a laborer in his father's mines and factories. Making suggestions that showed an aptitude for making money and succeeding in the world of mines and minerals. Coming home from college to work with his father in upper management, the brilliant young man who was going to turn things around for the company.

"I've heard he wasn't well-liked," she admitted to Terry.

"That would be an understatement. Maybe 'hated by all who knew him' would be a more accurate statement."

"So, are there a lot of suspects?"

"If he was intentionally poisoned? Yes, certainly."

"Have they found any contamination at his house or where he worked? That would explain him having mercury poisoning?"

Terry pressed his lips together, considering the question. "They have found fairly high concentrations of mercury and other heavy metals at a couple of the factories. But… there is some hesitation in saying that the levels of mercury would have been high enough to kill him."

"Even exposure over a long time?"

"Different experts will give us different answers. Or if he would have spent enough time at those facilities to be affected. And we're still waiting for confirmation from the medical examiner that it was mercury that killed him. And what kind of mercury it was. I guess there are different kinds of mercury, different sources it might come from. So we also need to know what kind of mercury poisoning he had, if that's what it was."

There were still a lot of unanswered questions on the cause of death. What if the medical examiner called back and said that it was a heart attack? Or some other cause of death that was either homicide or natural causes? Would all of the investigation that the police department had done be thrown out the window?

"So, do you investigate it as if it was intentional poisoning? Or an accident?"

"Right now, we have to treat it as a suspicious death. Possible homicide. That's the best we can do right now. We can't just *not* investigate and hope that the verdict comes back that it was natural causes. We have to gather the evidence while it still exists and talk to witnesses while their memories are still fresh."

"And how many of those witnesses are suspects?"

Terry leaned back into the couch and rolled his head and shoulders, working out the muscle soreness from the time he'd been spending at his desk. While he still did foot patrol and answered trouble calls while he was on shift, Erin suspected that the majority of his time had been spent moving the investigation into Fontainebleau's death forward.

"A lot of people had reason to dislike Fontainebleau. Including people that had quite a bit of access to him. We're not talking about a mobster or leader of state with lots of bodyguards around him to protect him from all of the people who hated him. He was pretty casual about security."

"I guess he figured being out in the middle of nowhere in backwoods Tennessee was protection enough."

"I guess so. And until now… it was."

CHAPTER 14

This time, it was a delivery that Erin knew about and had eagerly awaited. Not a delivery from some unknown man or woman watching her and sending her random gifts she couldn't understand the significance of.

"When is it supposed to get here?" Vic asked.

"I don't know." Erin hit the tracking number on her phone and waited for the details to come up. "Before five o'clock," she sighed.

"So it could be any time today." Vic rolled her eyes. "Sorry. You must be going crazy waiting for it."

"I am," Erin agreed. She felt like a little kid at Christmas. Back before she'd learned not to expect anything good at Christmas. Not the present she asked Santa for and not a magical Christmas miracle where she got a permanent family and the stable life she'd dreamed of. Despite all of the movies on TV and sermons at churches she attended sporadically, there was just no truth to Christmas being a magical time of wish-fulfillment. Those things only happened in movies and books. She'd never met anyone who'd actually experienced a Christmas miracle.

But she was excited. When the package finally arrived, it would be Christmas Day for her, no matter how high the Tennessee summer temperature soared.

She tried to lose herself in her work. There was plenty to be done, just like there was every day. When they finished baking the first batch of bread, it was time for opening and the morning rush, and then the customers eventually tailed off a little. She took a few minutes in her office to see if she could get a few more pieces of information entered into the computer system. She wanted to make sure she was caught up and then do a backup to ensure that she had a copy of all of her vital information in case she was ever in the position of having her computer stolen again. Or if it flooded, burned, or had some other kind of catastrophic breakdown. She never wanted to experience that heart-dropping moment of dread, thinking she had lost all of her information, again.

Charley came by for the afternoon shift. Erin had been hoping that by the time Charley got there, the delivery would have arrived, and she could test it out while Charley and Vic handled the bakery customers.

Mid-afternoon, there was a loud knock on the bakery's back door. Erin hurried out of her office to answer it.

"Someone at the door," Vic called, sticking her head into the kitchen and then grinning at Erin when she saw her running for the door. "I should have guessed you didn't have to be told twice."

Erin opened the door and greeted the deliveryman who stood waiting with several boxes on his dolly.

"Expecting a delivery?" Maurice asked. He brought in deliveries from the city regularly, one of the few delivery services that felt it was worth their while to make the trip out to Bald Eagle Falls.

"Yes!" Erin agreed.

He smiled at her excitement. "Well, then, these three boxes are yours." He looked at his clipboard and took three boxes off of his cart. Erin signed the clipboard to acknowledge her receipt. By the time she had the largest of the three boxes open, Vic was there to see. She helped Erin wrestle out the tight Styrofoam blocks that held everything firmly in place.

"There it is," she said in awe as she and Erin gazed reverently at the shiny ceramic glaze that coated the outside of the waffle maker.

"Thirty waffles at once," Erin murmured.

"Breakfast will never be the same again."

Charley was watching curiously from the doorway to the front of the bakery.

"I thought you only got runner-up in the waffle contest."

Erin and Vic exchanged looks.

"Yes," Erin admitted.

"Then how did you get the grand prize?"

Erin cleared her throat. "Well, I kind of had my heart set on it... so I had to buy my own."

Charley laughed. "Why bother entering the contest at all, then? Save yourself some time and just buy the waffle iron."

"Well, there was always the chance that I would win the contest and would be able to get it for free. Free is always better for the cash flow situation."

Vic and Charley both chuckled along with her. "Well, I guess it is at that," Charley agreed. "So why is it in three boxes? Just how big is this thing?"

"I guess there's some assembly required. And maybe some accessories, instructions, a recipe book..." Erin looked at the other boxes. "I'll get to them once I get this first box unpacked and assembled."

Vic helped her to assemble, floating between the front and the kitchen to make sure she covered both places as necessary. There were a number of accessories and manuals, as Erin had suspected. Erin nodded at the third box, which hadn't yet been opened.

"What do you think is in the last one? This looks like everything that was pictured in the assembly instructions."

"I don't know. Open it up and let's have a look."

Erin slit the packing tape on the last box and plunged her hand into the packing peanuts. "Okay, so what have we got here?"

She found the heavy, irregularly shaped object and pulled it out of the box, letting packing peanuts stream back down into the box and onto the floor.

"What's that?" Vic stared at the device, a sort of a plaque with several dials like analog clock faces on it.

"I... have no idea." Erin dug around in the box for any instructions or explanation. It didn't look like it was anything to do with the waffle iron. Maybe it had come to her in error. Maurice might have given her a box that wasn't hers. She bent down the flaps of the box to look at the address on it. It was definitely made out to her at Auntie Clem's Bakery. But someone might still have made a mistake, affixing the label to the wrong box. If there was a waybill, she might be able to get it straightened out for whoever was expecting the mutated clock.

But there wasn't even a scrap of paper in the box.

"What have you got there?" Charley asked from the doorway.

Erin turned it to show her. "I have no idea. Don't expect me to tell you the time on this thing. It looks like it came out of an airplane. Or a boat."

"Oh," Charley laughed. "My granddad had one of those. It's a barometer. Supposed to help you to tell the weather. Atmospheric pressure. It drops before a storm… or something like that."

"Huh." Erin looked at it. There were words around the big center dial like Rain, Fair, and Change. "Okay. I guess that's what all of this means. Cool, but… where did it come from and who needs to know the atmospheric pressure to make waffles?"

"That's a really cool one." Charley entered the kitchen to get a closer look at the barometer. "It looks like it's authentic. Like an antique, not just a knock-off."

Erin nodded. It was quite heavy in her hand, not just plastic parts fitted into particle board. "Yeah. Someone is going to be looking for this. I don't know how it got mixed in with my delivery." She looked at the labels on the boxes. The two that had contained waffle iron parts were clearly different from the one that had contained the barometer. "It has to be a mistake. I just hope we can figure out who it was supposed to go to."

CHAPTER 15

The next day, Erin and Vic had done the baking and opened Auntie Clem's when Erin got a call from Bella. Bella wasn't supposed to be on until the afternoon, so it was odd for her to call in unless something was wrong.

"Uh-oh," Erin intoned when she saw the caller ID. "Bella might be sick."

She slipped into the kitchen to take the call, leaving Vic to handle the customers.

"Bella, hi," she greeted.

"Oh, Erin, thanks for answering." Bella knew that Erin discouraged her employees from taking calls or even looking at their screens when serving customers, and tried to follow the same policy herself. Although she took special orders for the bakery, too, so she had to keep an eye on who was calling in case it was additional business. Bella's voice sounded different from usual. Erin figured that confirmed that she was calling in to say she was sick.

"No problem, Bella. What's up?"

"I need a favor, and... I don't really know who else to ask. I know you're working this morning, so I shouldn't, but..."

"What is it? Are you okay?"

"My car broke down."

"Oh, I see. So you won't be able to get in this afternoon."

"Well, that's one problem. But the other thing is, I'm supposed to be giving someone else a ride this morning, and now I can't, and she really needs to get in to *her* job, or she could lose it. And she has a family to look after, so… she can't afford to lose it."

"Who are you supposed to give a ride to? Just into town?"

"No." Bella sounded reluctant to go on, as if she'd decided that calling Erin was the wrong thing to do and she should try something else instead. "It's just… if it was just me, I would find a way to work it out. Or just get one of the others to cover my shift this afternoon. But she can't do that. They're very strict."

"Who?" Erin couldn't figure out who Bella would be giving a ride to. She and her mother lived alone on their goat farm. Maybe a neighbor out that way that she had offered to help?

"Well, you know Adrienne, don't you?" Bella's voice was tentative.

"Adrienne?"

"We've been helping her out. Her and her kids, so that she could go back to work. Now that the baby is bigger and can be left with someone, she needed to start working again. She lives a pretty thrifty lifestyle, but she still needs food and clothes for the kids and everything…"

"Of course. I know Adrienne; we've—" Erin cut herself off. She had been about to say that she had helped Adrienne with food from the day-old program before, but that would be breaking confidences. If Bella was helping Adrienne out, she probably already knew that, but it wasn't Erin's place to say so. "We've talked before. So you need to take Adrienne to her job?"

"Yes," Bella agreed. "And Mom's car is in the shop right now. We've got tractors, but I really can't take her to her work on a tractor. It was the worst time for my car to decide to break down. But we've done everything we could think of and can't get it started again. We'll have to get it towed into town to the shop. And *that* won't be cheap. We'll probably have Mom's back soon, but right now…"

Erin was thinking through the logistics. She could drive out to the Prost farm, take Adrienne wherever she needed to go, and bring Bella into town for her afternoon shift at the bakery, if she still wanted to do that rather than having someone else cover the shift. It would leave Vic alone for the time it took to drive Adrienne to her job, but that was probably in town and would not take long. Erin didn't like to leave just one person manning the bakery, so should she get someone to come in and help, or leave for a short time and leave Vic on her own for that long?

"Of course," she agreed. "I'd be happy to help. Where exactly does Adrienne work? In town?"

"No, at another place out here. It's kind of remote. If I was just trying to get a ride into town, I could probably find someone, but when she needs to go all the way out in the other direction…"

That probably answered the question of whether she should get someone to cover for her while she was gone. It could take a while.

"Okay. How far out is it?"

"Well, it's kind of… do you know where the Fontainebleau Homestead is?"

Erin shook her head. "The Homestead?"

"Yeah. I can give you directions. Or Adrienne can. But it's… like I said, it's remote."

And Bella said that as someone who lived in the country rather than in town herself. When someone on a farm said that a place was remote, it was remote. Erin remembered looking at the map when Fontainebleau's assistant had given her the GPS coordinates for the pie delivery. Fontainebleau liked to make people come to him. To inconvenience them and show them how important he was that he could make them leave the rest of the world behind to see him in his little kingdom.

"Yes, it is. Okay. Give me a few minutes to get the bakery covered, and I'll come out. What time is she supposed to be there?"

"Well, right now, actually, but we're doing our best to hold them off. You can't expect people to never have mechanical difficulties or run into traffic. As long as she gets out there ASAP, I think she'll be okay. She can work late to make up for it. Why don't you just head over here and, while you're on the way, I'll get Charley or someone else to come into Auntie Clem's. Vic will only be alone for a few minutes until someone can get over there."

"Okay. I'll do that. Thanks."

"No, thank you! I'll see you soon. Do you need any directions?"

"No, I remember where it is, and I'm pretty sure I marked it on my phone the last time I was out there."

"Okay, good. Just call me if you have any trouble. I can always come out on the tractor to guide you in."

Erin laughed at the image. "I think I'll be okay."

After letting Vic know what was happening, Erin got into her car and headed toward the Prost farm. She didn't mind doing a favor for Bella, an exemplary employee who never missed a shift and always offered to help Erin with other things. She wanted to get lots of business experience so that she could run her own business one day, and she had a good business mind.

And helping Adrienne to keep her job and take care of her little flock of children was important to Erin too. She had tried to befriend Adrienne in the past and to help her out in whatever ways she could. But Adrienne had remained remote most of the time and, like a number of the indigent families Erin had met in the area, didn't like to be offered "charity" by Erin or anyone else. Erin was glad that Bella had called her.

She got out to the farm as quickly as she could, *possibly* pushing her speed to slightly over the speed limit to cut down the length of time it would take to get there. Adrienne was already late, and she would be worrying over how long Erin took to arrive.

Adrienne was waiting near the gravel pad where the farm vehicles parked when Erin arrived. She stood like a wraith, her arms wrapped around her, unmoving, her clothes hanging off her skinny frame. Bella and the children were playing a game in the green field to keep them busy. When they saw the car arrive and Adrienne began to move toward it, they broke up the game and all ran to her like a little row of ducklings.

Hope grasped her mother's arm, starting to cry. "Mama, stay here with us. Please. Don't go."

"I need to go to work," Adrienne said sternly. She gave Hope a quick hug and a kiss on the top of her head, then nudged her away. "You be a big girl now, an example to the others. No tears. It's good that I have a job to go to. It means better food and new clothes for you." She smoothed the shoulder of the shirt Hope was wearing. "You're growing way too fast! You're just sprouting out of everything."

"Me too!" one of the younger children insisted. "I sprouting too!"

"Yes, you all are," Adrienne agreed, giving hugs and kisses and trying to herd the children back to Bella for her to take care of them. "Now you all be good for Bell and I'll see you tonight."

"You won't stay there tonight?" Hope sniffled.

"I hope not. But if I can't get a ride and Auntie Cindy doesn't have her car back, then I might have to. And if I do, you know the rules and go to bed for Cindy and Bella the way you're supposed to. Be good."

"I don't want you to stay!"

"If I do, it will just be one night. We'll get it sorted out. Now hush! It's time to help take care of the others, not to cause a scene. Be a big girl."

Hope wiped at her eyes and pulled the other children away from their mother, back toward the field where they had been playing. Erin didn't see the baby and suspected she was in the house, either sleeping or being cared for by Cindy.

As much as she hated Cindy's constant criticisms and innuendo, she was touched that Cindy would open up her house to Adrienne and all of the children to make sure they were cared for. She didn't think that Cindy was an actual "auntie," just a friend of the family.

Adrienne waved all of the children off and nodded to Bella. "Thanks so much. I'll let you know what happens."

Erin looked at Bella. "Aren't you coming too? You need to get to town for your shift, unless you're having it covered."

"Yeah, and if Mom's car is done, I can just drive it home from the shop. But you have to go all the way out to the Homestead and back. You can pick me up on your way back to town. I can look after the young'uns until then."

"Okay. I'll see you in an hour or so, then."

Bella nodded. "Thanks. I really appreciate you coming all the way out here to help."

Erin looked at Adrienne. She wanted to pat her on the shoulder, but restrained herself. "I'm happy to help out a friend."

Adrienne gave a stiff nod. She walked around to the passenger side of the car and climbed in.

CHAPTER 16

*A*drienne gave Erin directions for the quickest way to get to the Homestead from where they were. After Erin had driven a few miles, Adrienne sat back, her shoulders relaxing, resting her head back against the headrest.

"Thank you for coming to help," she said. "I didn't know what to do. Bella said that you would help, but... I know you are so busy. And it means you have to pay someone else to take your place at the bakery now. I'm sorry about that."

"No, it's okay. Don't worry about that. I'll just take one of her shifts another day. It won't cost me anything more."

"Except gas. And lost time."

Erin shrugged. "I think that if you can help others, you should," she said simply. "If more people did that... the world would be a kinder, gentler place."

"But most people don't see it that way. They want to know how to get ahead of everybody else. How to get more for themselves. There is so much greed and selfishness and corruption." Adrienne shook her head. "So much, Erin."

"I know," Erin agreed soberly. But there was good in the world too. She'd grown up in places where children had been prey, targeted by predators and downright evil people. And she'd lived in places where the children were ignored; they were just the means to a paycheck at the end of the month.

And she'd lived in places where she had been shown incredible kindness. There were still kind and generous people in the world, and she strove to be one of them.

But she wasn't sure how to tell all of that to Adrienne. Maybe the only way was by example.

"What's it like working at the Homestead?" she asked, rather than trying to put any of this into words. "I guess it's a pretty big place. Not like working in someone's home, not really."

"No, it's not like that. There are living quarters, but the whole place… it's run more like a hotel than a household. Lots of people, very busy all the time, trying to keep Mr. Fontainebleau and his family and favored staff happy. All the time." She nodded. "It's kind of stressful."

"I can imagine. Did you know Mr. Fontainebleau personally? Or just… you know… from a distance."

Adrienne looked out the passenger window, her face turned away from Erin. "Closer than I would like."

"Everybody I've talked to who knows him says he wasn't very likable. That he probably had a lot of enemies."

"I'm sure he did."

"You don't sound like you liked him very much."

"No. I work there. The best thing I can say about him is that he employed me. When a lot of people wouldn't. But that doesn't mean that he was good to me. I stayed as far away from him as I could, once I got to know what he was like."

"I'm glad he gave you a job, at least. That's what you needed right now, right?"

"When I came here, it wasn't just because he was offering a job. He offered residences for single moms with kids. I thought it would be so perfect, to be able to work here where my kids could stay. No commute. No worrying about finding childcare. Hope could look after Sarah while I was working, and I could still take breaks to feed her."

"But that didn't work out?"

"It isn't a good environment for kids. It wasn't at all like I had imagined it would be. I had to find somewhere else for them to stay, but I couldn't give up the job. I need the money. Even if you live as much as you can off the grid, you still need some money, raising kids, living in this world."

"Yeah, I can imagine."

"I don't know if you can."

Erin drove for a while without comment. Maybe she couldn't. Maybe she didn't really have any idea what it was like for a single mom like Adrienne, with all of those kids and no money and no partner. She thought she could understand, having been in desperate situations herself, and having been one of those kids from time to time, struggling to make it with a parent who didn't have the money or the time for children. But she hadn't been a mom. She hadn't experienced it from that perspective, with little people depending on her. Not just looking after herself but a handful of dependents.

"The entrance is up here," Adrienne pointed. "Just past the bend."

Erin slowed down as they made the wide turn. There was a split rail fence, all very old and rustic looking. Like something that might have been there a hundred years ago. There wasn't a guard booth or a security gate. No dogs or surveillance cameras. Erin was surprised. It was quite easy just to drive in. No one stopped them or demanded any identification.

Adrienne directed her to a parking lot to the side. She didn't get out immediately, and Erin waited, wondering if she were having second thoughts about returning to work. Maybe thinking of Hope and her tears, or the baby sleeping in the house at the Prost farm. It must be tough for her to keep going, to keep pushing herself despite what the children wanted. To be the parent who did what was best, even if it made them cry.

Adrienne put her hand on Erin's arm, as if stopping her from driving away. Erin waited for her next move.

"Your husband is the policeman."

"One of the policemen," Erin agreed. "But we're not married."

"Has he said anything to you about me?"

"No." Erin shook her head, wondering what Terry knew about Adrienne. Had she been caught shoplifting? Or just loitering or vagrant, the charges most often used as weapons against the homeless. "I didn't know that he even knew you. Or you knew him."

"Everybody knows who he is." Adrienne flushed a little and pushed a strand of blond hair back from her face. "Officer Handsome, with the dimple." She gave a little laugh.

Erin didn't know anyone else called Terry by that appellation, which she thought Vic had made up.

"He is a handsome man," she agreed.

"He hasn't said anything… about arresting me?"

Erin's brows went up and her mouth dropped open. "Arresting you? No, he hasn't said anything like that. Did he suggest that he might?"

"No. But I'm afraid he will. I'm afraid… they're getting closer."

"Why would he arrest you?"

"Well… here I am," Adrienne said, making a motion with her hands to indicate her place in the world or on the Homestead. "I'm pretty new here. I have access to all of the cleaning solutions and other chemicals. I don't like him. And then… he dies. They're saying it was murder. Poisoning. And who else could it be?"

"Well, literally anyone else who knew him, as I understand it," Erin pointed out. "And anyone who knew or had an idea where the Homestead is. They can just drive right in. So I don't know what would put you any higher on the list than anyone else."

Adrienne didn't explain why she might have more motive than someone else. "I didn't do it. I know that you've helped the police with other crimes. Figured them out before they could. And maybe… you could see that I didn't have anything to do with it. Maybe… spot who it really was. Figure it out before the cops decide to arrest me."

"Oh, I don't think so. This is a really big case. Fontainebleau had a lot of money and power and, from what I understand, there are a lot of suspects. They're not even sure it was murder at this point; they're still testing environmental contaminants and whether

Fontainebleau was poisoned. It could have just… been accidental contamination. Nothing that anyone did to hurt him."

"I don't believe that. Someone killed him. But not me."

"How can you be sure?"

"Monsters like him don't just die. They have to be killed," Adrienne said flatly.

Erin was taken aback by this. "Well… that's not really proof of anything. You think he was killed."

"He was."

"But you don't know who did it?"

"No. It was quick… since I started, I noticed a lot of changes. The way he acted. The way he talked. How he looked. I just knew… something was happening. I wasn't surprised when he died."

"But it wasn't instantaneous," Erin looked for verification. "He'd probably been poisoned over a period of weeks or months. It wasn't just… you know, that night."

Adrienne nodded. "I know. Like I said… quick… but long enough to notice changes."

"And… you don't know who poisoned him?"

"I don't know." Adrienne looked away. "Like you said, he wasn't very well-liked. So… it could be a lot of people. But people that he would allow near his food… I don't know. I don't think many people had access to his food."

"Or drinks," Erin said. "Or toothbrush. I don't know how easy it would be to poison him from something he touched…"

"There are a lot of people in the house. But I think people would notice if someone was somewhere they weren't supposed to be, like in the kitchen or his bathroom."

Erin nodded, but she wasn't sure she agreed. So far, she hadn't seen much indication of there being security at the Homestead. But maybe it was just discreet and well-hidden.

"Do you think I could see inside?"

Adrienne's brows drew down. "Why?"

"I just want to see how things are set up. How easy it would be to get close enough access to poison him."

She wasn't supposed to be investigating the case. She wasn't supposed to have anything to do with it. But it wouldn't hurt just to look around, would it? She could reassure Adrienne that there wasn't any reason to suspect her over anyone else in the household, because they all had access. And she could satisfy her own curiosity about the way Fontainebleau lived. See where her pies had been served.

She should at least see where her pies had been served, shouldn't she?

CHAPTER 17

It didn't really take any work to convince Adrienne to let Erin go along with her and have a look around the house. Maybe if Fontainebleau had still been alive, she would not have dared but, with Fontainebleau being dead, things were falling apart at the house. Adrienne wasn't really sure who her employer was anymore. The company? Fontainebleau's estate? His wife? But she was determined to keep working there and drawing a paycheck for as long as she could. Every penny she could put toward her children's expenses was important.

They entered through a side door, so there wasn't a great hall or a butler or a security desk like at a hotel or corporate building. There were just hallways and rooms for the household staff. People walked briskly like they had places to go and things to do. Erin was initially anxious, trying to put together a script to explain who she was and what she was doing in the house. But after the first few people just looked at her blankly and walked on by, she started to relax. Maybe she didn't need to give any explanation at all. People seemed to accept that if she was in those hallways or with Adrienne, she was supposed to be there. No one challenged her or asked for her identification.

"I do cleaning," Adrienne told Erin briefly by way of explanation. She tied on an apron and clocked in with a swipe card, then fetched a cart with a big garbage can and cleaning supplies on it and started making her rounds.

From the outside, Erin could tell that it was a big building. Lots of rooms. It took up lots of space. But she didn't really appreciate just how large it was until she started walking through the hallways. She felt like they had walked through miles of hallways before Adrienne had even begun her cleaning. Adrienne was not the only one providing maid service. There was no way one person could have kept on top of the cleaning, even working long hours every day of the week. Like a hotel, the Homestead needed a full complement of cleaning staff.

And then there were the other buildings that surrounded the main house. Garages and storage and living space like Adrienne had been given. They probably had to keep their own rooms clean, but the number of people who were needed to run the property was incredible. And all so that one man could show off his wealth. One man and his current wife, the children apparently all grown.

"You must feel like you've run a marathon by the end of the day!"

Adrienne nodded. "I get pretty sore and tired. And then I go home to the children!"

And that would take energy all its own. All of those children to corral and feed and get to bed. A baby to nurse, if Adrienne was still breastfeeding. Kids who all needed her individual attention and to roughhouse and cuddle and get all the physical attention children needed.

"It makes me tired just thinking about it. I think I'm tired when I get home from the bakery! And then I only have myself to prepare dinner for. And Officer Piper, if he's home. And the animals."

Adrienne looked amused as she started dusting the room they had landed in. "How many animals?"

"A very noisy cat. And a rabbit. And Terry's K9, a shepherd cross. And that's quite enough!"

"I guess so," Adrienne agreed. "The kids are always begging for an animal, but I don't need another mouth to feed. And it's hard enough to take care of kids without a roof over your head all the time. Animals…" She shook her head as she ran the duster over every surface. "I couldn't manage that too. Maybe someday, when we have our own place to settle down."

Would she ever actually achieve that? Erin knew how hard it was to scrape together enough money for the first and last month's rent to put down on an apartment. Even harder if you were looking for a house.

Adrienne opened the door to the next room and looked around to make sure it was empty before motioning Erin in.

"This is his private office. Or *was*, I guess. I don't know what they will do with it now." She shook her head. "I don't know how they're going to deal with anything. I guess there are ways to replace the president of a company, or the owner or shareholder. That's all legal stuff. But what do you do with a place like this? It wouldn't be dealt with under the company. Or would it, if the company owns it? Who decides what you do with a room now that he isn't in it anymore? I mean… you can't just install a new husband like you would a new president."

Erin pictured it and giggled. It was a funny thought. Interviewing a new husband, seeing if he would fit with the corporate and family climate. Dictating what he could use and what his duties would be. She followed Adrienne into the room and looked around.

As she had expected, lots of dark wood and heavy furniture. A vaguely nautical theme with ocean pictures on the wall and some complicated-looking measuring or navigating instruments on the desk and shelves. It was neat and tidy and didn't look like the place where he spent long hours working.

"Did he work out of this room a lot? Or just hang out here sometimes? Was he in some corporate office during the week?"

"He was here a lot. Liked to make other people come to him. Didn't even take meetings by video; he would tell people the internet coverage here was too spotty, even though he's got that satellite internet, which is really good. People had to come out here in person to meet with him. He would go to his other sites sometimes, but maybe… once or twice a week. And not all day."

She worked her way around the room, dusting and wiping and readjusting books or picture frames if they were not square. Fontainebleau's papers must be inside the desk drawers out of sight, or on his computer. Businesses needed paper. And it seemed like the bigger the business, the more paper it needed, even though people kept talking about achieving the paperless office one day.

The other door to the office opened, making Erin jump, and an unpleasant-looking woman looked down her long nose at Adrienne. "When you are done in here, I need to see you in the solarium," she told Adrienne. "Since Mr. Fontainebleau is not here this week, we have some other areas that require more attention than his suite."

"Okay," Adrienne said. "I'll be just a couple of minutes."

The woman looked at Erin without blinking or smiling, then withdrew again without asking who she was or what she was doing there. Did she know? Or did she not care? Maybe with everything disrupted and Mr. Fontainebleau dead and gone, people didn't think there was any need for security.

Erin looked at Adrienne. "She's okay," Adrienne said with a shrug. "She looks sour, and she can put on a mean face for the boss when he needs a heavy, but she's pretty nice."

"Oh." Erin nodded. She had judged the woman just by her appearance without even realizing it. "What are the rest of the staff like here? Are they all pretty friendly? I've never worked for someone like this. I've worked as a caregiver for old folks. Families that really couldn't pay much, but needed someone to live in and look after grandma or grandpa. So I never worked anywhere with a staff."

"They're mostly friendly. But if something happened to upset Mr. Fontainebleau or one of the senior staff… then it sort of goes all the way down the line and everybody gets treated like it was their fault, even if it wasn't anything to do with them."

"Did that happen to you a lot?"

"Sometimes."

Maybe that was why Adrienne was afraid of being accused of the murder. Because the blame got passed down and down until it landed on the lowest person. And Adrienne was afraid that was her.

"And did you know the family? What are they like?"

"His wife is hardly ever here. They have some fancy place in New York or some such, and she mostly stays there. The ex-wife is probably here more often than the current one. There are a few kids. I could never keep straight which ones belonged to who, but they're all grown up, so it doesn't really matter. I don't think any of them could stand each other. This place is so big that they don't have to see each other if they decide to stay here for a few days."

That was kind of how Erin had imagined a place like this and a family like Fontainebleau's would work. Maybe she relied too much on TV movies, but she couldn't think of one where the rich and powerful business magnate was a good guy with a close, happy family. But she supposed that movies needed conflict and friction for the story to move forward. There wasn't really material for a movie in a family that got along together and was blissfully happy in their little chalet in the woods.

"Speak of the devil," Adrienne whispered, slowing and putting a hand out to stop Erin. Erin stopped and listened. There was a loud conversation going on somewhere close by. Too far away to hear the words clearly, but there was definitely a woman's strident voice having a conversation with one or two men. "That's Marcelle," Adrienne said. "The ex-wife. Her office is over here. Maybe... I'll dust the anteroom."

Erin was going to protest, but it was too late; Adrienne was already on the move. She opened a dark, heavy door and reached around the wall to flick on the light switch. It was empty and looked like a little reading room in a library. Books lined one wall, and there was a small antique writing desk with a reading lamp. The carpet was deep and luxurious. It was a quiet, peaceful place where Erin wouldn't have minded sitting to read through Clementine's voluminous family history books, working on her planner, or writing a letter to a friend. Except for the fact that there was an argument going on in the next room. There was a door on the opposite wall and, though it wasn't open, it allowed enough sound through to hear most of what was going on. This was where Marcelle's assistant sat while she was there, or the room that visitors were shown into before they were allowed to see Marcelle. Or maybe where an employee sat when he was kicked out of a meeting so that the board could discuss his next year's salary. A room between rooms.

Adrienne slipped into the room and started dusting shelves. Erin didn't feel comfortable going in, but Adrienne pulled her in and shut the door, leaving her cleaning cart in the hall outside. It would have been pretty crowded with the two of them and the cart all jammed in there. Adrienne resumed her dusting. Erin leaned toward the door, eavesdropping on the conversation in the next room. Not intentionally, really; they were pretty loud. She couldn't help but hear them.

"The company is half mine," Marcelle insisted. "And since Clive is dead, that makes it all mine. I want to see the financials and any deals in the works. I want to know what he's been doing and how to get my money out of it. He's been making stupid business decisions lately. Everyone said that he was losing it. Everything he touched turned bad."

"The company is not all yours," a man's voice responded, smooth and oily. "The company is only half yours, just like it has been for decades. Or rather, forty-five percent yours. The rest of the company shares are held by Mr. Fontainebleau's estate until his will has been probated and the shares distributed per his wishes. And he did not leave the shares to you."

"That's ridiculous. I put my family money into the company to rescue it and bring it back from the brink, and Clive always promised me that I would get it back. Who is running the company now? I am the largest shareholder, so I should be running it."

"You do not own a controlling interest," the oily man, who Erin deduced was a lawyer, informed Marcelle. "That is held by the estate. And until it is distributed, I am the executor and trustee, and—"

"You're running the business? You don't know anything about it! You haven't set a foot in a mine or factory in your life!"

"I am not running the day-to-day operations of the company. That is being handled by the surviving management. They know what they are doing. They know all of the ins and outs you and I don't know. And they'll continue to run the company and to select a new president and continue to do what they're doing."

"What about that merger? Clive kept talking about the merger. I don't want it to go ahead. He didn't know what he was doing lately. I know it was a bad deal."

"That is for the current management to figure out. They'll probably put it on hold until they have hired a new CEO. There's no need to rush into anything new. At a time like this, it is important to stop and take a breath—"

"I want to see the financials. Why aren't they on my desk?"

It was a different voice that answered now. "Management is reviewing the current financials. They had some questions and changes to be made, so I can't give them to anyone at this point—"

"I'm the largest shareholder. If I ask for them, you have to give them to me."

"I can give you last year's financials, if you like?"

"I don't want last year's financials. I've *seen* last year's financials. They were pretty bad, but not as bad as what I've been hearing from my inside sources. Are you cooking the books?"

"Mrs. Fontainebleau!" the accountant's voice was higher and more strident. "Are you accusing me of illegal business practices?"

"Somebody is sucking this company dry. And that's *my* money going down the crapper. My family money that I was supposed to get back with interest. It was always supposed to be an investment. I would get it back when it had doubled or tripled in size. Instead, this company is foundering, and it is because of idiots like you!"

CHAPTER 18

"**M**a'am!" the accountant protested, stung.

Adrienne was beside Erin, not moving. They were both engrossed in the discussion going on in the next room.

"Where is my money?" Marcelle demanded. "Are you telling me it's all there, my little nest egg, nicely grown in all of the time you've managed it?"

"I am not in the company management, ma'am. I only do what I am told. Keep the books. The decisions were made by Mr. Fontainebleau and the management of the company…"

"And my money is safe?"

He didn't say anything.

"And my money is all still there?" Marcelle pressed. "Sitting in the bank waiting for me?"

"Of course not. Money doesn't do any good sitting in a bank. Mr. Fontainebleau put it to work. To leverage other acquisitions and operations. New partnerships and joint ventures. He had an outstanding business mind—"

"He *used* to have an outstanding business mind," Marcelle said icily. "That's why I was comfortable leaving the money with him until now. But after what I've been hearing over the last year, I told him I wanted it out. This company is hemorrhaging money, and I want mine out before it goes bankrupt!"

"Nothing can be done right now. Until Mr. Fontainebleau's shares are transferred to their new owners, and a new CEO has been elected, we really can't make any material changes to the way the company is operating—"

"Even though you know how badly it is doing."

There was no answer from either man.

"How bad is it?" Marcelle demanded. "Tell me it isn't as bad as I think."

"I'm sure that management will be able to stabilize—"

Marcelle gave a cry of rage, and there was a crash that made Adrienne and Erin jump.

"I will be coming back here with a court order," Marcelle told the men. "Do you understand that? I will be back, and I'll have an order that you can't touch my money until this is settled. I don't care if that means you have to fire every single employee and close the doors to every mine and factory. You need to cease operations until I get my money."

They heard a door open and then slam shut. There was a short silence.

"Continue as usual," the lawyer's oily voice said eventually. "She will not be able to get any kind of injunction against the company."

"Don't you think that we should at least—"

"No. Continue as usual. Let the management do what they like. As long as you are only taking orders, you don't have anything to worry about."

There was another period of silence.

"And if you *have* been cooking the books," the lawyer said eventually, "now would be an ideal time to disappear."

Adrienne looked at Erin, her eyes big and round. "Aren't you glad you're not her?"

"She must have sunk a lot of money into the company. It's

huge, and she owns forty-five percent? Do you think she's going to lose it all?"

Adrienne shrugged. "What do I know about stuff like that? I just know I'm glad I'm not in her place." Adrienne ran her dust rag over a row of books. "I might not have anything, but at least I'm used to not having anything! For her to lose everything would be a lot worse. Although… she probably doesn't actually mean *everything*."

"Yeah. Probably just that investment. It might hurt because it was her family money, but I doubt she'll lose her house or anything. She's had to have money that she's been living on since she gave Fontainebleau the investment if it happened years ago."

Adrienne worked her way around to the door they had come in, and they went back into the hallway to pick up Adrienne's cleaning cart and continue on the way. Erin was getting confused with all of the hallways and turns.

"Do you ever get lost here?"

"Not anymore. At least, not for long. But in the beginning, it was pretty confusing. It's not so bad if you're just going through the main guest areas; there are pretty obvious signs and routes. But when you're back here, going through the service hallways, you can get turned around."

"And… can anyone use them? I haven't seen much security."

"Well, anyone *could*." Adrienne considered the matter. "But I haven't ever seen anyone but the household staff and service people back here. The family and guests, they stay out there. Why would they want to come through this rabbit's warren?"

"Maybe to hide. To get from one place to another without being seen. Get access to Mr. Fontainebleau's food or drink and then disappear before anyone knew they were here."

"Someone is more likely to see you back here than out there," Adrienne dismissed. "If I was trying to sneak around, I wouldn't use the service corridors. You could run into anyone at any time."

They reached the solarium, which was a large, open hall with floor-to-ceiling windows and lots of lush plants, with a small waterfall and pond. Erin saw fish darting through the water. She looked at the roughly broken rocks that formed the pond and other "natural" features and wondered whether they came out of the mines, and what trace minerals they might contain. Mercury? Lead? Other heavy metals that would be just as effective for poisoning Mr. Fontainebleau? Maybe his poisoner didn't have to worry about any special preparation. Just dip a cup of water out of the pond every day or two.

There were a few other workers there. The woman who had talked to Adrienne initially, asking her to come to the solarium, saw her and approached again. "Great, thank you for coming to help, Adrienne." She looked at Erin and, this time, decided not to ignore her. "And I'm sorry… are you new…?"

Erin started to say, "I'm just visiting," and was trying to figure out how to explain her presence as she snooped around the house, listening in on other peoples' conversations.

"She's my ride," Adrienne said. "My car broke down today and she drove all the way over to drop me off. She just came in to cool down for a few minutes and wanted to see the place." Adrienne made a gesture to indicate the grandeur around her. "She's not staying."

"It is quite the place," said the other woman. She then ignored Erin and proceeded to give Adrienne detailed instructions on the jobs she wanted to be done. Erin drifted away from them as they spoke, enjoying the lush surroundings in the solarium. Although it was humid from the water, the temperature was pleasant. Plenty of air conditioning to keep the glass-walled room from becoming a sauna in the Tennessee sun.

In a few minutes, the woman walked away to deal with her other duties.

"I guess I should show you back to your car," Adrienne said. She looked around. "You'll want to get back to Auntie Clem's. You've got your job and I've got mine."

"Sure." Erin would have demurred and said she could get back to her car on her own, but she was not sure she could do that. She would need someone else to walk her out, unless she went outside and walked around the perimeter until she found it. "Thanks. It was… nice to see what the place looks like."

"It's big, isn't it?" Adrienne shook her head. "Can you believe that it's all for one family? One man? I don't even know what they will do with it now that he's dead. Will anyone stay here? It's out in the middle of nowhere. Maybe the family, one of the kids?" She shrugged at her own question. "They'll probably sell it. I don't think anyone will want to live out here and look after everything."

They took a different door out of the solarium from the one they had entered through. There was what looked like a lecture hall, with a few workmen handling long coils of cable, calling each other as they worked on whatever they were wiring. Erin didn't know if it was for a sound system, network cabling, or something she hadn't even thought of.

"Pull that over here, and we'll—" The man who had just crawled out from under a table stopped talking when he saw Erin and Adrienne walking by. Erin froze.

It was Willie Andrews.

$\mathcal{W}$illie's mouth was open and he looked as stunned to see Erin there as she was to see him. Erin walked toward him.

"What are you doing—"

He tried to wave her away before she could draw any attention to the two of them, but Erin shook her head. Willie had said that he had not been to the homestead. If he considered Fontainebleau to be an enemy, then what was he doing there, working for the guy? Or working for his estate or his company, since Fontainebleau was dead?

"Willie, what are you doing here?" Erin demanded. "What's going on?"

Willie eyed Adrienne as well, shaking his head at Erin again. "Erin, why don't you just go… back to Bald Eagle Falls. I'll talk to you tonight when I'm done. Explain all of this."

But Erin wasn't about to be put off. "I thought you couldn't stand Fontainebleau. So what are you doing here? Why would you be working for the guy?"

"I'm just doing a little subcontracting. It doesn't matter who it's for. Just a job that needs to be done. They pay their bills, so why should I care who it's for?"

"You said that he was a competitor. Why would you be working for a competitor?"

Willie opened his mouth to respond.

"And you said that you'd never been out to the Homestead, and now here you are! Why would you say that?"

"I didn't." Willie looked at Adrienne and opened his mouth, then changed course. "I didn't say that I'd never been here. I said that I'd seen pictures of it."

"You led me to believe you hadn't ever been here." Erin looked back and forth between him and Adrienne. They seemed to know each other, which was just one more confirmation that something was going on that Willie wasn't telling her about. "Are you going to tell me this is the first time you've ever been here?"

Adrienne raised one brow, interested in Willie's response to Erin's question. She wasn't going to let Willie get away with lying to Erin. She owed Erin for having driven her to work, leaving her own work at her own shop to do so. If there was a disagreement between Erin and Willie, Erin figured Adrienne would come down on her side.

"I've been here before," Willie growled. "Yes. Not that it is any of your business or anyone else's."

"Why would you tell me you hadn't been?"

"I didn't."

Erin rolled her eyes. She'd given Terry similar excuses for not having told him about Brandon Quayle. She'd said that she hadn't ever seen him around Bald Eagle Falls, implying that she had never seen him before at all. When she had not only seen him, but knew him way too well. Was Willie doing the same thing with her? Covering up because he and Fontainebleau were connected, not just by both being in mining, not just by a little subcontract cabling job that Willie had taken on, but because they knew each other?

"What was the real relationship between you and Fontainebleau? Did you know each other? I mean really know each other?"

Willie stood there looking at her. The other men he was

working with had stopped what they were doing and were watching and waiting.

"Erin, I'll talk to you about this later. Right now… I have work to do here. You're holding me up."

"Are you setting up a computer network?" Erin looked around at the cables, hoping she was at least close and didn't sound like a complete idiot.

"Just some electrical." He waved off the question as if he couldn't be bothered to go into more details. "Which you already know that I do, since you asked me to help the crew at Mrs. Peach's house. But if I'm going to get it done today, I need to get back to it. So…"

"Fine." Maybe he would tell her more when she was back at home and no one was there to overhear their conversation. But she suspected he didn't intend to tell her anything. At least, nothing that got close to the truth. "I'll talk to you later, then."

Willie nodded. Erin started walking down the hall again, in the direction they had been going when she had spotted him. Adrienne pushed her cart a couple of inches, her eyes on Willie.

"You okay?" Willie asked her.

Adrienne nodded and started again to walk with Erin. They held eye contact for too long.

Not only did Willie have something to do with Fontainebleau that he wasn't talking about, but he knew Adrienne and something to do with her as well. They'd both been around Bald Eagle Falls; there was no reason they couldn't know each other. One of Adrienne's previous camps had been close to one of Willie's mining claims. Maybe they had run into each other there. Maybe he'd told her kids to stay away from the caves or had helped out when one of them got into trouble. He certainly didn't seem confrontational with Adrienne, like they'd been at odds before. Instead, he appeared to be worried about her.

And maybe he should be. Maybe Erin should be too. Adrienne was pretty sure that they were going to accuse her of Mr. Fontainebleau's murder. There was a reason for that. And maybe Willie knew what it was.

Erin and Adrienne walked together without saying anything for a few minutes. Adrienne didn't ask Erin how she knew Willie, and Erin didn't ask Adrienne about how well she knew him and how often he'd been around the house before Fontainebleau's death.

They went through a door, and Erin found herself stepping back out of the building again, to find her yellow bug parked and waiting for her. "Oh! I didn't even know this was the way out." Erin laughed.

"Sometimes what you're looking for is right in front of you."

Erin shook her head. "Yeah. You never know."

"Thanks again for helping me out. I really appreciate it."

"Of course. And… let me know if you need a drive home at the end of the day."

"Oh, I couldn't expect you to come all the way out here again. If Bella doesn't have her car back, I'll stay here overnight. There's a room for me if I need it."

"Still…" Adrienne's place was with her children, not stranded out there on the big property like she was a prisoner there.

"It's fine," Adrienne assured her. "I'll be fine. It will work out okay."

Erin put her hand on Adrienne's arm for a moment. She wasn't to the point where she felt comfortable hugging her, but she wanted some kind of physical contact to show her feelings toward the woman. To show that they were a part of a sisterhood, even if they were living very different lives.

Adrienne pulled away, nodding. "You'd better get going, then. You know the way back out?"

"Just keep taking the bigger roads until I'm out to the highway."

Adrienne nodded. "Pretty much, yeah."

Erin went to the driver's side of the car and let herself in. Adrienne stood by, waiting for her to leave. Erin rolled down the windows while she waited for the vehicle to cool. Another woman similar in age to Adrienne came out the door and saw her standing there.

"Oh, Adrienne! Hi!" She pulled out a cigarette and lit it

quickly. "Just gotta get my nicotine hit while I can. How is everything?"

Adrienne shrugged. "It's been a day. My friend's car broke down this morning so I couldn't get in. Miss Erin there drove me." Adrienne nodded toward her.

"Well, you're lucky!" The other woman gave Erin a breezy wave with the hand that held the cigarette. "They'd dock you if you didn't show up."

"Yeah. I need all the money I can get."

"How are the kids?"

"Fine. Full of energy."

"I wish they were still here. They're so much fun. And Hope? How is she?"

"She'll be fine."

The woman nodded. "Kids are flexible. Isn't that what they say? They bounce back fast."

CHAPTER 20

It felt so good just to sit and cuddle with Terry on the couch and relax with him. It seemed like they had been missing each other all week and this was the first time they'd actually had to sit down together and have a conversation. They needed to relax together for a while before they could talk about anything meaningful, and they hadn't been able to do that, trying to fit hello and goodbye in between all of the shifts.

Erin gave Terry the highlights of the day, going to get Adrienne and taking her to the Homestead.

"And then you brought Bella into town?" Terry asked. "Did her car get fixed so she had a way to get back out to the Prost farm?"

"No, but Cindy's was fixed, so Bella grabbed it and drove it back to the farm. And then, I assume, went out to the Homestead to get Adrienne so that she could be together with her kids."

"It's nice of them to help her."

"Yeah, it is. I'm glad she's got someone to help them out. It would be really hard to have all of those kids and no home and no way to go out and get a job. I don't know if I could face that kind of hardship."

"Well, you face what you have to. You went through rough patches too."

"Yeah… but I never had kids to look after. I can't imagine doing all of that with kids to look after too. And not just one or two kids. I think she's got… five? Six?"

He laughed. "That's a lot of kids, alright. And all of them in the Prost house? That wasn't a very big farmhouse, if I remember correctly. How many bedrooms does it have?"

"I don't remember. Two or three. And they are pretty small. Maybe Cindy and Bella in one room, and Adrienne and Hope and the baby in another, and the rest of the kids in another. Or in the living room on the floor and couch. It's not a mansion like Fontainebleau's place out there."

"That place is really something, isn't it?"

"Wow." Erin sipped her tea and put it back down on the table. "Yeah, it's pretty amazing. I kept forgetting that no, it's not a hotel or convention center. It's actually one person's home. It's huge."

"Did you see the kitchen?"

"No, I didn't get that far. A few offices or meeting rooms, the solarium. And miles and miles of hallways."

"It's at least twice the size of Auntie Clem's. And I don't mean of the kitchen of Auntie Clem's. I mean twice the size of the entire place. It's very large and modern, with lots of ovens and other appliances that I don't even know the names of or what they are for."

"Oh, I wish I'd seen it. I didn't even think to ask."

"Maybe another time. You can volunteer to drive Adrienne out there again. See if she'll take you on a tour of the kitchen. Or maybe they'll ask you to cater the desserts for the funeral, and you can drive out there and take them to the kitchen. Or tell them that you'll bake them on site."

"Oh, wouldn't that be fun." Erin laughed. "I'd love to see it, but I'm not sure I'd want to use someone's kitchen other than my own for a big job like that. I wouldn't know where anything was or the eccentricities of their ovens. I'd screw something up and then I'd be in trouble."

"I'm sure you would do just fine. I've seen you at work."

"Hmm." Erin decided to take the compliment, but she wasn't sure Terry was right. He tended to see her abilities in the best light, and she often felt the need to correct him and point out the realities of the situation—which tended to just make him tense about the whole thing. She needed to take his compliments in the spirit in which they were given. "You don't think that Adrienne did it, though?"

Terry raised his brows at the change in subject. "Did what?"

"Poisoned Fontainebleau. She says that she's afraid she's going to be arrested for it, and she isn't the one who did it."

"Why were you talking to her about that?"

"She brought it up. I didn't. She's afraid. Especially about her kids and what would happen if she was arrested."

"Well, I don't think she needs to be worrying about that yet."

Erin leaned against Terry's shoulder and listened to his breathing. "Yet?"

"She is not in imminent danger of being arrested. We don't even know for sure that he *was* poisoned yet. Or that it was at the hand of a murderer rather than just an accidental environmental exposure."

"So you don't think that it was actually murder?"

"A determination hasn't been made yet. The medical examiner's office has done their preliminary work, but they need all of the lab tests to be interpreted before they can say for sure that it was intentional poisoning."

"Does that mean you think it was or wasn't?"

"It just means we have to wait. And while we're waiting… we have to investigate as if it were murder. We don't want evidence to be missed because of sloppiness or waiting around."

"His ex-wife thinks he was running the company into the ground, and she owns forty-five percent of it. That's a good motive."

Terry looked down at her. "Yes," he agreed, sounding amused. "That's a good motive. But I don't need you investigating over there. You need to stay out of the way and leave that to law enforcement."

"Oh, I am. I just overheard something when I was over there.

And I didn't go over there to investigate," she reminded him, just in case he'd forgotten that part. "I was just helping out a friend."

"And why does she think he was running the company into the ground? He's always been a shrewd businessman."

"She said he's been making all kinds of bad decisions lately. That everything he touches turns into lead instead of gold. Like in that myth."

"The Midas touch."

"Right. Except every time he touched something lately, he made it fail."

"So his behavior has changed lately."

"Yes. She was afraid he was going to bankrupt the company, so she wanted her money out—"

"Don't you think it was probably the mercury that affected his cognitive ability and decision-making?" Terry suggested.

"Oh. Well, yes, that makes perfect sense. It *must* have been the mercury," Erin realized.

"It doesn't exactly make sense for her to poison him, causing him health and cognitive issues if she wanted him to continue to handle her investment properly, does it?"

"Uh… right." Erin had to admit that made sense. It wouldn't be smart of Marcelle to start poisoning her ex-husband while he was still managing her money. If she'd wanted him out of the way, it would make more sense to kill him quickly—being hit by a car, or in an industrial accident—so that her investment didn't lose any value. So maybe she *wasn't* the best suspect in the murder.

But there were still lots of other suspects.

Willie, among others, had said that Fontainebleau was not well-liked and there would be no shortage of suspects.

Willie among them.

CHAPTER 21

Without meaning to, Erin turned her head to look toward the back of the house, even though she couldn't see the backyard or parking pad from where she was sitting in the living room. Terry looked down at her.

"What?"

"Oh, nothing. I was just wondering if Willie is over. With Vic."

"I don't know. Why? What's up with Willie?"

Erin hesitated, not knowing whether she should say anything or not. She didn't want to get Willie in trouble, and she knew that Terry was always quick to suspect him of being involved in any crime he investigated in Bald Eagle Falls.

"Nothing. I just wanted to talk to him. Maybe I'll pop over there."

Terry raised an eyebrow, maybe doubting that she was being completely open and honest with him.

Which was fair, since she wasn't. But she didn't like it when he saw through her.

"He was over at the Homestead today," Erin admitted. "I didn't get a chance to talk to him while he was over there. We were both busy, but I wanted to talk to him tonight."

"What was he doing over at the Homestead?" Terry sat up straighter, scowling. "He said that he hadn't been there."

Erin didn't correct him. Willie hadn't lied, exactly, but he'd certainly misled them. She shrugged. "He was doing some kind of electrical. He didn't say what it was, and I guess it's none of my business exactly what he was doing. Wiring a conference room."

"Well, that's interesting, isn't it? Why don't you see if he is over there? Maybe he would like to come in for a beer."

Erin pushed herself up from the couch. She did want to see if Willie was there and to talk to him, but she didn't want there to be any trouble. "I'll see if he's there, but…"

"Ask him in for a beer. If he doesn't want to come, he won't come."

"I just don't want a big thing. The two of you don't always… see eye to eye."

"It's not an interrogation," Terry assured her. "I'll mind my manners."

Erin still wasn't so sure. But she walked into the kitchen so that she could see out the back window. Willie's truck was on the gravel pad. She texted Vic rather than Willie.

You guys want to come over for a drink?

It was a few minutes before Vic texted back an emoji confirming that they were, in fact, interested. Erin went to the fridge to get out the cold drinks and put on the tea kettle for herself. In a few minutes, she saw Willie and Vic both crossing the backyard. Vic was in first, with a cheery greeting. She grabbed one of the bottles of beer and handed another to Willie.

Willie was slower, bringing up the rear. He looked at Erin and probably read in her face that Terry already knew about his being over at the Homestead. He shook his head, looking resigned. He grabbed another beer and walked into the living room to give it to Terry and find a seat. Soon, they were all sitting around the room, looking as relaxed as possible. Vic was the only one who didn't seem to realize that there was an agenda. She made casual small talk while Terry watched Willie as if waiting for him to make a move.

Vic's chatter eventually tapered off and she looked at Terry and Willie. "What? Am I missing something here?"

Willie took her hand and squeezed it. "Erin and Terry weren't just interested in a drink."

"Well… no. I thought we'd have a visit too. It's a nice day. The temperature is dropping. We should be sitting out back instead of cooped up in here."

"Erin probably wants to follow up on a discussion we had… or didn't have… at the Fontainebleau Homestead this morning."

"What? What discussion?" Vic looked at Willie. "What were you doing over there?"

"I had a small electrical job."

Vic frowned at that, then shrugged. "Okay, then. You had an electrical job. They called Erin to do the catering and you to do some electrical. They're hiring out small locals. That's nice."

"And it wasn't the first time you'd been out there," Erin deduced.

"No. I've been there before," Willie admitted.

Terry took a long drink of his beer. "So you had a prior relationship with Fontainebleau. Even though you told me that you'd never been out there before."

"I didn't say I hadn't been out there."

"You said that you and Fontainebleau were competitors. And that you hadn't been to his place; you'd only seen pictures of it."

"I said I'd seen pictures of it. And I have."

"*And* you've been out there."

"Sure."

"How many times?"

"I haven't kept track. A few times."

"To do wiring jobs."

"I've done various jobs over there."

"I would think they would already have pretty good electrical at a place like that. And that they would already have their own guy. A live-in handyman or a general contractor they called on. A property manager."

"Or maybe they're interested in hiring small local labor. More economical and gives the local economy a bit of a boost."

"You and I both know Fontainebleau couldn't have cared less about helping the little guy in Bald Eagle Falls get ahead."

Willie chuckled. He pointed his beer bottle at Terry to acknowledge this point.

"So why not stop with the games," Terry said, "and talk about this like two adults who get what's going on. Why would you do work for someone you considered a competitor?"

"Just because we were competitors in the mining business, that doesn't mean I couldn't milk money out of him for something else. And why wouldn't I? He'd be just as happy to pick my pocket, so why not?"

"You're a savvy businessman. And you're not known for being particularly tolerant of anyone you feel is interfering with your business. That tells me there's more to it than just helping out with some small jobs that needed to be done at the Homestead."

"You have a pretty smart boyfriend, Erin." Willie brought Erin back in on the conversation, even though she was trying to stay out of it. It might be her fault that Terry knew about Willie's latest business activities, but she didn't want Willie to think that she was against him or informing on him.

She was inclined to agree with Terry. She didn't think Willie was doing work at the Homestead because it was a way to get money out of Fontainebleau, someone trying to take money from him. The little bit of money that he would get for something like that was not enough to be a motivator.

Willie tipped his beer up again and then sighed. "I guess I should have known that there are too many people in and out of that monstrosity for me to stay below the radar. I wasn't expecting Erin to show up there. But it could just as easily have been you." He nodded at Terry. "I knew it wasn't secure."

"It doesn't seem like there's any security over there," Erin said, shaking her head. "I don't understand how someone as rich as Fontainebleau and with that many enemies could live like that. Didn't he know that he was a target?"

"There is a lot of security in just being someplace as remote as the Homestead," Terry said. "That will deter ninety-nine percent of outsiders. And they'll assume that he has a lot of security. Most people won't chance it."

"And there is more than you think," Willie said. "Just because you can't see the security, that doesn't mean it isn't there."

Erin thought about what she had seen and shook her head. "Okay. Maybe there is. I didn't see a single guard, though; they don't check identification. Anyone can just walk in there. Maybe they have some electronic surveillance, but I didn't see any cameras."

"Cameras can be so small now that you won't see them. You don't know what security measures you trip when driving into the property because you don't see anything. But they don't need a guard in a booth at a security gate to get your license plate number and pictures of everyone in the car as soon as you cross the property line. By the time you get to the house, security knows exactly who you are. They don't have any reason to worry about the town baker wandering in with a maid. They're better off focusing on people who might still have evil designs against the Fontainebleaus even though the figurehead has been removed."

"So what were *you* doing there and how do you know anything about their security system?" Terry asked.

"I know the security system because I designed parts of it."

Terry gave him a half-smile. "Then why isn't it secure?"

"Because they weren't looking for a completely secure system. They don't care about something that is airtight. They just wanted something... casual. An early-warning system if some known enemy of the company or Fontainebleau himself arrived intent on committing harm. The thing about a very tight security system is that it keeps the protectee in a cage. And Fontainebleau knew that. He wanted to be free to roam without being the subject of scrutiny. To come and go on his own property as if he were free, the lord of the manor."

Erin looked at the burglar alarm panel at the front door. She appreciated that it helped to keep her safe, especially on nights when Terry might be on shift. But she hated having to disarm and rearm it all the time. She hated the feeling of being forced to live like an animal in a cage, as Willie had suggested. She could understand why someone like Fontainebleau would want to spend his money in a way that kept him safer, yet still free. So that he didn't have to deal with the bars that she did.

"And when you were there today, was it to upgrade the security system? To close up the holes that might have led to Fontainebleau being poisoned?" Terry suggested.

"No. In fact, not." Willie let the silence draw out for some time before going on. "My reason for being there today, aside from the stated purpose of the wiring I was doing, was to remove listening devices that had been previously installed."

CHAPTER 22

*H*e knew that he was stringing them along and had played his cards right. Willie sat there looking pleased with himself, enjoying their stunned expressions.

"Someone was bugging Fontainebleau's house?" Vic demanded.

Willie nodded. His face remained calm and collected, as if it should not have surprised anyone that Fontainebleau had been under surveillance. And maybe they shouldn't have been surprised by it, since they had just finished discussing the fact that the Homestead was not secure, and Fontainebleau had known that. Had made it a conscious choice.

"Who was bugging the house, and how did you find out about it?" Terry asked.

Willie shrugged. "Like I said, I designed some of the security measures."

"So you knew where the weaknesses were. Kept your eyes out for them. Maybe swept the place for bugs once every week or two. Or when you heard that Fontainebleau had died."

Willie shrugged again.

"Or," Erin said slowly, thinking it through, "you're the one who put the bugs there in the first place."

"Erin!" Vic reprimanded, sounding shocked.

Willie chuckled. At the offended expression on Vic's face, it grew into a belly laugh. It was a couple of minutes before he managed to rein in his laughter, taking another swallow of his beer and wiping at the corners of his eyes.

"No need to be offended for my sake, Vicky. Erin hit the nail on the head."

"What?" Vic demanded.

Both she and Terry looked stunned by this.

Willie nodded slowly. "Yes. I'm the one who placed the listening devices initially. So no need to spot the holes in the security system or sweep for bugs to find them. I already knew they were there. And that it was time to pull them down. Since they were not needed anymore."

"You were bugging Fontainebleau," Terry said.

"Yes."

"Why?"

"They were competitors," Erin said. "He wanted to know what Fontainebleau was up to. Industrial espionage."

"Of course," Willie agreed.

"Why would Fontainebleau hire you to work on his security system in the first place if you were competitors?" Erin asked. "Isn't that like asking the wolf to babysit the sheep?"

"I wasn't big enough to be a concern to him. He could take all of my business easily enough. Wipe me out. But I couldn't do the same to him. If we fight over a mining claim, it's my livelihood. But it's just another in a long list for him. Maybe not even a mine that he'll end up working in the next ten years. Or twenty. He just wants it in his back pocket for when he decides to exploit another area. And to have a legal way to keep little guys like me from trespassing on what he sees as his mountain. As far as he's concerned—was concerned—the whole mountain was already his. He was just wiping out some irritating little fleas."

"So he would hire you to do electrical or security work, but didn't care that you were one of those fleas?"

"No."

They all sat in silence for some time, absorbing this.

"What did you find out from bugging him?" Terry asked. "I'm sure there must be things that are relevant to the investigation of his death."

"Not very much," Willie said. "The guy was off his rocker, but I'm sure you'll find that out from other people. He was making business decisions that didn't make any sense. But his managers did what he said because they thought he was a genius. Everything had always worked out before, and they didn't seem to get that things had changed."

"And you must have heard the reactions of some of the people around him to the way he was behaving."

"They tended not to speak up around him, and the locations I had listening devices were the areas where he would tend to be conducting business. So, no, I didn't hear a lot of the doubts or concerns that must have been expressed."

"And you didn't hear anyone plotting his murder?" Vic teased.

"At this point, if he was already making rash decisions, then someone was already poisoning him," Terry said. "Or he was already being poisoned by something in his environment. Anyone planning to kill him once he had already been poisoned was late to the party. They probably didn't have time to put anything in motion."

"They could have," Erin pointed out. "They could have picked a faster-acting poison. Cyanide or belladonna. Something that would kill him right away instead of taking weeks."

Terry shrugged. "Possible, but I think that's unlikely."

"Look at how many different ways they tried to kill Rasputin before they succeeded," Erin pointed out. "I mean, the guy was poisoned multiple times, stabbed, shot, drowned…"

"It happens," Terry admitted. "Especially with longer-acting poisons. People get impatient and decide to shortcut the process."

"I didn't hear anyone plotting to kill him," Willie said, shaking his head. "People upset with him, yes. But no murder plots."

"I would hope that if things reached that point, you would call the police department and let us know what was going on," Terry suggested.

Willie tapped a finger on the side of the beer bottle he was holding. "I can't say what I would have done in different circumstances, since that's not what happened."

"Do you have a suspect?" Erin asked him. "Someone that you think might have done it?"

"I don't know anything about anyone poisoning him."

"But who do you *think* might have done it? Who had motive? Who was really likely to follow through?"

"I don't know."

She studied his face for some sign that he did have a suspect in mind. Willie was good at hiding his thoughts. "What happened to Hope?"

He wasn't *that* good. Willie betrayed surprise at the question. He blinked and looked away from Erin, focused on some distant object that wasn't visible to her.

"What do you mean, what happened to Hope? Who is Hope?"

"Adrienne's little girl. Or her biggest girl, to be more exact."

He shook his head slowly. "I don't know what you might have heard…"

"Adrienne had planned to have all of the kids there with her to start with. That's why she took the job. Because it included a room or a couple of rooms so she could board there with her kids. But something happened that made her decide it wasn't a good place for the kids, so she had to move them to the Prost farm. Where she can't be with them all the time. And Hope has been acting… I don't know. Clingy. Traumatized. And one of the other staff members asked how she was. Talked about how kids are flexible and bounce back. So… what happened to her?"

There was a long silence. Vic's expression was concerned. Willie's and Terry's faces were more carefully masked.

Erin supposed it wasn't any of her business what had happened to Hope or what Willie knew about it. But she felt bad for Adrienne and whatever she was going through. She had enough to deal with without whatever had been going on at Fontainebleau's house. And little Hope deserved to be treated like a person who had been through a trauma, not just written off as a little child who would be fine if no one acknowledged what had happened to her.

"I wasn't there," Willie said eventually. "And I never picked anything up on my bugs about it. That's something you'll have to take up with Adrienne."

"But you know," Terry said, "or you've got a pretty good idea."

"I don't have any evidence. I'm not a witness. I can only tell you that there have been rumors and whispers. And I'm not the kind of person a young woman would confide in. Someone who knows her better will need to get the story out of her," he told Erin, meeting her eyes. "Or someone with some expertise, who she would trust." He looked at Terry. "I'm not the type that inspires confidences."

"She has no reason to trust me," Terry said, shaking his head. "Her type rarely trusts officials for anything. She lives outside the law; she doesn't rely on it."

"And she thinks you're going to arrest her," Erin said.

He nodded and didn't say whether she was on his list or not. Maybe when he'd gathered enough evidence…

"I'll try to talk to her another time," Erin said finally. "See if I can get anything from her, help her out at all. But she's still pretty wary of me too. Maybe Adele can talk to her. Or Bella."

"I'm sure they probably already have," Vic contributed.

But would either of them urge Adrienne to go to the authorities? Or to seek professional help for her little girl? Erin thought there was a good possibility that Bella would. It was good that she and her mother were helping Adrienne out. Hopefully, they had a good enough relationship that Bella would be able to help them in some way.

Willie shifted in his seat, stretching his muscles and arching his back. He massaged his shoulders. "Must be a weather system coming in," he groaned. "I don't think this is just from a wiring job. I don't usually stiffen up this much from something like that. Plenty of stretching and pulling, but no heavy lifting. It doesn't usually bother me."

"I think they were predicting rain," Vic agreed. "Hey Erin, this is the time to break out your glass and see if it says what kind of weather to expect."

"My glass?" Erin repeated.

"Your barometer. It should be showing a change in pressure."

"Oh, that!"

"Your barometer?" Willie asked. "When did you get a barometer?"

Erin didn't even have an outdoor thermometer to tell her the temperature outside, so she could understand Willie being surprised that she had suddenly acquired a barometer.

"It's not actually mine," she said. "It was a mistake. I'm trying to figure out who it belongs to."

"It sounds like there's a story there," Terry shook his head. "You accidentally got someone else's barometer?"

"Well, yes!" Erin laughed. "When I got the waffle iron for the bakery, you know, the new one that I've been waiting for, then it came in three boxes. Only, two of them were the waffle iron parts and manual, and one was not. It was… a barometer. We don't know how the mix-up happened. Someone must have packed the boxes wrong."

"Someone sent you a barometer."

"Yes… or no. I don't think that someone sent it to me. I think that was a mistake. They packed the deliveries wrong. The barometer was obviously to go to someone else, because it doesn't have anything to do with waffle making. But there was no packing slip or waybill, so I'm having a hard time figuring out who it was supposed to have gone to. And I'm not sure if calling the company will do any good. Some fulfillment company picked the wrong item or combined two orders. Whoever was supposed to get the barometer will probably have to order a new one."

"So are you going to keep it?" Vic asked.

"I don't know. I guess I'll call the company if I can't figure something out. Find out if they can trace who it was supposed to go to."

"You brought it home, right? We should see if it works."

"I shouldn't use it if it isn't mine…"

"You're not playing with it. You're just checking to see if it shows a pressure drop. The pressure is going to go up and down without you doing anything. You don't even have to touch it to see if the pointers are pointing in different directions than before. You can just open the box and have a peek."

Erin could see that Vic wasn't going to give up on it. For some reason, she was eager to look at the barometric pressure to see how it had changed. Was that what Willie could feel in his joints? Or had something else affected them?

She rolled her eyes. "Fine. I'll go get it and we can check, but we're not playing with it."

"There's nothing to play with. We're just going to look at the dials."

Erin went to her room, where she had stowed the box

containing the barometer with some other boxes she had to deal with. Parts being returned. Some genealogical research that Naomi had thought Erin would find interesting if she could connect it up with Clementine's research. But Erin hadn't gotten around to searching for that part of the family yet. One day she would do it. Maybe she would have some time tomorrow, if the day stayed quiet.

She returned to the living room and reached to hand the box to Vic. Terry motioned for her to stop.

"Hold on. You got this delivery when?"

"Yesterday."

"And it didn't have any markings on it? No delivery address?"

"It had my address on it," Erin said, shaking her head. "And my name."

"And the name of the waffle iron company."

"No. Not the name of The Kitchen Crew. There wasn't any sender identification on it that I could see. That's why I don't know exactly how to handle it. If it was from the same company, then it should have their label and return address on it."

"So maybe it's another delivery from your secret admirer.'"

Erin had still been reaching to hand it to Vic, but now she pulled back. "Really? Why would my secret admirer send me a barometer?"

"Why did he send you newspaper clippings? We're still trying to figure out what's going on in his mind. He hasn't made a whole lot of sense up until now."

"Let me see," Vic begged, even more interested in looking at the barometer now that there was some question about where it had originated.

Erin cleared a space on the coffee table and put the box down. She opened the flaps of the box so that they could see inside. They all gazed at the instrument, brass and glass and dark wood, like it might explain itself. It looked exactly as it had the last time Erin had looked at it. How could it have changed?

But now, it gave Erin a knot in her stomach to look at it. It had been interesting before but not portentous. Now she wasn't sure what it meant, but she didn't think she would be able to look at it the same way again.

"It didn't change," Vic observed with disappointment. "It's still pointing at Fair. And the other pointers haven't changed either, as far as I can tell."

"It's just something interesting to put on your wall," Terry said. "There are a lot of pieces of junk like that. Just an executive toy. Something to attract comments. 'Oh, my grandfather used to have something like that.' You know how people are."

Erin nodded. She should be disappointed, but she wasn't. It wasn't hers anyway. She'd known that from the start.

"Like Fontainebleau had," Willie said.

"What?" Erin looked at him, not understanding.

Willie pointed to the barometer. "Fontainebleau had one in his office. You saw his place. Lots of nautical-themed nonsense. Not like he was ever on a ship or would need a barometer. Or a sextant or anything else he had in his office."

Erin tried to envision his office. There had been a number of nautical-themed items, as Willie said. But she couldn't remember a barometer. And she thought she would have noticed one, after having received one in a delivery the day before. It would have jumped right out at her. She shook her head. "I don't remember seeing one. Where was it in the room?"

It wasn't like she had searched his office. It could have been on a wall that was out of sight from the door she'd been standing in.

"What if this *is* the one in Fontainebleau's office?" Terry asked. "I remember seeing one there too. One that was... pretty similar to this one."

"But how would the restaurant supply company have ended up with it?" Erin asked, shaking her head. That didn't make any sense at all. From Fontainebleau's office to the restaurant supply company, then mispackaged and sent to Erin.

"Why would the restaurant company send you a barometer?" Terry asked, pointing out the illogic. "You just think it was from them because you got it at the same time as the waffle iron packages. Right?"

"No, it was one of three boxes. I had to sign for all three from the courier company."

"That doesn't mean they were all one delivery. Just that the total number of boxes was three. If they weren't labeled the same way, they didn't all come from the same sender. And where would it have come from? Who has been sending you strange gifts by courier lately?"

"My secret admirer."

He nodded his agreement.

"Really? You think that my secret admirer sent me a barometer?"

"Right."

"Mr. Fontainebleau's barometer?"

"I don't know. But he sent you the clippings about Fontainebleau, didn't he?"

"Well, yes. At least, we think that everything came from him. It's always possible that... they came from two different sources."

"What all did you get?" Willie asked, not having heard the details before this. Or maybe they just hadn't been of any interest before. Now that they were potentially connected to Fontainebleau's death, it was a different matter.

"Um, a small bouquet of flowers. With a note saying that I was sweet. And then..." Erin's face heated. "Lingerie. No note. Then I got an envelope in the mail here. Not at Auntie Clem's. And it was articles about Mr. Fontainebleau when he was younger. Like, real newspapers from decades ago."

"And you don't know where they came from?"

"I thought someone might have taken them from the library or historical society, but they said no, nothing was missing from their collections."

"Then maybe it came from Fontainebleau's house. Just like the barometer."

"Are you saying that it came from someone else? Not the secret admirer?"

Willie shrugged. "It's possible, isn't it?"

"I... guess so."

"The first two deliveries are personal, romantic type gifts. The other two are directly tied to Fontainebleau and are not personal or romantic in any way."

Erin thought that the barometer might be argued to be somewhat personal. Maybe significant of travel or a romantic getaway. But she let it pass. Willie had a good point.

Terry was nodding slowly. "It's possible. But it would be awfully coincidental to suddenly have two separate people sending her anonymous deliveries at the same time. Unconnected? There must be some kind of connection. I mean, you haven't gotten any other deliveries like that in the time that you've lived in Bald Eagle Falls, have you?"

"No. Nothing else."

"I'll need to take the barometer. We'll want to dust it for fingerprints. See if there is any sign that it came from Fontainebleau's office. His assistant or someone at the Homestead should be able to tell us if it was his. Or if his is missing."

"It could be his assistant. She's the one who reached out to you about catering the party, isn't she?" Vic asked.

"Yes." Erin's head was whirling. "I really don't understand how it is all connected."

"You've become known as an amateur detective. Maybe she expects you to put all the clues together to solve Fontainebleau's murder. Maybe... the romantic presents mean that it's something to do with his wife or a romantic partner. And the clippings, obviously, are connected and might have something in there to lead you to the killer or his motive. And then the barometer is meant to..." Vic shook her head, trying to find something that fit. "Tell you they're fair. I don't know. I don't know what the barometer means. It's a captain. It's someone who travels. It's a fair-weather friend. The barometer doesn't work, so maybe that means..."

"The barometer doesn't work," Willie said suddenly.

Erin nodded. "Right...?"

"Do you have any idea how an old barometer operates?"

Erin shook her head. "No."

"Like an old thermometer... some of them use mercury."

CHAPTER 24

They all considered this, staring down at the barometer.

"There wouldn't be enough mercury in there to kill a person, would there?" Erin asked the obvious. "And you wouldn't be able to just put straight mercury in someone's food. You'd have to… do something with it, wouldn't you?"

Terry nodded slowly. "I would think you would notice little silver balls of liquid rolling around in your food. I don't know if eating elemental mercury would have the same effect as methyl mercury in your food. I assume you'd want to process it somehow if you were going to feed it to someone. But… if you have elemental mercury to start with, I imagine you could find out on the internet how to process it into something you could sprinkle into someone's food without it being detected. And there are enough people in his company with knowledge of chemistry who probably wouldn't need to look it up."

"Who would even know that there could be mercury in a barometer? I didn't know that. I didn't even know what a barometer was until this thing showed up."

"He had it in his office, if this is the same one," Willie pointed out. "People ask about it as a part of small talk. Or he brags that his great-grandfather was a pirate and this was his barometer. Who knows. But anyone who visited his office would probably learn what it was and could look up how it worked."

"Nobody is saying this *was* the murder weapon," Terry added. "It may have stopped working years ago. It may or may not have mercury in it or ever have had. The police lab will have to check. But maybe it was supposed to make you *think* about mercury being used to poison Fontainebleau. That whoever sent it to you knows something about how he was killed."

"So now my secret admirer is the killer?" Erin asked. "Is that what you think?"

"I think that someone wants you to know what is going on. Or to get involved."

"Or they want to make you look guilty," Vic said, pointing to the barometer. "Put the weapon into your hands."

And Erin had blithely played into his hands, taking the barometer home with her. Putting it under her bed. What if she hadn't said anything about it and Terry had found it there? Would he have suspected her? Would he have known that it had come from Fontainebleau's office?

"Did you see it there?" Erin asked him. "At the Homestead when you went up after Mr. Fontainebleau died? Was it in his office then?"

Terry nodded. "I told you I saw it there."

"Then you know I didn't have anything to do with it. I hadn't ever been to the Homestead before today. I didn't… I don't know, bring it home with me after visiting him a few months ago, get the mercury out of it, mix it with something that I could put in his food, and then give it to him a little at a time."

Terry blinked at her. "I never would have thought that you did. That's ridiculous."

"Yeah, it is," Erin agreed, the muscles in her stomach relaxing a little. "So if he's trying to make me look like a suspect, he failed."

"I don't think that was ever his intention," Terry said, looking at Vic and shaking his head.

Vic shrugged. "We're just brainstorming here. Coming up with ideas. No one knows what's actually going on in this weirdo's mind."

"No." Terry nodded. "I think that we can all agree on that. Whoever this guy is… none of us really knows what it is that he has in mind. What he wants Erin to do, or if he is taunting us, or thinks he's being clever. We don't know if he had anything to do with Fontainebleau's death, or if he knows who did, or is just a prankster. We don't know if this is the barometer that came from Fontainebleau's office. Just that it looks like it. And a lot of people could know that."

"Was it in the pictures?" Erin asked.

"What pictures?"

"The newspaper clippings. There were pictures of Fontainebleau at the Homestead. Was the barometer in any of those?" Erin took out her phone and tapped through to her photos.

Terry raised an eyebrow. "You took pictures of them?" He had, of course, taken them as evidence in the investigation. But Erin had taken photos of them first. They had been sent to her. Why shouldn't she have copies?

"I wanted to be able to look at them later. Read through them. See if there was any clue about who it was that did this. Who sent them, or who killed Mr. Fontainebleau. I haven't had a chance to read through them yet." Or, more accurately, she couldn't bring herself to read through all of that crap about the up-and-coming businessman and his family history and where everyone thought he was going. The densely written newsprint was daunting, especially to read through on her phone, and she hadn't been able to make herself go through it when she'd had the chance.

She flicked through the articles and zoomed in on a couple of photos taken in an office in the Homestead. She couldn't tell whether it was the same office or not, but there *was* a barometer on the wall.

～

Of course, Terry took the barometer into evidence to be examined and disassembled at the police lab in the city, and Erin had to make a lengthy report on how it had come into her possession. She felt a little silly that she had thought that it had been part of the waffle maker delivery. It had not been packaged or labeled the same way. And, of course, there was no packing slip because it wasn't some mass-produced decoration ordered through a fulfillment company. She had made assumptions at the time because she had been excited about the arrival of the waffle maker and getting it assembled. She hadn't been thinking about the secret admirer or the murder.

She was pretty sure by now that it *was* a murder. There was no way that it had just been accidental exposure to mercury, even if there was mercury contamination at some of Fontainebleau's work sites. Maybe that was why someone had decided that mercury would be an appropriate murder weapon. Maybe they thought that because of the contamination, it would be seen as accidental causes rather than murder. Or perhaps they thought that was what Fontainebleau deserved after exposing his workers to a dangerous toxin.

Erin had a restless night, her brain constantly going over what Willie had said. How much of what he said was the truth? And how much of the truth was he sharing? He knew more than he was prepared to share. It had been difficult to even get the little bit they had. Did he know who had plotted to murder Fontainebleau? Had he heard something on one of his bugs or through other people working at the Homestead? It was a big place; a person could work there all day and never even see Fontainebleau. Just because Willie had been there and planted listening devices, that didn't mean he knew anything more than anyone else.

And Adrienne. What exactly had she and her children been through while they had been there? Surely Adrienne wouldn't still be working there if it had been anything too bad. She knew that there were other jobs, and that she was at least taken care of if she didn't find something right away. Bella and Cindy would help her with the children and provide shelter. Erin could help with food. It wouldn't be ideal, but if things were too bad at the Homestead, she could choose to leave.

Erin tossed and turned. She tried to stay still so that she didn't keep Terry up. He needed his sleep if he was to be any help in cracking the case. But she was so restless, and her brain so busy with all of the ideas she had gathered the day before, that it was late into the night before she managed to get to sleep.

CHAPTER 25

The next day was Sunday, which was good, because Erin could have one of her employees manage ladies' tea and she could rest and relax after her long night. Maybe even get in a nap during the day if she needed it.

But, of course, she knew it was hopeless. She wouldn't have a nap during the day. And if she did, she would end up with a headache, and she wouldn't be able to fall asleep at bedtime because she'd slept during the day. It was better to just push through the day and be sure to be good and tired when bedtime rolled around.

So when she started to get drowsy in the afternoon, she decided it was time to get out and go for a walk. Getting out of the house would wake her up and ensure she didn't give in and have a nap.

It was a lovely day out. It was nice to have a break in the weather where it wasn't quite so hot. A little cloudy, but it didn't look like it was actually going to rain. She should be safe going out. She would go on a walk through her woods. Maybe see Adele and make sure that everything was going okay with her. It had been a long time since they'd had a good chat. Then she could decide whether to go any farther or return home. Maybe make some nice iced tea and relax with Vic if she were around, or work on her plan for the next week if Vic and Willie had gone to the city.

Then Terry should be back for an early supper and a relaxing, sleep-inducing evening.

She had it all planned out.

The woods were warm but shaded, dappled light filtering through the treetops to the ground below the canopy. Birds sang, squirrels ran across branches, and there was no one else around. She had the whole woods to herself.

She didn't run across Adele as she had expected to. She even stopped at the little summer cottage and knocked on the door to see if Adele was home, but there was no answer. Erin wasn't as bold as Vic would have been, so she didn't try the handle and poke her head in to call a yoo-hoo to Adele before entering. If Adele didn't answer the door, Erin didn't think going further was necessary.

Maybe Adele had caught a ride into the city and was doing some shopping or other errands. She didn't spend much time or money on food or worldly goods, but even someone like her needed to buy something now and then. A new cast iron frying pan or big soup pot.

Erin chose a trail she didn't normally use, because she knew it eventually ran out on a paved sidewalk, and she usually didn't want to walk through the neighborhood on the street when she had the option of walking in the woods. It was just so much more relaxing.

She saw a shape through the trees and squinted, trying to make out the figure.

"Adele? Is that you?"

The figure paused and turned toward her. Erin saw immediately that it wasn't her gamekeeper, but a man. She opened her mouth to apologize and then slink off in the other direction in embarrassment, when she thought she recognized the man.

"Uh, hi." She took a few steps along the path to get a better look. "I don't think I've seen you around here before."

He looked like he would flee, but then his body relaxed and he gave Erin a shy, slow smile. "No, I haven't been around here before. I've driven by and always thought it looked like a fine place to explore, so…"

As Erin got closer to the man, she knew it was him. "This is actually private property," she told him. He should have seen the Private Property sign at some point, no matter which direction he came from. The perimeter was well-marked so that Adele could more easily get trespassers to leave or call the police if they refused.

"Oh. Well, I'm sure the owner probably doesn't mind people taking a walk through as long as they don't mess anything up. There are a lot of pathways, so people use it often enough."

"It's *my* private property. A lot of the pathways are actually game trails. I can't exactly keep the deer and other animals from trespassing."

"Oh." He looked at her, now that they were close enough to see each other's features. "You're Erin Price."

"Yes. And I think… you delivered a package to me last week."

"Well, that's what I do," he admitted, smiling.

Erin gazed up into his friendly brown eyes. "It was strange, though; there was no address on the package."

"Sometimes there isn't."

"How can you deliver something if it doesn't have an address on it?"

"When they call it in, they give the address. If it isn't on the package when I get there, that doesn't really matter."

"How do you keep them straight? Most courier companies would put their own label on it."

"Nah. Never bothered to get one of those mobile label-makers. Not enough business here to worry about it. I just put a sticky note on it. Put the order number on it. Then there's no danger of mixing them up. Everything is marked."

"But what if the sticky notes fell off?"

He shrugged and shook his head, bemused. "I haven't ever had any trouble with my system. Don't see why it should matter to you."

"Well, I'm not sure that the package I received was actually meant for me. There was no packing slip or waybill, and it wasn't anything I was expecting…"

"You think I gave you the wrong package?"

"Well… maybe. There was no note, and… no one I know

would send me…" Erin shrugged, her face burning. Even though the deliveryman had not seen what was inside the package, she was still embarrassed. It was clear from the packaging that it was a gift. And it was small enough that he could guess at the contents. It hadn't been heavy enough for a book or a box of chocolates. There were other possibilities, but she was afraid he had probably guessed what the package was without being told.

"If you didn't think it was for you, then why didn't you call to let me know there had been a mix-up?"

"Call where? I don't know your name or your company name. I'd never seen you before. There's no waybill. So how, exactly, am I supposed to get ahold of you to find out where it came from?"

He nodded slowly. "Well, that is a puzzler," he admitted.

"So I'm talking to you now. Who was it that sent me that package?"

"I don't recall."

"But you have records, right? You can look it up and find out."

"I don't keep anything for short-term deliveries. If it had come all the way across the country, that would be different…"

"But it was local, and you don't keep records for local deliveries?" That didn't sound right to Erin. "What about taxes? Don't you have to prove to them what work you have done? Where your income came from?"

"I keep what I need to."

"But you have no idea who sent me that package."

"No, sorry. A friend or family member. It shouldn't be hard to figure out."

"It didn't come from a friend or family member. That's just the problem. It came from a…" Erin paused, trying to decide on the right word. She didn't want to scare this guy off if he did remember who had sent the package or if he was the one who had been sending her things himself. "A secret admirer. I'd really like to know who it is and to talk to him."

"Oh, that sounds exciting. How interesting." The man looked at a watch on his wrist. "I have to get going. There's somewhere I'm supposed to be. It was nice chatting with you, Erin Price. Enjoy your day."

"No, wait." Erin stepped forward and tried to block his way. "I need to know who is sending me things. If it is you, then I need to talk to you about… what you sent and what it means. Because I'm not getting it all. The messages that I'm supposed to get from each thing."

He held her gaze for an instant, then shook his head and raised his hand in farewell. "Sorry, I can't help you."

"What's your name?"

He turned and walked away. Erin followed after him a few steps, but then stopped. What was she going to do? Lay hold on him and pull him back? Even if she had the physical ability to control him, he had already said that he didn't know who the sender of the packages had been. He wouldn't change his tune just because she said she really *really* wanted to know. Even if it was related to the Fontainebleau murder, she didn't see him having anything else to say to her about it.

CHAPTER 26

Erin called Terry to tell him about the man in the woods. He drove over and tried to spot him but was unsuccessful. She called Adele and left a message about him, hoping that he might come back to walk in the woods again. But she suspected that he hadn't been there just to take in the wilderness, but had been looking for her. And even if he had been there to enjoy nature, she had told him that it was private property and he was trespassing, so what were the chances he would return?

Monday, she was back on shift at Auntie Clem's as usual. The gossip surrounding Fontainebleau's murder seemed to have quieted down without any new information having come out. Erin was mostly thinking of her brand-new waffle iron and what she would do with it first. Probably a couple of batches of her pumpkin spice waffles, something people could keep in their freezers and pop in the toaster in the morning. Like the mass-produced commercial stuff, only better. Suitable for sweet or savory toppings. And the family restaurant might want some of them too, so they had another offering for those who came to the restaurant hoping for a gluten-free meal.

And then she could branch out and start making blueberry

waffles. And chocolate chip. And whatever else she thought people might enjoy. She was really looking forward to putting the new waffle iron to good use.

"Your phone, Erin," Vic pointed out.

Erin noticed the vibrating in her apron pocket. "Oh, thanks. I'll get it when I take a break. They can leave a message."

But it kept ringing and ringing after it should have gone to voicemail. Eventually, Erin ducked into the kitchen to see who it was and why they either kept calling her back or the phone had decided not to go to voicemail. Whoever it was, they were being very persistent.

Adrienne.

Erin looked at the name on the face of the phone and tried to decide what to do. She had already decided to call back, of course, but she was in a quandary. She always told her employees to deal with personal calls later, when they weren't on shift. And whatever Adrienne wanted Erin for was undoubtedly personal. She wasn't calling with a catering order or special birthday cake request.

But Erin had truly meant it when she told Adrienne to call her if she ever needed anything. It wasn't just an empty, trite offer for Adrienne to get in touch with her.

And Adrienne had taken her up on it.

She owed it to Adrienne and the children to see what was going on and to help if something was wrong.

Sighing, Erin swiped to call Adrienne back and brought the phone up to her ear. "Adrienne? Is something wrong?"

"I need to get back to the farm. I need to see what's going on. Bella can't come out to get me because she's looking after the kids. And they've only got one operating vehicle right now. It isn't big enough for everyone."

"Okay. Okay, well, what's going on?" Erin asked, hoping for more information. It sounded like Adrienne was already at the Homestead, and she usually would work there until late afternoon or evening, so she shouldn't need a ride until the end of the day.

"Our camp. Someone was there and messed things up. I have to see how bad it is and what's salvageable. All of our stuff is there! Who would go all the way out to the Prost farm to mess with my stuff?"

"Your camp?" Erin repeated.

"My tent and the whole set-up. We moved out to the Prost farm so I could be closer to the kids, and Bella and Cindy could help out when I wasn't there. My camp. My house."

Understanding washed through Erin. She had seen Adrienne's camp a couple of times before. Once when it was set up in Erin's woods when they had been squatting on her property without her knowledge. A big army-surplus tent and another canopy with her kitchen things under it. Coolers for food and various cookery implements and pots. A smaller tent that was probably for the older children. And there were probably other necessities out of sight. An outdoor shower and a latrine. Everything the family needed to survive in the wild, as independent from other people as they could be.

Erin had assumed that Bella and Cindy were putting them up in the house, but it sounded like they had instead allowed Adrienne to set up her usual camp on their property, where she could be independent, at least while she was there to look after the children.

"Okay. Um, when do you need me? When do you want to go back—"

"Now. I need to go now. I need to see how bad it is."

Erin looked toward the front of the bakery. She would need to arrange for someone else to come in and help Vic. Erin didn't like to leave any of the employees on their own. It was safer if they worked in pairs, and a lot easier to keep track of additional baking in the ovens and make sure that nothing burned while managing the customers in the front.

"Okay. I'll be out as soon as I can. It will take me a little while to get there."

"I know." Adrienne let out an audible sigh. "Thank you. I didn't know who else to call. I didn't know what else to do."

"I'll be there as soon as I can."

"Thank you."

~

Erin puzzled over who could have a grudge against Adrienne and be so angry that they would go to all of the effort of driving out to the Prost farm to wreck what little Adrienne had. It wasn't like she was taking anything away from anyone.

She crossed the property line onto the Homestead and remembered Willie talking about her license plate and picture being logged as she did so. She looked around, but couldn't see any sign of surveillance cameras. Wherever they were, they were well hidden.

When she reached the parking lot she had previously used to drop Adrienne off, she pulled out her phone to let Adrienne know that she had arrived, but didn't need to. Adrienne opened the door and exited the building, making a beeline for Erin's car.

"Thank you so much," she said breathlessly as she climbed in. "I don't know what I would have done if you hadn't come. I don't know who else I could have called."

"I'm glad I could help," Erin told her. "I'm sorry that it had to be under these circumstances, though. I hope… that everything is okay."

"It's everything I have," Adrienne said. "I can't believe that anyone would want to destroy my life like that. How screwed up is that?"

Erin shook her head. She had found, when in dire circumstances herself, that people didn't really see the homeless and indigent as people. People acted as though they were animals, another species. They wouldn't treat someone in their own social strata that way. But someone who was homeless? Who had no friends and no resources? Someone who wouldn't go to the police with her problems? That was different.

She followed the road back out to the highway and toward the Prost property. Adrienne was texting on her phone. Probably telling Bella that they were on their way. That she would be home in just a few more minutes.

It seemed to take twice as long as it should to get to the Prost farm. Erin knew it was just because she was in a hurry, and kept looking at her speedometer, thinking that she couldn't be going fast enough. But she was over the speed limit, not under it.

133

CHAPTER 27

Finally, they reached the familiar farm. By the time she stopped on the gravel parking pad, the children were all running toward their mother, Bella trying to keep up behind them with the baby in her arms.

"Mama, you have to see," one of the smaller girls insisted. "Somebody wrecked everything! Our camp! Why would they do that?"

"I don't know, honey." Adrienne gave them all hugs and kisses, trying to comfort them. Her expression was one of dread. How could she face losing everything she had tried so hard to build? She looked at Bella and took a deep breath.

Erin expected her to ask how bad it was, but she apparently couldn't bring herself to do so. She just climbed out of the car and headed toward the dense woods. Erin wasn't sure whether she should follow but, eventually, she did. It wouldn't make sense for her to sit in her car waiting to be told how bad it was. Or to turn around and return to Auntie Clem's without waiting to hear the news.

She had to move quickly to keep up. The children were running, Adrienne close behind them.

Eventually, they got to the clearing where their camp had been set up. The tents were flattened. Clothing and cooking implements were scattered around. The coolers that had held their food had been kicked open and dumped—maybe trampled. Adrienne looked around, her face stricken. She went to the main tent and lifted it, examining it to see how bad the damage was. A couple of the children were crying, snot running down their faces. Bella jiggled the baby and didn't say anything, waiting for a report on the disaster. Adrienne looked around and then inside the tent.

"I don't think any of the poles have been broken, and the canvas is intact," she said, her voice devoid of emotion. "It just needs to be set up again." She dropped it to the ground. She looked around at the other items that had been scattered. "It's a mess. But I don't think anything has been destroyed. Some of the food. But most of our stuff is either in cans or in the house in the fridge."

"So… it isn't so bad?" Bella asked tentatively.

"No." Adrienne sat on the ground and looked at the chaos around her. "I think… everything is actually okay. It will take some work to whip it into shape, but the kids can help. They know what to do."

Hope, rubbing red eyes, perked up at this. "We can help, Mama."

"Yes." Adrienne rubbed the head of one of the children closest to her. "You guys are good workers and you know how to set up camp. You can help."

She produced a crumpled tissue from her pocket and wiped noses. "Enough tears. That's not how we get things done."

"Samuel Andrew," Hope said with authority, "you get the food and put it back in the coolers. If it is still good. If it is mashed but still okay, put it in a pile on the picnic table. We will make a casserole. Jeffey and Samantha, you get all the clothes and sort whose they are. I'll help fold later. Mama and me will get the tents back up." She looked at her mother for approval.

Adrienne nodded. "That's my big girl."

"Wow, you're a really good organizer," Erin told Hope sincerely. "What can I help with? I don't want just to stand around and watch."

Hope considered. "You're the baker, so you can help Samuel Andrew with the food."

Erin nodded. She picked up one of the overturned coolers and snapped the lid back onto the box where the hinge had popped. One of the young boys wandered over and picked up another cooler.

"You need to tell me what to do," Erin told him. "Do certain things go in each cooler?"

He considered her, sucking on his finger, and she didn't think he was going to say anything at first. "Fruits and veg'tables go there," he told her finally, indicating the cooler she had readied. "Carrots and potatoes. Most fruit you have to eat the first day. The cans don't go in a cooler. They go over there." He indicated a pile of striped canvas. "The pantry. When Mama puts it back up."

"Okay." Erin went to work, picking up what food was salvageable and putting it either in the coolers or on the picnic table, wondering what kind of casserole they would make with the motley assortment of ingredients. But she was sure they would manage it somehow. It was clear that the family was well-practiced in how to manage their camp. It was probably not the first time they'd had to deal with wanton destruction. And certainly, they had to move around often to avoid trouble, so they knew how to take everything down and put it up again with the minimum amount of fuss.

"What about me?" Bella asked. "I could help too."

"You take care of Sarah," Hope told her, looking at the baby in Bella's arms. "If she settles, you can fold clothes."

"I can put her down on a blanket. She can help me with socks."

Hope laughed. "Babies can't sort socks!"

"Maybe not, but she'll be interested enough in them if I give her some to hold and play with."

"Don't let her put my socks in her mouth," Hope shook her head at this thought. "Wet socks are bad. They give you blisters. And baby drool socks are gross!"

Bella laughed. She found a blanket, spread it out on a flat, unused spot on the ground, and sat down to help fold clothes as the young children sorted them into piles.

~

"You've got really good kids," Erin told Adrienne as they all worked together to get the camp whipped back into shape. "They're very smart and know how to work together."

Adrienne nodded. "We depend on each other. They know how to do lots of things, even the little ones. We can't depend on people like Bella or you to provide for us and do things for us. We want to be self-sufficient." She rolled her eyes. "I know it might not look like it right now, 'cause the car doesn't work, so I need help getting around, and we're using the Prost land, but we try to do for ourselves. Don't rely on government or programs to help us out. One day that will all be gone, and anyone who relies on them is going to be out in the cold."

Erin wasn't sure if she believed in the eventual collapse of the government and social programs, but she nodded anyway. She could understand Adrienne's desire not to depend on anyone else, and knew that those who relied on social programs were often left in the lurch when there were cutbacks or they no longer qualified for services. It was best for Adrienne to do for herself if she could.

Adrienne and Hope worked together efficiently to sort out the tents and shelters that had been knocked down. It could have been a lot worse. If the vandal had broken the tent poles or slashed the canvas, it would have been difficult for Adrienne to recover but, as it was, within an hour, things were looking pretty good again.

Chairs and stumps had been set up for seating, and Adrienne ordered everyone to sit down and have a drink of cold water after working hard in the heat of the day. The water bottles the children handed out before sitting down to drink had obviously been reused. Erin wondered whether they had been filled in the house or in a nearby stream. The water was cool, but not cold, having been dumped out of the cooler and left scattered across the ground by the vandal.

"It's safe," Adrienne told Erin, catching her hesitation about drinking water from an unknown source. "They bottle water from mountain streams and sell it for hugely inflated prices. This here is 'artisan' water." She took a long swallow to show that it was safe to drink and wiped her mouth with the back of her hand. "It's been certified as free of dangerous bacteria or environmental contaminants, and we've been drinking it for a few weeks. Nobody's gotten sick."

Erin forced herself to open the water bottle and drink to show that she took Adrienne at her word. It was very refreshing and not flat and stale like water that had been sitting on shelves in bottles for months before purchase.

"What about heavy metals?" she asked. "I know some of these mountain streams can contain high levels of arsenic or lead…" Or mercury, but Erin didn't want to suggest that. Adrienne was already worried enough about being accused of poisoning Fontainebleau without bringing that up.

Adrienne rolled her eyes and shook her head. "It's perfectly safe," she repeated, but didn't answer whether it had been tested for any heavy metals.

The children seemed healthy enough after drinking it for several weeks, but Erin didn't know how long it might take for them to show effects from lead or mercury. She planned to only have a few sips of the water until she could leave. Maybe she would take it home and get it tested herself. Though she wasn't sure Adrienne would let her take one of her bottles away with her.

Once the children had rehydrated, Adrienne sent them off to play. She didn't give Erin any sign that she hoped to be taken back to the Homestead to finish her shift.

"Do you have any idea who would have done this?" Erin asked, once the children were out of earshot. "Vandalized your camp, I mean? It seems like such a random thing to do, and you're all the way out here; someone actually had to come here intending to mess things up. They didn't just stumble across your camp like they might if it was in the woods in town."

Adrienne didn't say anything, but she smoothed out a couple of crumpled papers that had been in her pocket and handed them to Erin. Erin looked at the block letters on the two notes in disbelief.

*KEEP YOUR MOUTH SHUT AND GET YOUR CHIL-
DREN OUT OF HERE*
   LEAVE BEFORE SOMEONE GETS HURT

Erin shook her head. "Who would do this? You're not hurting anyone by camping out here. Why would someone want to run you off?" She looked around her uneasily for any sign that someone was watching them. She had assumed that the vandal would be long gone but, if he wanted to drive Adrienne off the property, maybe he was watching to see if he had succeeded.

"I don't know," Adrienne admitted. "We've run into this before, when we were squatting on a property without permission or too close to town. But out here…? Who cares that we're here?"

"You're not camped anywhere near anyone's property line? And the kids aren't playing on someone else's land?"

"No. This is all the Prosts'. And if Cindy didn't want us here anymore, she isn't one to mince words. She wouldn't do something like this. She'd just tell us we'd worn out our welcome."

Bella nodded her agreement. "We actually like having you here. Mom loves hearing the kids play and helping to look after Sarah. She likes getting to play 'grandma.'"

It was hard for Erin to picture critical, sour Cindy doting on the little children. But everyone had good and bad points. Maybe a love for children was a good thing about Cindy that Erin had not previously known about.

CHAPTER 28

"*H*ow is Hope doing?" Erin asked Adrienne. "She seems happier when she has a job to do."

Adrienne looked at Erin, frowning. "Hope is fine."

"What happened to her?"

"I don't see how it's any of your business."

"It's not," Erin admitted. "I just wondered what it had to do with Mr. Fontainebleau. If it did. And how… it might come up in the investigation."

Adrienne scowled and shook her head. "It won't come up in the investigation if everyone keeps their mouths shut. But that isn't going to happen if you are asking questions. You should just leave it alone."

"Did he hurt her? Or did he just scare her? Or did she see something that upset her?"

Adrienne didn't answer. Erin looked at Bella, wondering if she knew the details. Not that she would share them with Erin with Adrienne sitting right there telling Erin it was none of her business. Erin just wanted to make sure that someone knew. That Adrienne had support from someone. Maybe she wouldn't ever willingly deal with the police or a social worker, but Erin hoped she at least had the support of her friend.

"You can trust Erin," Bella said, which was not what Erin had been expecting. "She's a good listener and she wouldn't do anything that would hurt Hope."

"But your boyfriend is a cop," Adrienne addressed Erin directly. "And you'll talk to him about it. I don't want cops involved. I promised not to involve the police."

"I won't talk to him about it if you don't want me to. But he needs to know what was happening in that house if he's going to solve Mr. Fontainebleau's murder."

"I don't care if they ever solve his murder. Whoever killed him did the rest of the world a favor. They should get a prize, not go to prison."

"Well, maybe they'll get off if there were mitigating circumstances. If they did it to protect children like Hope…"

Adrienne chewed on her lip. "I don't really care why they did it. I'm just glad they did."

Erin shook her head. She didn't know what had happened at the Homestead, but Adrienne was clearly pretty bitter toward Fontainebleau, even though he was already dead.

"You don't know," Adrienne said. "So don't judge."

"I'm not."

She couldn't know what she wasn't told. It was up to Adrienne to decide whether to tell her about it or not.

Adrienne took a few long swallows of her water. "It's a big house. You saw that. And you might expect it to be wired like an airport, with microphones and cameras everywhere, so that no one could get away with anything. Walking off with a Tiffany lamp or some Monet. But it's not. Mr. Fontainebleau didn't like all of that monitoring. Not because he trusts people and thinks the best of them. That's not the way it was."

Erin nodded. She was already aware of some of this because of her discussion with Willie. She knew that Fontainebleau had only done the minimum necessary to protect himself and his property. Maybe he *did* think that people were inherently good, no matter how Adrienne perceived it.

"I'll tell you why he didn't want any electronic monitoring,"

Adrienne said darkly. "It was so that no one could prove what *he* was doing."

A knot of dread formed in Erin's stomach. She hadn't anticipated that perspective. There were a lot of shady things that someone rich and powerful like Clive William Fontainebleau III could get away with. But the fact that it was something that had traumatized Hope made Erin's chest hurt, like she'd actually been stabbed in the heart. She was having trouble catching her breath.

"I thought that it was so nice that they would let me bring all of the kids and move in there. To have our own little place and make it easier for me to work and still be close to my kids. He and his assistant talked about how important it was for them to be able to employ single moms and people who couldn't get jobs in other places because they weren't able to accommodate children or parents with responsibilities." She stopped for a moment and cleared her throat. "He was friendly with the kids and told them to call him Uncle Gus and gave them little treats or acted like they were important. He knew their names. I told the kids that they had to stay out of the way. That they weren't supposed to be around the big house when I was working, but had to stay in our rooms in one of the small houses. I didn't want them getting underfoot and wrecking things for us."

Erin nodded. It was a windfall for Adrienne to land a job like that, where she could take care of her kids the way that she wanted to. Erin could see how enticing that would be. To be able to be independent and work to build up the savings to get a place of her own eventually. Not having to worry about shelters or trespassing or other people wandering into their camp.

Adrienne went on, "But Hope said that she'd been in the house. Helping Uncle Gus. That he gave her money to do things for him, so she was working like Mama."

"What was she doing for him?"

"I thought just following him around, helping to tidy his desk, things that little kids do to try to be grown up. Maybe he gave Hope her own duster. I told her I wanted her to stay in our rooms, that I would do the work and it was her job to do her schoolwork and help look after the other kids." Adrienne swallowed. Her jaw worked, clenching and unclenching. "I went back the next day partway through my shift to check on them. The baby had been fussy and I wanted to make sure she was okay and that Hope was where she was supposed to be. But she wasn't. One of the other women, one who works in the kitchen, said that Fontainebleau had come looking for her. He had told her that Mama needed her, and she needed to come with him."

Erin cleared her throat but didn't know what to say. She could barely breathe, anticipating the story. She didn't need to be told. She had lived around enough predators to know how the story went. How it always went.

"It's such a big house." Adrienne's eyes welled up with tears.

Erin could see her frantically searching through the house, looking for her daughter and the man who had taken her. Asking people desperately if they had seen either one of them, where they might be.

"It took forever to find them. Everyone just looked the other way. They knew what was going on, and they just looked the other way! I found them together. My poor baby. You know that what she was doing for him had nothing to do with dusting the shelves or straightening his desk."

Erin shook her head, her own eyes burning. "Adrienne… I'm so sorry." She couldn't help adding, "Why wouldn't you go to the police? Why not have him arrested for what he did? He couldn't be allowed to just go on doing that."

And Adrienne had kept working there. Why would she work for someone who she knew had assaulted her daughter? Erin could see why Adrienne was afraid this would leak out and she would be accused of murdering Fontainebleau. Anyone with a heart would have wanted to kill Fontainebleau after that. And a mother! She must have wanted to cut out his throat. Slow poisoning by mercury would be too easy for him.

"I wanted to. I was going to. But…" Adrienne swallowed, fighting back the tears and outrage, "they said that he would never be charged. No one would believe me. They would say that I was just trying to embarrass him, or that I was trying to extort money out of him. It *wasn't* the money. It was never about the money."

It was Bella who leaned forward, her brows knotted, and asked, "What money?"

"I could stay there. I could keep working there, with nothing changed, and if I didn't say anything, didn't do anything to blacken his good name, then I would get a bonus. Enough for a stake. To buy our own land." Adrienne sobbed and couldn't go on for a minute. "Our own land, where we could build, where we could live without anyone bothering us or ever being kicked out again. He'd make sure that we were looked after. That the kids never had to go hungry. That I could have a running car. The nightmare would be over and I could live like anyone else. Like *you*," she looked at Erin, "with your own house in town, and a car and a business. Respectable. With friends and everything you need." She scrubbed at her eyes with the palms of her hands. "He had the money to do it. He had millions. Kicking a few dollars in my direction would be nothing for him. Just a drop in the bucket. All I had to do was keep working there and keep my mouth shut."

Bella moved closer to Adrienne and rubbed her back soothingly. "Adrienne, honey… you never said. You never told me all of that."

"I didn't want to tell anyone. I'm ashamed of myself. What a terrible thing to do to my baby. To say that what happened to her doesn't matter, if it means that I can get the money to start us out on our own. She matters more than a piece of land and a few dollars."

"Of course she does," Erin agreed. "You want to give them all the stable life they need. You want all of them, not just Hope, to feel safe and secure and have their own place in the world." What Erin would have done for a family who loved and protected her and kept her forever when she was a little girl. It had been a dream that she knew she would never achieve.

Adrienne nodded. "I want the best for her. Kids recover and they bounce back. I'm giving her memories and a life that will wipe out all of that other stuff. She won't remember any of it. Going to the police would just keep stirring that all up. She'd have to talk about it. To keep telling about it over and over. A court case would just destroy her. To have them say that she was lying and just making things up, just doing something I told her to go get money out of him. This way… it's over and done. She doesn't have to think about it or talk about it anymore. She has her family and a safe place to sleep, and she can grow up to be healthy and strong and just forget about Uncle Gus and what he was doing. She won't even remember it when she's older."

Erin wanted to hug Adrienne, or to pat her shoulder and rub her back like Bella was doing. She wanted to go find Hope and assure her that everything would be okay and squeeze her hard to let her know that she was safe and that wouldn't ever happen again.

Though the truth was that there was no guarantee it wouldn't happen again. Children who were abused were often re-abused over and over again throughout their lives. They ended up in bad situations and relationships and gave off a "vulnerable" vibe that attracted predators like bees to honey. At least Hope wasn't in foster care, where predators loved to lurk, seeking out the most vulnerable. At least she was home with her mother and siblings and had been removed from the Homestead.

And Fontainebleau was dead, and would never again be allowed to molest another child.

CHAPTER 29

*A*drienne sighed and drained the remainder of her bottle. "I know you think I made the wrong choice. I know you think that you would choose something different if it happened to you. But you don't know that. You don't know how you would have reacted when they presented you with the two choices, and you saw how it would rip your child's life apart if you went to the police. It wasn't the money. It wasn't the land and the house and the car. It was Hope. Giving her a better life. Protecting her from what would happen."

"I can't say. It wasn't me," Erin agreed. She might think she would have gone to the police, but she knew that in the past she had avoided talking to them, even when her own boyfriend was a cop. Even when she knew and respected every cop in town and knew that they would treat her as fairly as they could.

"Well, it's over now," Bella said. "This is what happened, and now it's over."

"Of course... Hope wasn't the first," Adrienne said, her voice tight with barely controlled emotion. "This scumbag had been able to do whatever he wanted to for years. Preying on single moms. Their children. The wives of employees. People he had promised to keep safe and take care of for decades." She shook her head.

"Decades! Do you know how many victims that means? Some of them never told their parents or spouses, just suffered in silence because he was so rich and powerful and could make anyone shut up and do what he wanted them to. Because his people would keep writing checks, making threats, and doing whatever it took to keep everyone quiet. Leaving a trail of victims behind him..."

"Did you talk to other people that it had happened to?" Erin asked. "Other victims?"

Adrienne shook her head. "Everyone keeps quiet. They all get paid to keep their mouths shut and not say anything about it, even to each other. Even if they all know what kind of a person he is —was."

"That's really too bad," Erin commented. "It's an environment like that that lets him keep abusing people." She looked away, not wanting to put too sharp a point on it, because Adrienne had joined the ranks of those who had agreed to stay quiet about it. Even after his death, she was still keeping it quiet, refusing to come forward and tell what had been going on. She was still part of the problem instead of the solution. Erin could understand that she didn't want Hope to be traumatized more by the system than she already had been at the hands of Uncle Gus. But that wasn't a solution and didn't help the next child.

"I heard them talking," Adrienne said, following some segue that her own mental processes had led her to. "Matthew, one of the guys who had been working with him for years. Decades. He'd been loyal, one of Fontainebleau's biggest supporters. He had just found out... his son did one of those DNA tests. The ones that give you stuff about your ancestry and who you're related to. Only, none of Matthew's family showed up as being related to him."

Erin's eyes widened. "What?"

"It shows his cousins, aunts, uncles, and anyone who has done one of those DNA tests. But it didn't. Instead, whose family do you think it showed?"

Erin tried to clamp her jaw shut, but it sagged open again in disbelief. "Fontainebleau? It showed his family?"

Adrienne nodded. "So all along, this boy he thought was his

son, turns out he isn't. Not biologically. It was Fontainebleau. He slept with Matthew's wife and no one ever told him. Never gave him a clue that the baby might not be his."

"What did his wife say about it? He must have confronted her?"

"His wife is dead," Adrienne explained. "Been dead for years. Depression. Suicide, as far as I can guess."

"Oh, my. Oh, that poor man. And his son!"

"Yeah. Imagine finding it out now, twenty years later. Finding that he put in however many decades for this guy, loyal to him to the end, just to find out that he had forced his wife."

"Did he know the circumstances? Whether it was... you know... she didn't just have an affair?"

"After working for this guy for that long, do you really think he had any doubt? He must have heard all of the stories about Fontainebleau. He knew it wasn't just an affair."

"What did Fontainebleau do about it? What did he say?"

"What he always says. Money talks. He sends them to the purser and lets her take care of them. Money if he'll keep his mouth shut about it. And do you really think he wants to have his dead wife's name dragged through the mud? Or his son's parentage broadcast all over the state? Best thing to do is to hold out for as much money as he can get... and keep his mouth shut."

"I can't believe that he wouldn't talk about it. If he was one of Fontainebleau's top guys, he must have already made a lot of money. I wouldn't think..."

"That it would be as easy to talk him into it as it was to shut me up?" Adrienne finished bitterly. "Yeah, he probably had to pay Matthew a whole lot more. Give him early retirement, so he never has to work again. He's a nice-looking guy. Tall, distinguished, dreamy-looking eyes. He could easily get married again. Settle down with another family. He's still young enough."

Erin blinked, a face popping into her mind at the description. "Wait—what did he look like?"

Adrienne looked surprised. She tried to describe him in more detail. Erin thought she recognized him from the description.

"And who's this person he was supposed to go see? Mrs. Purser?"

"The purser. Like on a ship. The person who pays the bills, looks after the financial stuff, and ensures everyone is comfortable and happy. She's supposed to keep all the discontents quiet. Pay them off and make them sign nondisclosure agreements."

"Is that all she does?"

"No, she does other stuff around the Homestead, too. Keeping everything running smoothly. Like the head of the household staff." Adrienne shook her head. "She told me... that he'd never gone after a child before. Only young women. She promised me... she said she'd make sure it didn't happen again. That I should sign the agreement, but she would make sure that he was dealt with. I guess I should have realized that it was all just talk. She was never going to go to the authorities with what she knew. She was just telling me that to make sure that I signed the agreement, so I was legally bound. So I couldn't... do what I'm doing now and tell you or anyone else. But he's dead and gone now and I don't care if people know what a terrible person he was. They can come after me for slander or whatever they want to. If the cops arrest me for murder—I'm going to spill the beans. I'm going to tell them everything I know."

A person could be pushed only so far, and it would seem that Adrienne had reached her limit.

CHAPTER 30

Erin had promised not to tell anyone about what had happened to Hope, especially not the police, so she couldn't go to Terry and use him as a sounding board. She couldn't point him in the right direction and hope that he just figured it out himself.

Back at her office at Auntie Clem's, she wrote notes in her planner, trying to map out a path that would allow her to find out more and, hopefully, find something that she could give to Terry and the Bald Eagle Falls police department. She couldn't prove who had killed Fontainebleau, but if she could find some proof… then she could give it to the police, and they could make an arrest, and Adrienne would be safe. She wouldn't have to worry about being arrested for the murder herself. What would happen to all her kids when they took her to prison? Even if she was found not guilty, the children would have to be in someone else's care for years if she were charged. Jury trials didn't go that quickly and, if Adrienne made a plea, who knows how many years she would get? As much as Erin would like to think that the law was just and the sentence she received would be appropriate, she didn't believe it.

But would Erin want the real killer to end up in prison? The person who had decided that Fontainebleau deserved to die for all of the damage he had done? For all of the broken hearts and broken lives? Would that really be justice? After all Fontainebleau had been allowed to do because his money and power could silence anyone who got in his way?

∾

"How did things go with Adrienne today?" Vic asked as she and Erin worked together on clean-up and closing at Auntie Clem's. "Is she okay? What happened?"

Erin tried to focus on the question. Vic knew nothing about what had happened at Adrienne's camp or the revelations about Hope and Fontainebleau's history. Erin knew Vic could keep a secret, but Adrienne had asked her not to talk to anyone about the attack.

But Vic didn't need the details about Hope. She was just wondering about Erin's trip to the Homestead to rescue Adrienne and take her home to the Prost farm to see what had been done there.

"It looked pretty bad to begin with, all of Adrienne's tents and their belongings scattered all over the place. Everything knocked down and destroyed. But it wasn't actually as bad as all of that. Some of the food was wrecked, but the clothes, tents, and everything were okay. If someone had really wanted to wreck everything, they could have broken up the tent poles and slashed the tents and the clothes. Poured bleach on them or lit them on fire. But they didn't do any of that. Just scattered everything around. It took work to clean it up and get everything organized and set up again, but there wasn't any permanent damage. Her kids are smart and good at working together and getting their camp set up."

"That's a relief," Vic said, blowing out her breath. "I don't understand how anyone could do that to someone already down on their luck. To anyone, I mean, but especially to someone like Adrienne, who is struggling so hard to keep her head above water. I feel awful for her. How could someone be that cruel, just throwing everything around for no reason?"

"I know," Erin agreed. "It burned me up. I'm glad it wasn't as bad as it looked at first, but I still think it was nasty. It isn't like Adrienne is doing anything to bother anyone. She is living where she has permission to; it isn't on public property or trespassing on private property. She looks after her kids, works hard, and keeps her mouth shut. So I don't understand why someone would try to run her off like that."

"Run her off?"

"Yeah. There were a couple of notes... telling her that she should clear out. But where do they think she's going to go? She doesn't have a working car. Doesn't have a permanent home. It isn't like there is a shelter to go to in Bald Eagle Falls even if she *would* agree to go to one. And she won't go anywhere like that because she says it isn't safe for the kids. Where exactly do they think she's going to go?"

Vic shook her head as she poured out the batters that were to soak overnight. "Why would anyone want to run her off? She's such a hard worker. She's not some drunk or deadbeat."

"I don't know. People don't like to have to look at the poor and the homeless. They don't want them anywhere near their properties. They're fine with social programs that help people out, as long as it doesn't mean the homeless people are in their backyards. Try to help addicts or single-parent families by actually giving them a home in your neighborhood..." Erin shook her head. She'd seen too much of that kind of self-righteousness. "Where exactly are they supposed to go? You can only have shelters and halfway houses in the slums? How does that help get people away from that life?"

"If you have an answer, I'd love to hear it."

Erin just shook her head. "But I can't even figure out who doesn't want them there. They couldn't be much more out of sight. It isn't like anyone has to see them out there. And they had to seek out Adrienne's camp and target her. It's in the middle of nowhere!"

"People can be really cruel."

"Yeah."

They worked in silence for a while, used to the routine. It was rare that any of the employees needed to refer to the procedural checklists anymore. Erin kept them all up to date so that it was easy to open and close Auntie Clem's, and that all of the recipes and till codes and other procedures were all in one reference binder.

"Do you think…" Vic started and then broke off.

Erin waited, then, after a moment, turned and looked at Vic, whose brow was furrowed as she wiped down counters and started running through the last few checks before leaving.

"Do I think what?"

"You've been over at the Homestead and probably heard things from Terry. About what things were like over there, what kind of person Fontainebleau was and everything. I mean, everybody says how much he was disliked. He was rich and arrogant. But I mean… I just wonder what kinds of things he was involved in."

Thinking back to what Erin had discovered about Fontainebleau, she wondered if there was anything she could reveal to Vic without breaking confidences.

"What do you mean?" If Vic was already halfway there, Erin couldn't be blamed for confirming her suspicions.

"I mean… organized crime."

"Oh." That took a turn in a far different direction from what Erin had been expecting. She didn't know what to say. "Well… I don't know. I haven't really heard anything about that."

"A lot of big businesses, they're involved with organized crime. Directly or indirectly. You know how you always hear about the construction industry, how it's so intertwined with the mob? Maybe that's just on TV. I don't know."

"I don't either," Erin admitted. "It makes for good TV, but it's probably exaggerated. Not *all* construction companies are involved with the mob. Or protection rackets. Money laundering or hiding bodies in the foundations of new buildings. I don't think much of that happens in real life."

"No," Vic agreed. "But on the other hand… I know how the clans are. They mean business. And they *do* get involved with other industries. Not just drugs or money laundering. Around here… it could be things like mining. Lots of money in it. Big industry."

"You're thinking… that the Jackson clan might be involved with Fontainebleau's business? They might have some kind of claim on it?"

Vic bit her lip, pausing in her work. "I was thinking about the Dysons, actually."

Erin was startled. She had thought that maybe Vic had heard something about Fontainebleau or his business through her family connection with the Jackson clan, even though she had nothing to do with anyone in her family but Jeremy anymore.

But her only connection with the Dyson clan was…

Willie.

$\mathcal{E}$rin looked at Vic. "What makes you think Fontainebleau might have been involved with the Dysons?"

Vic looked away, shaking her head. "I just... wondered what was going on with him. Like I said, everyone keeps saying what a terrible guy Fontainebleau was... and... is it really just that he's competitive? Buying out claims that the independent miners think should be theirs?"

"You'd have to ask Willie about that." After saying it, Erin clamped her mouth shut and tried to figure out how to take the conversation in another direction. She hadn't meant to throw it back at Willie, who Vic was obviously already worried about. And not just Willie himself, but the possibility that the Dyson clan might be involved.

It was a long time since Willie had been a soldier for them, and he now lived and worked independently of them, except for doing supposedly legitimate work for Nelson Dyson, who had split off from the main part of the clan. This might be worse than working for the main clan, putting Willie between two warring factions as well as at risk from the law.

"I mean about the mining," she said. "Not about the clan."

"You think he is involved with the Dysons, though, don't you?"

"Well, with Nelson." Erin shook her head. "But I don't know anything about it. Doing computer work for him doesn't necessarily mean that he's doing anything to break the law or anything that would involve money laundering through Fontainebleau's company. It could be completely innocent, like he says."

"Yeah. Or it could be a complete lie and he's up to his eyeballs in clan stuff." Vic made an angry noise in her throat. "I thought that when I left my family I was done with anything to do with the clans. And then I find out that Willie is still… I don't know what he's doing. But he's had some blow-ups lately. I thought it was just stress over some mine or claim jumper. But it seems like he was more than just a competitor to Fontainebleau. I think it goes a lot deeper than that."

"Going into Fontainebleau's home and planting bugs?"

Vic rolled her eyes and nodded. "Yeah. That's pretty hard to stomach. If he was afraid that Fontainebleau was sniffing around his mines, then why not just protect his mines? Like he's always done? Why go into Fontainebleau's Homestead and plant bugs there? He just wants to keep one step ahead of the guy? Make sure that he's not doing anything against Willie's interests?" She shook her head, sighing in frustration.

"Well, at least he was open about that. Admitted to what he'd been doing."

"Don't count on it. That's what he confessed to when you had him in a corner, because you'd seen him out there. Is it really the truth? I mean, did you see him removing listening devices?"

"No… I saw him pulling wire. With other workers."

"Right. *Not* covert surveillance. Willie out there in the open with other people."

"Then…" Erin was confused. "That doesn't sound like anything too bad. What's the big deal if he was just doing an electrical job? Something Fontainebleau hired him for?"

"Because he's covering something up. Something worse than planting or collecting bugs. He's trying to distract everyone from what he was really there for."

"What do you think he was there for?"

Vic didn't say anything. She went to Erin's tiny office to grab her purse and get ready to go.

"Something worse like poisoning Fontainebleau?" Erin demanded. "I don't think Willie had anything to do with that. Not for a minute."

"No?" Vic sounded slightly relieved at Erin's vehemence. "You don't think he would do something like that? No matter what the reason?"

"Not because of work. Not because he thought that Fontainebleau was acting against his interests. No."

But would Willie do it if he knew what had happened to Hope? He hadn't answered her when she had asked for information on what had happened, but that didn't mean that he didn't know. She suspected he knew a lot more about it than he had let on, but he was leaving it to Adrienne to manage the information. Giving her privacy.

But that didn't preclude his deciding to do something to end the problem permanently. Erin knew how protective he was of her and Vic. She could only imagine how protective he would be toward a little girl like Hope, who had been harmed.

"So I'm probably just blowing things out of proportion," Vic said. "It isn't anything to do with the Dysons."

"What made you think that it was?" She couldn't see Vic jumping right from the impression that Willie wasn't telling her something to assuming it was because it was the Dysons. That might be their biggest moral conflict, but that didn't mean that every one of Willie's secrets had to do with the Dysons.

"Well, just… every now and then, something that I hear him say on the phone. Or that comes up on his screen. I don't think that he's doing anything *really* bad. I mean, up until now, I just figured… it's his business. How he manages his business and what he chooses to do with Nelson Dyson, whether honest or shady, is up to him. And if he doesn't want to talk to me about it, then fine. I'd rather not know if it is something that could potentially get him in trouble."

But if it was something to do with a murder, that was different.

Vic and Erin headed for the back door. "I don't think Willie would poison Fontainebleau over a business deal," Erin assured her. "He's not that kind of guy. He finds other ways to deal with his problems. Like bugging the Homestead."

"Somebody was asking him, I think, about what he found out at the Homestead. He kept saying that he would deal with it later. That there wasn't anything to report."

"And you think that was Nelson or someone from the clan? Then you *do* think that Willie was planting bugs? Or retrieving them?"

"I don't know. I wish I did. I think… that's the kind of thing that he would do for Nelson. Think about it. If he was setting up networks and security for Nelson, then it's not a stretch that he might set something up at the Homestead under orders from Nelson. And then Nelson wants to know what he's found, demands to know what Willie's discovered so far…"

"You know, I think there was something in those newspaper articles."

"What?" Vic looked at Erin as they got into the yellow VW. "You think there was *what* in those newspaper articles?"

"I don't know. I have to look at them again. I just have…" Erin shook her head, frowning and trying to catch the fleeting impression that had just tugged at the back of her brain. "Sorry, I didn't read the articles carefully, just glanced over them, and then looked at them again when I was looking to see if the barometer showed up in any of the pictures. I just think… there's something I should have seen."

"That has something to do with Nelson?"

"I don't know."

Even without looking at Vic, Erin could tell that the younger woman was rolling her eyes. And she couldn't blame her. She wasn't sure what it was she was trying to say or what her brain had caught hold of. But she knew she needed to read through the puff-piece news articles about Clive William Fontainebleau III to tease out what she had missed. The key was there.

~

Vic was there to offer moral support, since they couldn't read the articles on Erin's photo roll simultaneously. Even zooming in and scrolling down each column without losing her place in the articles was difficult. It was not exactly how newspaper articles were meant to be read. But it would have to do because they were the only copies she had.

The articles were from decades before, when Fontainebleau was entering the family business as a young man, having gotten whatever business degrees his family's money had bought him. He was joining his father in the industry, acclaimed as the golden boy who could turn the company around and put it back on the track to success.

Erin read a few articles this way, then leaned back on the couch and closed her eyes, relaxing her shoulders and trying to process what she had read and whether there was anything there. She reached out to hand her phone to Vic.

"Why did he need to turn the company around?" she asked.

Vic took the phone from her hand and started flicking through the articles. Her reading speed was much faster than Erin's, or maybe she was just focused on answering that one question instead of absorbing everything the articles had to say.

"Yeah, they allude to it a few times," she confirmed. "Turn the company around. Return it to its former glory. Taking over the reins of the family fortune from his father. I guess... his father didn't have the same business acumen as he and his grandfather had?"

"It sure doesn't sound like it."

"They were expecting Fontainebleau the Third to be a business genius. When he hadn't actually had anything to do with business yet, he had just finished school. But everyone figured he was the answer."

"So his father must have been really bad. And the company was in pretty poor shape."

"Maybe business just wasn't his father's thing. Maybe he was the artistic type and had never wanted to be part of something like that."

"Maybe," Erin agreed. "Or maybe he had a specific vice. He was a drinker or a gambler."

"Oooh…" Vic drew the word out in realization. "If he was a gambler and got in with the wrong people…"

"Or tried to cover up by taking out a loan from a… less legitimate source. Someone who charged a high lending rate, say."

Erin opened her eyes. Vic was nodding vigorously. "And if Fontainebleau the Third had to run the business the way that the Dyson clan said to, because they were hugely in debt to them…"

"I mean, it was decades ago," Erin said, pointing to her phone to indicate the articles. "But if he had to work hand in hand with them to get out from under… once you've been in business with organized crime, it's pretty hard to get out."

"And then, more recently, Fontainebleau the Third starts making questionable or unwise business decisions. The clan starts to get concerned. Wants to know that he's still the right guy to run the company…"

"But that would be the clan, not Nelson. Nelson has split off. He doesn't have anything to do with the historical business of the clan, right? He wouldn't have anything to do with an old debt by Fontainebleau's company."

"I don't know. He could have bought that debt. Or maybe since he was a Dyson, Fontainebleau went to him when things started to falter again. Figured that he just needed a little cash, and things will turn back around again. Because he'd done it before. He had all of these other plans and something was bound to work out."

"It could be." Erin took her phone back from Vic. "But of course… this is all speculation."

"But it would explain Nelson Dyson wanting to know what's going on. He needs ears on the inside and knows Willie is good at this kind of thing. And Willie's interests are aligned, because he wants to know what Fontainebleau is doing too, wants to make sure he is staying away from Willie's mines."

CHAPTER 32

*E*rin tapped through the photos again, but wasn't reading them this time. She was just skimming over the headlines and the titles. And there was more she hadn't read yet. Her secret admirer/stalker/informant had picked each one carefully and sent it to her for a reason. What information did he want to give her that she hadn't figured out yet? The barometer. Fontainebleau the Third coming back from school to save the company from the hole his father had put it in, whether that had involved deals with the local leg-breakers or not. And what else? Were there clues there as to the young Fontainebleau's skirt-chasing?

"If we can figure this out from the articles, then the police can too," she reminded Vic. "They have the originals of these articles."

"But they don't know Willie has been getting calls from Nelson. And there's not actually anything in there that says that Fontainebleau the Second had anything to do with the Dyson clan. That's just our speculation. There's no proof of anything. Not in those newspaper articles, anyway."

"Are there clues in the other things that he sent?" Erin cast her mind back over the other gifts. "If the newspaper articles and barometer were to tell us about Fontainebleau and his killer and maybe something about why Fontainebleau was killed, then do the other gifts mean something too? I thought that they were just… romantic gifts from a secret admirer when I got them. But what if they were supposed to tell me something right from the beginning, only I missed the significance?"

"Well, I guess they could be," Vic agreed. "Flowers and lingerie. Could be something to do with a wife or girlfriend. Someone he had an intimate relationship with. They could point toward a suspect. If the newspaper articles and barometer are the why and the how, then maybe the flowers and lingerie are the who. His wife or ex-wife. Someone else he's seeing. It shouldn't be too hard to narrow down who he's been seeing, even if it is a mistress on the side."

Erin grimaced. She didn't want to tell Vic everything she had learned from Adrienne. But finding out everyone that Fontainebleau had been intimate with, even just going back a few months, might be more challenging than Vic expected. "Actually… from what I gather, Fontainebleau was… very active. That might be a pretty wide pool."

"Oh." Vic gave a little laugh. "I didn't know. I guess that's part of why he isn't very well-liked. Maybe the details of the flowers and lingerie are important clues? They might point to someone specific?"

Erin pictured the flowers. Just a small bouquet of colorful flowers. They had not been ultra-romantic. Not a dozen red roses. But also not black roses. Or white lilies that might be more funereal. When she had seen them, she had thought that they might come from Peter or the Foster family as a thank-you for helping get Mr. Foster the job at the bookstore. They could even have been from Naomi, for that matter. There hadn't been anything creepy or stalkerish about them. But nothing that she could see that would point to a specific person. Unless they were someone's favorite flower, a particular gift that Fontainebleau had sent to her, or they were code for someone's name. Daisy or Susan or Iris. Erin knew few flower names. She couldn't have named most of the flowers that had been in the bouquet.

"I don't know much about flowers, do you?"

"I know there's a whole 'language of flowers' thing, where different flowers and colors represent different messages, but I don't know anything about it. Other than red roses being love and yellow roses being friendship."

"You know more than I do. Maybe we can look them up online. But I'm not sure what flowers were in the bouquet, and I didn't take a picture."

"They must have been ordered from somewhere close by. We might be able to find out more from the flower shop they were ordered from."

"Yeah. Though we'll have to come up with a good story, because I don't think they'll give us any information like they would to the police."

"I guess they'll already have been around asking who ordered them and if they were charged to a credit card."

"Maybe," Erin said doubtfully. "Terry never said he was going to, and we didn't know at the time that they were anything other than… an anonymous gift. It wasn't until later that things started to get weird."

"He must have after, though. When you got the lingerie and then the newspaper articles. He must have looked into it."

"I guess. Probably."

"And then there's the lingerie…"

Erin nodded. She immediately started blushing. Why should a little lace negligee be so embarrassing? Especially if it was a clue as to the identity of the murderer rather than a romantic gift from Terry or a secret admirer? It wasn't anything to do with Erin. Certainly not a statement about how the man who had sent it felt about her. It might not even have been sent by a man. There was no reason it couldn't have been sent by one of the women at the Homestead who knew what was going on and wanted to point Erin in the right direction.

Vic giggled at Erin's blush, which just made her more embarrassed.

"So what kind of clues could the lingerie give you?" Vic asked. "I never saw it, so you'll have to describe it in detail for me."

Erin opened her mouth, sure that her face was lobster red.

"And I mean in detail," Vic reiterated.

Erin put both hands over her face. "I didn't really look closely. I mean… it was a negligee. Lacy, sheer. Not like something I'd wear around the house."

Vic laughed at the thought. Erin didn't usually even wear a nightgown, like Vic. A t-shirt and shorts were more her speed. Maybe yoga pants on a cooler night.

"What color?" Vic asked.

"White, with some baby blue trim."

Did the blue mean something? A clue to point them toward Fontainebleau's illegitimate son?

"And what about the cut? Was it… slim? Busty? Like it was bought for you, or someone else?"

Erin thought about it. She hadn't tried the negligee on. From the time she had first seen the foil stamp on the box, she had known in her gut that it was not from Terry. She had not taken it out of the box when she'd received it at Auntie Clem's. She had taken it out of the box only once at home, to hold it up and get the full effect when Terry was not in the room to see. It had been longer than a camisole or baby doll, but not floor length. Somewhere around knee level on Erin's short frame. Mid-thigh for someone taller like Vic. And the cut? Had she noticed? Had she held it up to herself to see how it would fit?

"I don't really know. I guess… It was maybe bustier than I could wear. Maybe for someone a little taller and better endowed than me."

Vic nodded.

And what did that tell them? They didn't know anyone at the Homestead other than Adrienne. It would not have fit her thin frame. But it wasn't a glass slipper that would be a perfect fit for one woman who worked at the Homestead. Or that Fontainebleau might have had contact with at some other location.

"There's nothing that says that the secret admirer—or whatever he is—picked out the size to represent a particular woman specifically. Or that he was any good at eyeballing a woman and knowing what size of negligee to get," Erin pointed out. "In my experience… men can be pretty ignorant of things like cup sizes."

Vic started to giggle. "I haven't had much experience with sexy lingerie myself," she said, "but yeah… I don't think most guys are much more advanced than 'big or small.' Maybe if he's a lingerie designer or salesman. But not Joe Blow off the street."

"Or Willie?" Erin guessed.

Vic giggled even louder, and this time she was the one turning red. "I have to admit, my situation is a little more confusing, since I have a variety of… *options* and may change from one day to the next. But yeah. The man is hopeless."

Neither one of them could speak for some time. Erin had to get herself a glass of cold water when she started hiccuping. Every time she tried to get back on track with a serious study of what clues the secret admirer might have been giving her that they might have missed, she just started laughing again.

Poor Willie.

CHAPTER 33

*E*rin had not told Vic about the woman Adrienne had referred to as the purser, who handed out the checks to keep people quiet. And she hadn't told Adrienne that she had recognized her description of Matthew, the man who had been talking to Fontainebleau about his son.

She wondered what kind of payment that warranted. Not only had Fontainebleau assaulted Matthew's wife, but he had fathered a child who might have some claim on his estate. The boy could come forward at some point and demand to be acknowledged. Fontainebleau had another son, but there was plenty of money to go around. However much the purser had given Matthew, it probably wasn't as much as he would have gotten in court for all of those years of parental support. Or enough to even touch what Matthew's son would receive if he were to inherit after Fontainebleau's death. There wasn't any amount that would compensate him for the loss of his wife to depression, which would certainly have been exacerbated by the assault, the birth of her son, and keeping the secret from Matthew, who continued to work for Fontainebleau for years after.

Erin waited until Charley came in to take the afternoon shift, and then once more drove out to the Homestead. Not to see Adrienne this time, but Freda Jones, the woman known as the purser.

What if Jones refused to see her? She didn't have any reason to talk to Erin. And probably a hundred reasons not to. She had enough work without having to deal with a nosy baker from town who wanted to know all of her secrets.

Or at least, one of them.

And not only did Jones not have any reason to see Erin, but she also had no reason to reveal the identity of the man Adrienne had seen. She had paid him to be quiet, so why would she disclose the information to Erin? Erin would need to be smart about it. To prise the name out of Jones without her knowing why or that it had any real importance to Erin.

But she didn't know how she was going to manage that. Jones would know she hadn't driven all the way to the Homestead to gossip over a cup of tea and reminisce about the various people she had paid off over the last year.

Erin hesitated at whether to park in the same place as she had when she had dropped off and picked up Adrienne. Maybe she should park out front like she was an expected guest instead of sneaking in a side door like one of the staff. But she didn't know the protocols, who was allowed to park there and how to convince the receptionist to let her talk to the purser. Her chances were better if she worked her way in from the back.

Erin let herself in the door, which was not locked. She was amazed every time she got there at the lack of security. Or visible security. She looked around the entryway for cameras. There should at least be cameras at the outside doors, even if Fontainebleau did not like them in the inner rooms. She couldn't imagine how the security staff could keep track of who was coming and going without them. But Willie had said that they could be hidden, that she wouldn't even see them. Maybe someone was watching her arrival.

She walked into the Homestead with no idea how she would even find the purser. She didn't know her way around in the rabbit's warren of back hallways. And she had no idea whether the purser's office was conveniently beside Mr. Fontainebleau's office or buried somewhere else in the maze.

She didn't have far to go before she came across a couple of women chatting as they walked down the hallway. They stopped talking at looked at Erin curiously, apparently knowing she didn't belong there.

"I got turned around," Erin told them, smiling warmly. "Can you tell me which way to go to find Mrs. Jones?"

The two women exchanged glances, then directed Erin down an adjoining hallway, with a series of turns she should take to find the purser. Erin nodded as if this all made sense and went down the hall they had indicated. The process was repeated several times, Erin getting closer to Freda Jones's office each time, until she finally arrived.

She knocked tentatively on the door, unsure whether Jones would be on the phone or with a visitor, and if people normally walked in or had to be called upon and have an appointment set ahead of time. There was a "Yes?" from within. Erin opened the door and poked her head in uncertainly.

"Uh—Mrs. Jones?"

A woman sat at the large, heavy desk. Perhaps fifty years old, with red hair bobbed at her shoulders, graying around the roots. She wore glasses and was dressed in conservative business attire, a modest gray dress with a classic cut. "Come in. Can I help you?"

She set aside the file she had been looking at and gave Erin her attention. Erin entered the room, hesitated, and pulled the door closed behind her.

"I'm sorry to disturb you without an appointment. My name is Erin Price, and I work in town—"

"At the bakery."

"Yes." Erin nodded. "Auntie Clem's. I don't think I've ever seen you there…"

The woman did not look familiar. She knew most of her regular customers, but wouldn't necessarily remember if Jones had been there only once or twice in the time that the bakery had been open.

"No, I haven't had the pleasure," Jones agreed. "Although I have had the pleasure of eating some of your baked goods. They are very good."

"Oh, thank you. I didn't know if... I thought you probably get your groceries for the Homestead delivered from the city."

"Yes, usually. But we occasionally have other goods brought in from Bald Eagle Falls or other towns close by. For a while, we were able to get these locally crafted jams." She smacked her lips. "Jam Lady. Did you ever have those?"

Erin laughed. "Yes, I know the Jam Lady. Both the brand and the person. It's too bad that they aren't able to make them anymore. They were really good. Though maybe... there's always the possibility they could take it up again." Erin knew the secret identity of the Jam Lady, though she would never reveal it.

"That would be wonderful. You'll have to tell me if they do. They were very good." Jones motioned for Erin to take a seat in one of the large leather chairs in front of her desk. "Please. Have a seat." She adjusted her glasses. "What can I do for you today?"

"I'm looking for some information on a man who works here. Or used to work here; I think he has retired now. I don't know his last name, only his first name. And maybe he didn't even work out of the Homestead. He might have worked at one of the company's other locations."

"Yes...?"

"His name is Matthew? Around fifty years old, I think. Graying hair. Rimless glasses. Pleasant looking."

Jones nodded. "Matthew Harris," she offered.

And Erin had his name. She hadn't had to be sneaky about it at all.

"What do you want Matthew for?" Jones asked.

"He has some information that I need. I ran into him the other day but forgot that I needed something else..."

"What would you need someone with his expertise for? I know that bakers need a certain amount of understanding of basic chemistry, but I wouldn't think that there would be a lot of overlap between the chemical processing that Matthew is an expert in and the chemistry of rising dough and protein structures."

Erin's heart quickened at the revelation that Matthew was knowledgeable in chemistry. He could probably transform elemental mercury into something that could be hidden in Fontainebleau's food without a second thought.

"Well, no, it wasn't actually anything to do with chemistry, more with… history. He's been around these parts for a while. He has a lot of knowledge about… the history of the area."

Jones's eyes were quick and discerning. Did she know more than she was letting on? Were Erin's answers more revealing than she had meant them to be?

"Well, I hope Matthew can give you the information you need. He was always a very good employee. I was sorry to see him go."

"Do you know what he's doing now that he retired from the company? Is he just fishing and enjoying life? I know he has a son…"

"Yes, I think he's planning on spending more time with his family. After putting in so many years with the company, he deserves it. But I wonder how he will enjoy retirement. Some people are never really able to slow down and adjust to it."

Matthew might be forced to slow down more than he expected to.

"Does he live in the city now? I don't have his address."

"Actually, he's in Bald Eagle Falls. The two of you are practically neighbors."

"I don't suppose you have his address?" She might be pushing her luck asking for it. And she was sure that Terry would have access to Matthew Harris's address through DMV records or other government sources.

"Well, let's see…" Jones tapped her computer keys and clicked busily on her screen. "You're Adrienne's friend."

Erin swallowed. She nodded slowly. She hoped that her being there would not cause Adrienne problems. She didn't want Jones to associate the nosy baker with the hard worker who really needed to keep her job at the Homestead.

"I know Adrienne, yes. Helped her out by giving her a ride a couple of times lately. She's… very appreciative of her job here. I'm not here because of anything to do with her."

Jones looked away from her computer to meet Erin's eyes for a moment, then looked back at the computer again. "Yes. The job seems to be very important to her."

"It's hard for a single mom to find something stable. And Adrienne… faces a lot of challenges."

"It's too bad that she's run into problems."

That was too subtle for Erin to know whether Jones was hinting at the assault on Hope, or Adrienne being homeless and a mom, or a gentle warning for Erin to stay out of the way and not cause any more problems for her.

"I hope that… nothing will change with Mr. Fontainebleau's death. That she'll still be able to work here like she has been."

"Maybe things will be better now."

That was reassuring. They at least weren't planning on booting Adrienne out the door with the change in management.

"If she abides by the terms of her agreement," Jones added, still looking at her computer screen.

Her employment agreement? Or the nondisclosure agreement that kept her from talking to anyone about what Fontainebleau had done? Adrienne would have to take better care. If she had been overheard talking to someone about what had happened, even someone in the Homestead who already knew, she could be in trouble. Erin made a mental note to give Adrienne a heads-up. She didn't want to lose her job or the money she had been promised that would allow her to move into a place of her own.

"Of course," Erin agreed.

Jones looked away from the screen and made eye contact again. She gave a nod. "Good. Matthew's address…"

Erin dug her planner out of her purse and flipped to a fresh page to take down the address. Jones read it out.

"I enjoyed working with Matthew," she said. "We were both here for a long time. I enjoyed getting to know him and his family over the years. Give him my regards…"

"Sure, of course. I'll let him know that you were thinking of him."

CHAPTER 34

𝒜rin's thoughts were whirling as she drove home. Matthew was living in Bald Eagle Falls and she knew where to find him. Jones knew who Erin was and that she was friends with Adrienne. She still wanted Adrienne to keep working there but Adrienne had to abide by the terms of her NDA. Jones and Matthew were friends. Jones knew things would be better for Adrienne with Fontainebleau out of the way. She had known Matthew's family, saw what Fontainebleau had done to them. Yet she had stood by and let Fontainebleau destroy the family.

And Adrienne? Had Jones made the same false promises to others as she had to Adrienne? Said that she would take care of things and see that no one else was put in danger, and then let the same thing happen again time after time, family after family?

Erin knew that Terry would not be home yet, and called to see whether he was at the police department offices or out on street patrol. He liked to be out and about so, if there weren't anything pressing on the Fontainebleau investigation, he would probably be out with K9.

"Erin. How are you doing?"

"Good. Are you in the office? I have some information for you."

"Uh, no. But I'm not far. I can meet you there. What's this

about?" He was using his *have-you-been-poking-your-nose-where-it-doesn't-belong* tone of voice.

"I'll tell you about it when I get there."

"Hmm. Okay. See you in a few minutes."

By the time she got to the police department, Terry was standing in the reception area, talking to Clara while he waited for Erin to arrive. She appreciated not having to get past the gatekeeper to see him. He just ushered her into his office and cleared space for her to sit down. He sat behind his desk and K9 lay down on the floor beside him with a sigh.

"So… what have you got?"

"I think I have the name and address of my secret admirer." She didn't know why she was still calling Matthew her secret admirer when she knew that his reason for contacting her had nothing to do with how he felt about her, but only to pass on clues about Fontainebleau and his killer.

"Really. Where did you get that information?"

Erin pulled out her planner and passed it to him so he could copy Matthew's information. "I just… Adrienne had heard him talking to someone at the Homestead, and when she described him, it sounded like the man who delivered the lingerie. And I talked to him when I ran into him in the woods. I just… I suspected that he was the one who had sent it, not that he was just the deliveryman."

"But you don't know for sure. He might just be a courier."

"Maybe. But the man that Adrienne saw at the Homestead… well, obviously he had access to Fontainebleau. And if he worked at the Homestead, then why would he be a courier? If it's the same guy, he retired from Fontainebleau's company, but I don't see a scientist like him rushing out to get a job as a courier. If he did want to work, I would think it would be in… academics or as a consultant in the mining industry. Not delivering parcels around Bald Eagle Falls."

Terry nodded. "You seem to know a lot about him for someone Adrienne just happened to mention that she saw at the Homestead that sounded like someone you had seen here in town."

"Adrienne knew a little bit about him. That he had just retired, and some other stuff. And when I talked to the woman who's in charge over there, she was the one who said that he was a chemist."

Terry's eyebrows went up. "A chemist?"

"Yeah. I figured… someone like that would know how to mix up the kind of mercury you could add to food."

"Yes, he probably would. And exactly when did he retire?"

"I'm not sure exactly when. And… if he took the barometer from the Homestead, he could get in and out, even if he doesn't have a legitimate reason to be there. You know that their security is… not very good."

"Who is this woman you talked to who is in charge?"

"Her name is Freda Jones. I don't know all of her duties, but she knew Matthew's last name and where he lived. They've both worked there for a long time, so she knew him quite well."

"And didn't have a problem with giving you his personal information?"

"Well… I was a little surprised at that too. I figured she'd turn me away, or I'd have to find a good reason why I should have access to it. But all I had to do was ask. She seemed happy to give it to me."

"Maybe she suspects him of having had something to do with the poisoning. Although, you would think that if she knew something, she might want to talk to the police investigating it."

"Maybe she doesn't know anything, so she didn't want to throw accusations around, but she still has her suspicions." Erin shrugged. "I don't know. It seems like a lot of people just don't want to talk to the police."

Terry nodded. "Welcome to my world. 'We want you to keep the peace and arrest all of the criminals in the area, but we don't want to give you any information that will allow you to do so.'"

Erin chuckled. "Yeah. That sounds frustrating."

She knew that she should probably leave. She'd given Terry the information that she had come to give him. It was up to him to follow up on it.

"How are you going to… you know…" Erin motioned to the address he had written down, "make contact with him?"

"Knock on his door. Tell him that we have some questions for him. Follow up on the anonymous deliveries. Hope that it leads us to something about Fontainebleau's death."

"I was thinking… wouldn't it be better if *I* contacted him? I mean… he picked me out as the person to send his deliveries to. He obviously wanted to tell me about it, for me to figure it out."

"You are not a law enforcement officer."

"Well, I know that."

"We can't involve a civilian in an investigation."

"But you have before. I've helped before. Answered questions. Helped work through possibilities."

"Not the same as sending you in as an agent of the police."

"Well then, maybe… it will take you a while to get your stuff together, and I could just happen to go over there first."

"Erin."

"You use informants. You do that all the time."

He raised his brows.

"Well, okay, maybe not all the time. But they do on TV. And you use information that civilians bring you."

"I'm not sending you in to talk to this guy by yourself. There's every likelihood that he is a killer. Now he may have done the world a favor by getting rid of someone like Fontainebleau, but someone who has killed once is that much more likely to kill again. And people who are trapped tend to fight back."

"I just think… he'll talk to me. He's been trying to give me clues as to what happened. So let him. Let him give me the final clues so that you know who it was and can make an arrest."

"Clues are not the same as proof. I need proof before I can arrest someone."

"Maybe he'll have it. He had the barometer."

"And we don't know whether the barometer actually had anything to do with the poisoning of Fontainebleau. The medical examiner says he was not poisoned with elemental mercury. It had to be made into a compound and sprinkled or stirred into his food or drinks."

"But Matthew is a chemist. He could have done that."

"We'll need proof. Not just talking to him. A search warrant for his home or workshop, wherever he might have mixed it. Witnesses who can put him in proximity with Fontainebleau. Motive."

Erin opened her mouth and closed it again. Terry looked at her, waiting.

"Motive?" Terry suggested again.

"I… this is unverified."

"As is everything else at this point. Don't hold back on me."

"Fontainebleau assaulted Matthew's wife. Years ago, without Matthew realizing it. Matthew just recently discovered that his son is not his biological son, but Fontainebleau's."

"Well… yes, that would certainly be a motive. What is the wife's story? Does she confirm this? That it was an assault rather than an affair?"

"I think that either way, it gives him motive to kill Fontainebleau. But the wife is dead. Suicide some years ago."

"Ouch."

"So Fontainebleau really screwed up Matthew's family. And was never punished for it. That's a pretty good motive."

"Yes, it is," Terry agreed. He leaned back in his chair, staring at his computer screen. "I'm going to have to discuss this with the others. Work out a plan. Make sure we've got all of our ducks in a row before approaching him."

"And tell them that I should be the one to talk to him. Because I'm the one he reached out to."

Terry scowled. "I'll talk to the others."

CHAPTER 35

"Stand back and to the side until I tell you otherwise," Terry reminded Erin. He was not standing directly in front of the door himself as he reached over and rang the doorbell. He formed a fist to knock on the door loudly, as cops did, then relaxed it and just waited. The point was to keep it as informal as possible so that Matthew would feel comfortable talking to them instead of clamming up because Terry was a law enforcement officer. Things had taken longer to arrange than Erin had expected but, after the many hours it took for the police department to formulate a plan that everyone could live with and make all of the arrangements, they were finally standing on Matthew's front step.

The door opened slowly, and the familiar face peered out. The man looked at Terry, K9 standing beside him, and then his eyes slid to Erin and he smiled.

"Erin Price," he greeted pleasantly.

"Matthew?"

He nodded. He opened the door the rest of the way and motioned them in. Terry stepped forward and glanced around inside, then made a slight motion for Erin to follow him. He was the first one in the house and was keeping a close eye on Matthew and for any other sign of danger in their surroundings.

There didn't seem to be anyone else in the house. If Matthew's son lived there, it would seem he was out. The house was quiet and still.

Matthew ushered them into a comfortable-looking living room, one that had seen use and was not just preserved in pristine condition for someday in the future when somebody important might visit.

"Have a seat, please," Matthew invited, motioning to the couch in the living room. He swept several magazines off the surface, stacked them, squared the edges, and put them down on the coffee table, which was already thick with reading material. "Sorry. Just getting caught up on some reading."

They sat down and K9 lay at Terry's side.

Erin looked over the magazine titles. They all seemed to be professional magazines. Chemistry, engineering, mining, mineralogy. Way over Erin's head. Was there anything in there on the latest methods of processing with mercury? Erin had done a couple of internet searches and found that mercury was used in processing gold. She had always thought of the mines in Tennessee as being mostly coal, as attested to by Willie's darkly stained skin, but there were other precious minerals mined in the area.

Erin looked at Terry. He gave a little nod. "I should introduce myself. I'm Terry Piper from the Bald Eagle Falls police department. We haven't met before, I don't think."

He wanted to be sure that Matthew could not claim that he had been tricked or coerced into giving a confession to a police officer if it turned out that he said something they wanted to use in court. It was not an undercover operation.

Matthew nodded his understanding, not appearing to be put off by this information. "Yes. Nice to meet you."

It was Erin's turn. She was a little tongue-tied facing her secret admirer, and uncertain how to start the conversation. She hoped to be able to get a lot of information from him and, if she goofed up, they might be kicked out with nothing but denials. Matthew knew something, and it might take some delicacy to get all that information from him.

"So, you know who I am," Erin said with a little laugh. "But you have the advantage over me because we've never been introduced. You're Matthew Harris."

"Yes."

"And you're my secret admirer. The person who has been sending me packages."

"I've been delivering them."

Erin gazed at him steadily. "I think you're more than the deliveryman."

He looked away after a few seconds. "What makes you think that?"

"You used to work with Fontainebleau. At the Homestead. You had access to the newspaper clippings and the barometer. Those couldn't come from just anyone."

"A lot of people might have had access to those things. And I don't work there anymore. I'm retired."

"It's pretty easy to get in and out of there. There isn't any security guard or gate. Maybe if they thought you were a threat, they would do something about it, but people walk in and out of there all day. I've been in a few times, and no one has ever challenged my right to be there. I've never had to talk to any security personnel."

"There is plenty of security that you don't see. They would get rid of you fairly quickly if they didn't want you to be there."

"But they didn't. Someone was able to poison Mr. Fontainebleau without getting caught. And you were able to get the newspaper clippings and barometer out of there without being stopped."

He shrugged. "So you say."

"I think… you want to tell me about what happened. You want someone to know what you did, and you picked me out to be the one to tell. That's why you've been sending me these gifts. Because you want to tell me what happened."

"Someone should know. But there are certain… barriers to telling anyone the full story of what has been happening at the Homestead."

"Well… I'm here. So why don't you tell me about it?"

He sat back and looked at Erin with an expression of consternation. "I said that there were barriers."

Erin nodded. Until he said what those barriers were—whether he was afraid to talk in front of the police or had some ethical dilemma, she couldn't do anything to encourage him to tell the story. She could maybe prompt him, talk about what it was that they knew so far, but Matthew needed to break through a few of those barriers before they were going to get anywhere.

Matthew looked at Terry, and back at Erin again. "I'd like to be able to talk to you about what I know… but I can't. I'm sorry."

Erin hadn't expected a flat-out no. "You sent me those things for a reason."

"Yes, obviously," he agreed.

"And it wasn't just because… you admired me and wanted to give me a barometer."

"No."

"I think that you gave me the barometer to point out that mercury was involved."

Matthew said nothing.

"You know that Fontainebleau was killed with mercury poisoning," Erin said.

"I imagine the symptoms line up," he said mildly. "I'm not a medical examiner, and I can't tell you what they found in the autopsy."

"The medical examiner has determined that mercury toxicity is the cause of death. And since there wasn't enough mercury at his work sites to cause death by casual exposure—and his employees who are there every day would succumb to it first—the manner of death was homicide."

Matthew spread his hands. "Then you already know that," he summarized.

"The paramedics and medical examiner immediately noticed the rashes. And the descriptions of his behavior in the weeks before his death suggest heavy metal poisoning."

Matthew nodded.

"You're familiar with mercury, aren't you, Mr. Harris?" Terry asked. "Handling it, toxicity, compounding it."

"Sure. It was my job to know all of that stuff."

"Why don't you tell us what led you to poison him? I suspect you would really like to get it off your chest. What Fontainebleau did that deserved death."

"I can't do that. For one thing, I did not poison him."

"You had good reason to hate him."

Matthew shrugged, not disagreeing.

"You gave him years of your life. Decades. And he had betrayed your trust. The impacts on your family were catastrophic."

Matthew swallowed. He looked around. "Can I get you something to drink? I didn't offer you a drink."

Even though both Terry and Erin immediately shook their heads, he got up and headed to the kitchen. Terry made to get up and go after him, but Erin put a hand on his knee to encourage him to stay there. He looked at her and stayed. But he gazed toward the kitchen as if he could see through the walls and waited for Matthew to make a wrong move. K9 was his mirror image, ears pointed toward the kitchen.

CHAPTER 36

They could hear the familiar sounds of a kettle being put on and the clinking of cups. No indication that Matthew was leaving through the back door or getting a weapon. Erin hadn't felt unsafe with him from the moment they'd walked into the house. Maybe part of that was Terry being there. She knew that he wouldn't let anything happen to her. But she didn't think Matthew would do anything violent. If he were the murderer, he had killed with good reason, and he hadn't shot Mr. Fontainebleau, but had poisoned him. Murder from a distance, over time, patient and waiting.

Eventually, Matthew returned with a tea tray. He set it down and poured water into each of their cups, motioning for them to help themselves to the tea bags, cream, and sugar. Erin reached for one, and Terry touched her arm, warning her. She looked at him. He gave his head a slight shake.

Taking tea with a poisoner? Maybe not the brightest possible move. While Erin felt sure there was nothing wrong with the teabags, commercial teas she'd used her whole life, there was the possibility of tampering. That they had been soaked in some poison, injected, or opened and closed again. Matthew looked from one of them to the other.

"They're perfectly safe. I told you I didn't poison Fontainebleau."

"You could have more mercury around here," Terry pointed out. "You could have prepared these ahead of time for just an occasion like this. We would be fools to drink them."

Matthew shook his head. "Hand me any one of them."

Terry selected a teabag and handed it to him. Without any apparent concern, Matthew plopped it into his cup to steep. That was a pretty good indicator that there wasn't any poison in the bag or any of the others that awaited them on the tray. Erin looked at Terry to see if this had convinced him.

Terry didn't take one. "They could all be poisoned. You might not care if you die. That might be your plan. If cornered, you take the coward's way out."

"You have a high opinion of me," Matthew said sarcastically. "I can assure you I have no intention of dying. Or of being arrested." He turned abruptly to a side table and picked up a photo frame. He turned the picture toward them. "My children," he explained, showing them the photo of the three of them standing together, arms around each other, smiling at the camera. Matthew, a daughter, and a son. The daughter a little shorter than he was, and the son almost a head taller, a gangly teen. "My daughter just had a baby. My first grandchild." He got out his phone and fiddled with it for a few minutes, finally turning it around to show his daughter, older in this picture, with a swaddled newborn in her arms. Swiping the picture, he showed them another, with proud grandpa holding up the baby for the camera. "Do you think I could leave them now? They need me. And I didn't raise them by myself just to abandon them for something like this. Their mother committed suicide. I could never do that to them."

He used his spoon to squeeze the teabag against the cup a few times and then lifted the teabag out and set it on his saucer. He took a sip of the tea and exhaled a long sigh.

"But he's not your son," Terry said. "You recently found out that he isn't actually biologically yours."

Matthew looked surprised that he knew this. "That doesn't

make him any less my son. I raised him from infancy. I was there for the ultrasounds and doctor's appointments before he was born. I was at my wife's side and held him first." He swallowed hard, eyes shining. "Of course he's my son."

"And you wanted to punish Fontainebleau for what he had done. For what he did to your wife. For his complicity in your wife's death."

"Of course I wanted to. But what good would that do? How would it change anything? I wouldn't risk my life with my children and grandchildren for that despicable man. I should have turned him in. But after this long, I didn't think there was any chance of him being charged. Not after this many years, and with his power and wealth. His influence would keep him safe, just like it always had."

"You knew about other cases?"

He looked away. "Of course I'd heard the rumors. We all had. I never saw any proof of it, and I was happy to keep it that way. Better that it was an unfounded rumor than that I knew the truth." He snorted and shook his head at himself, sounding disgusted. "All of us should have been more interested in the truth and stopping a predator than in preserving our own jobs and reputations. Letting him operate in the dark like that, year after year, was tacit approval of what he did. We were all complicit in those assaults on those young women."

"Then why are you keeping quiet?" Erin asked. "Even after his death? Why would you keep protecting him and his reputation?"

"What difference would it make now? He has been stopped. He won't ever do that again. There's no reason for me to give up my... security to talk about what kind of a monster he was."

"You'd rather have the money," Terry said.

"I would rather be able to give my children and grandchildren the things that they need. To make sure that they never want. I took early retirement. I was owed every penny. I worked for him for years and earned every cent."

"You let him buy your silence."

Matthew shook his head, his jaw clenching and unclenching. "I haven't said a word. And I'm not going to. But there were things I *could* do." He made a motion toward Erin. "Ways that I could communicate without words."

"So you started sending me the anonymous deliveries," Erin said. "That was your way of telling the story."

He shrugged and sipped his tea.

"But you haven't told us anything," Terry pointed out. "Was the lingerie supposed to symbolize his sexual assaults? Or is that just the spin we're supposed to put on it when you realized that you didn't have any chance of courting Erin? The flowers? Were they supposed to symbolize something? Innocence and purity? And there's nothing in the news articles to indicate what he had done. Just puff pieces about the golden son coming back to save the company from ruin. There was nothing there about his predatory behavior or what he did once he took over the company. You didn't even pick any modern pieces that talked about what he had done over the years. You picked old articles that said nothing."

"Anything modern, the police could get off the internet, and I assumed you were already doing that. The old articles… you'd have to go to archives to find. And why would you, since all of his history was included in the current press? Or a version of it, anyway."

"I thought you picked those articles to show his father's involvement with the Dyson clan," Erin said. "How his father got the company into debt and what Fontainebleau the Third had to pull the company out of. Or his ongoing involvement with them."

Matthew raised his brows. He had another sip of tea and wet his lips. "There were always rumors of his involvement with organized crime. But I never saw any proof of it. I wasn't involved in the financial stuff. Just in the operations of the mines and the chemical processing. Anything on financing and debt and how he got his money… that wasn't anything to do with me."

CHAPTER 37

"So you won't talk about what Fontainebleau did to your wife or how she was involved with him," Terry stated.

"I can't. I signed an agreement."

"You would have to if called to testify in court."

"But that isn't going to happen. I'm not going to court."

"If we find evidence that you were involved in poisoning Fontainebleau, you certainly are."

Matthew set his teacup down and folded his hands. "I was not. You won't find anything to prove that I was. In the weeks before Fontainebleau's death, I wasn't even here. I was visiting my daughter. Helping her to get settled with the new baby. Making sure they had everything they needed."

"We have a warrant to search this house."

Erin's secret admirer looked a little surprised by this, but raised his shoulders in a shrug. "You won't find anything."

Terry stood up. He reached out a hand to give Erin a hand up as well. "This is your exit cue," he told her. "And I call the others in to do the search."

Erin nodded. She had been expecting this, though she hadn't expected the interview to end so quickly or that she would be left confused about whether Matthew had really had anything to do

187

with the poisoning. She had thought that by the time she left, Matthew would be under arrest, and she would know for sure that he had been the one to kill Fontainebleau. If it had been a TV show, he would have confessed his involvement, and there would be plenty of evidence to back his story up. As it was… maybe Terry and the other law enforcement officers would find something in the search.

Matthew stood, putting his teacup down carefully. "I have one more delivery for you, Miss Price."

Erin's eyes went to Terry to gauge his response. He shook his head. "No more games. If you have something to say, then say it."

"This isn't from me. As I said… I can't say anything. I can't afford to lose my retirement funds."

Terry didn't look happy about this. But what were they going to do? Refuse to accept a piece of evidence that was offered to them? If it was like the rest of Matthew's gifts, it probably wouldn't solve the case, but it was possible that it would at least push them in the right direction.

"Just wait here," Matthew instructed, and headed for the hallway.

Terry's hand shot out, and he grabbed Matthew by the shoulder. "You're not going anywhere." K9 growled a warning.

Erin's heart was in her throat. She couldn't help thinking of the TV shows she had seen where the perpetrator of a crime walked out of the room to get a wallet or some other possession, followed by an off-screen gunshot as they committed suicide.

"Matthew," she protested.

He looked back at her. "I just want to get that delivery for you."

"You can tell us where it is and we'll grab it during our search," Terry told him sternly. "You sit back down there and stay put. We don't like suspects walking around a scene while we are conducting a search. Things get damaged, destroyed, flushed down the toilet. I would tell you to leave until we are finished, only I don't want you out of sight."

Matthew sighed and pulled gently away from Terry. He sat back down in his chair. Terry nodded at Erin.

"Out you go. Send the sheriff in."

Erin walked out of Matthew's house and nodded to Sheriff Wilmot, waiting at the edge of the property line. "He's ready for you."

Wilmot and the others walked up to the door, Wilmot flourishing a sheet of paper folded lengthwise at the door. "Search warrant," he announced, and then was inside the house and Erin couldn't see or hear any more of what happened. The law enforcement officers entered and shut the door behind them.

Erin waited outside of the house.

This hadn't been part of her agreement with Terry, who expected her to go home once her role in the investigation was completed. But she wanted to be there when they retrieved the item Matthew had intended to deliver to her. Or when they found traces of mercury or lab equipment in the house. Or maybe a written confession of what he had done.

Though she wasn't sure now that he had actually done anything.

Murderers lied all of the time, of course. Matthew still wanted to be able to see his children and grandchildren, so he didn't want to be arrested. He would say he hadn't done it even if he had. And if they could verify that he had, in fact, been visiting his daughter and new grandbaby, and couldn't have gotten back to the Homestead to poison Fontainebleau during that time, then they would have to admit that he was not the poisoner.

They didn't come out again within a few minutes like Erin had hoped. It couldn't take them very long to find whatever Matthew wanted to give her, but Terry also wouldn't know that she was still waiting outside for him to bring it to her. They had arrived in Terry's truck, so she returned to it and sat waiting.

~

Eventually, the Bald Eagle Falls police department exited Matthew Harris's house. They didn't carry very much with them. A few items to be tested for mercury residue, Erin assumed. Maybe some personal correspondence or a journal that they wanted to examine at length. And whatever it was that Matthew had planned to give her, if that hadn't been a ruse to get out of the room before the search was performed.

The law enforcement officers clustered together outside the house to discuss proceedings. Maybe they needed to search the backyard and whatever garage or shed Matthew had, if they hadn't already.

Looking away from the others as he talked, Terry's eyes focused on his truck, and he saw Erin inside. He shook his head and walked over to her.

"You didn't need to wait around. You should have gone home."

She couldn't exactly complain that she hadn't had her own vehicle to get home in, since everything in the town was within walking distance.

"I wanted to see what you found out. And what Matthew had for me."

He held up an envelope with Erin's name hand-printed neatly on it. "That is apparently the last delivery."

"Did Matthew write it?"

He looked at the printing and shrugged. "I don't know. He won't say a word about it, of course. Keeping his agreement not to say anything to anyone about the whole affair." He rolled his eyes heavenward. "If he was so concerned about justice being done, he could break his NDA and speak to us."

"But then he would lose the money he has to live on for the next few years. He's too young to start drawing on a 401K or pension."

"What is more important? Seeing justice done or having money? I thought that he was concerned with right and wrong."

"I think the most important thing for him in all of this is family. And he needs to take care of his children. Does his son still live with him?"

Terry nodded. "Searched his room. Nothing of concern there."

Erin let out a breath. "Good. I was afraid that he might be protecting someone in his family."

"That doesn't mean that it *wasn't* his son who poisoned Fontainebleau. But he would have needed access to the man at the Homestead. And I think that the staff out there would at least be able to tell us whether his son ever came out for visits in the past few weeks. Even if they aren't in the habit of kicking out anyone who doesn't belong."

"But how old is he? Eighteen? I doubt if he would plan out a crime like that. Mercury poisoning isn't something an eighteen-year-old would necessarily think of or have the patience to carry out. Teenagers are impulsive. A shooting or stabbing, maybe. Not something that took place over a period of weeks."

Terry made a gesture that was half nod, half shrug. "I don't think the son had anything to do with it. I'm just saying that there isn't any evidence one way or the other right now. I want to interview him to see what he has to say about his father's behavior over the last few weeks. If he's noticed any changes. Any odd smells coming from behind closed doors. Talk of getting back at Fontainebleau or someone who has done him wrong."

"You don't think he would tell you anything, do you?"

"No, probably not. But you never know. Maybe he's had some concerns. Sometimes kids need someone to talk to..."

She didn't like the idea of his acting sensitive and empathetic toward the young man just to get incriminating statements about his father out of him.

Erin reached for the envelope. "So, can I see it?"

"We need to take any fingerprints or trace evidence, and then open and read it. After that..."

Erin rolled her eyes. "*Then* I can see the note that was intended for me?"

He shrugged, having the grace to look slightly embarrassed. "Maybe. You know that we're not able to release evidence in an active investigation."

"Without me, you wouldn't have that evidence. I can't even see it? You can open it now. Let me read it. Or take a picture and send me when you open it at the police department offices. You can't just push me out of my own..." She trailed off, realizing that she was going to claim it was her own investigation. But she was a baker. Not a police officer or private investigator. She didn't have an investigation. Just curiosity about what had happened to Mr. Fontainebleau. It wasn't *really* any of her business, even if Matthew had tried to bring her in on it.

The corner of Terry's mouth quirked up, and the dimple appeared on his cheek. "It's not your investigation."

"I know. But I really want to know. I think I deserve to see what's in a letter that's addressed to me. I didn't have to bring you into any of this. I could have just gone to see Matthew on my own without telling you. Then he would have given that to me and I could have read it. And *maybe* shared it with you, if I felt like it." She gave him an impish smile, teasing him.

"I will *try* to get you a copy. I can't open it here, but at the police department offices… I'll share it when I can. If I can."

"You've got a camera. Someone has to take pictures of it."

"You are relentless."

"But that's what you love about me, right?"

Terry shook his head. "Do you want me to drive you home on the way back to the office? Or do you want to walk?"

K9 gave a little whine at the word "walk." Erin laughed and scratched his ears. "Sorry, boy, I think you're going to be sitting in the office for the rest of the day." She looked around. It had been hot sitting in the truck. She hadn't wanted to run the air conditioner the whole time Terry was in the house, idling the engine, so she had only turned it on for a minute or two every now and then to take the edge off. But out in the open air, it actually wasn't too bad.

She would go for a walk and think about what she had learned about the case so far. Maybe she wouldn't need the final delivery. Maybe she'd be able to figure it out herself if she put her mind to work while she walked.

CHAPTER 38

 𝓔rin didn't have any brilliant insights on the way home. Matthew Harris could be the poisoner. Maybe. Even if he had an alibi for the weeks that Fontainebleau had been suffering from mercury poisoning, he might have poisoned the man before he left, and it just took him that long to die. Mercury was a slow killer.

Or Matthew might have put it into something that Fontainebleau would continue to consume while Matthew was gone. Teabags, coffee grounds, a daily vitamin, cigars or some other indulgence that he would take dose by dose the entire time that Matthew was away, slowly poisoning himself until he succumbed.

Maybe he was supposed to die while Matthew was still out of town instead of waiting until he came back so that Matthew could declare with authority that he hadn't even been there when Fontainebleau had died. That he was totally in the clear.

But so many other people had just as much or more opportunity to poison Fontainebleau. And just as much motive as Matthew did. Fontainebleau had hurt a lot of people, broken a lot of lives.

There was nothing else Erin could do about it. She didn't have anyone else to ask questions of or any other avenues to pursue. She had exhausted all of her leads. Terry held the final piece of evidence. He and the rest of the police department would be examining it as Erin worked on the next day's plans and made herself supper. Sorting out all of the clues and coming to a landing on it without any input from Erin.

She was surprised to hear Terry come home as she was putting her supper dishes in the dishwasher. She looked around, realizing that she would have to get everything out again to dish up dinner for Terry. He would be tired and hungry after a long day of investigating.

Terry didn't relax and release K9 from duty when he walked in the door. He didn't even glance toward the kitchen or sniff at the air and say that something smelled good. He looked at Erin and gave her a nod of acknowledgment.

"I need your help."

Erin laughed. "You need my help? Well, that's the last thing I expected to hear from you. Was the last clue a recipe that I need to make? Some mercury-containing ingredient that you need me to identify?"

"No. I need to know if you can identify the author of the note."

"It wasn't Matthew?"

He shook his head. "No, not as far as we can tell. We're at a loss as to the author, but since you are the intended recipient, we assume you will know who the sender is."

Erin nodded. She sat down on the couch to get comfortable and waited for him to give her or read her the note. Terry sat on one of the chairs, perched on the edge as if ready to jump up the instant she told him what he wanted to know. He reached into the zippered portfolio that he held against his body under one arm and withdrew a plastic document holder with a single sheet of notepaper in it.

Blank white paper, nothing identifiable about it. As far as she could see, no name, address, or watermark for the company. Torn from a tablet on someone's desk rather than taken from a ream of copy paper. Erin focused on the words on the page.

I told A that I would take care of it, and I did.

I have watched the man ruin so many lives and helped him to do it. But I couldn't let it go this time.

I couldn't let him attack a child and just cover it up.

It was in the fish that Fontainebleau ate at least once a week for his health. I didn't poison it. He did that himself by dumping wastewater into bodies of water that he hoped would not be tested. He knew that it was not safe and would poison the wildlife and anyone who depended on the lake for their water source.

He knew it would poison someone. It seemed only fitting that it should be himself. All I did was provide the kitchen with the fish he had contaminated.

Erin stared at the words on the paper in perfectly formed cursive handwriting. Something that the younger generation could barely read or write anymore. But for the older generations, it was natural, and it looked like the author had practiced until her formation was perfect, all with regular slant, size, and spacing, even though there were no lines on the page.

"Do you know who wrote that?" Terry asked.

"I… don't know the handwriting. Sorry."

Erin hoped that he would leave it at that. She couldn't help him. He would have to figure it out himself, and he wouldn't be able to because everyone had agreed not to talk.

"Erin."

She raised her brows and shook her head. She handed it back to him.

"Don't try to put me off by not answering the question directly."

Erin cleared her throat. "Would I do that?"

He chuckled. "Of course you would. You're a master at deflection."

Erin couldn't help the embarrassed smile that spread across her face. She had done it to him too many times lately. He was on to her. She wasn't going to be able to distract him from the fact that she hadn't actually answered the question he had asked.

"We can go to the Homestead and ask questions about who

provided the kitchen with fish, if that is really how he was poisoned. But that will tip everyone off, and we'd rather go in there knowing who our target is. So," Terry's voice was stern and all business. "Who wrote that note?"

Erin sighed. "They call her the purser. She's the one who is in charge of writing the checks to pay off Fontainebleau's victims to ensure their silence. She's the one who… would know where all the bodies were buried, so to speak."

"What's her name?"

"Freda Jones."

"She's the woman you said gave you Matthew's information. His name and address."

Erin nodded. "Yes."

He frowned. "Why would she give you that information? Especially if Matthew was the one who had this note? Why would she send it or give it to him and then send you to talk to him?"

"I don't know. I'm… a bit lost."

"She's confessed. It wasn't signed, but she knew you would understand where it came from."

Erin nodded. Her heart started beating faster. Earlier in the day, she had been worried about Matthew's intentions, afraid he would harm himself either by self-poisoning or by walking out of the room and shooting himself. But he wasn't the poisoner. At least, not according to this note. And if Jones was confessing, what were the chances that she was just sitting at the Homestead waiting for Terry or one of the other cops to go out there and arrest her?

"You don't think… Do you think that she's done something? She must have written this right after I went out to see her, and then asked Matthew to give it to me. You don't think…?"

"I don't know. You stay here, and I'll head out there and find out. Hopefully…"

Did he hope that he would find her and be able to arrest her? Or did he hope that she would have dealt justice to herself as well as to Clive William Fontainebleau III?

"I'm not staying here," Erin objected. "I'm coming with you."

"This is a police action, Erin. You can't."

"I'll follow you out, then. You can't stop me from coming."

"Why would you want to go out there? The news isn't going to be good. You know that. Either this woman is arrested for killing a truly despicable character and saving countless other people harm, or she's already dead. Neither scenario is one you want to be a part of."

"I'm already a part of this. She sent me the letter, and I told you who wrote it. I'm already all mixed up in this."

"There's no need for you to go out there. I can tell you what happens after it is all over. You don't want to see anything. And you wouldn't be allowed to. All that you'd be able to do is sit outside the house waiting for me to tell you what we find."

"That's all I want. I need to be there. I know I won't see anything and wouldn't want to. But you can't stop me from being a part of this."

"Apparently not," he agreed dryly.

"Do you want something to eat on the way?"

"What?" Terry looked distracted.

"A sandwich. Have you had anything for supper?"

"We ordered in at the office. Thank you, though." He met her eyes for a moment and nodded his thanks. "You're always looking out for me."

"No more than you do for me."

He reached out a hand to her to help her to her feet. Erin handed him the note in its plastic envelope instead of giving him her hand.

"That's not what I—"

"I know," Erin agreed. "Let's go."

Terry shook his head and led the way back out to his truck. K9 stuck close to his side, though he looked back at Erin once or twice to ensure she was following.

CHAPTER 39

They didn't have much conversation on the way out to the Homestead. Terry was busy on his phone, talking to the other law enforcement officers and ensuring everyone was on the same page. The Homestead was a big place and not secure. They would all head out there and try to cover the exits to ensure that Freda Jones couldn't slip out of their grasp, but they all knew there was no way they could cover every escape route. They didn't know what roads might run from the back of the property, through narrow country trails, before eventually coming out onto the highway. They could block the main road, but there were too many other possibilities.

"You need to stay in the truck," Terry told Erin again. "I mean it. No coming to check on me or anything else. You stay there until I tell you otherwise, which means you're going to be there for a while."

"I will."

Would she be able to see Freda one last time? Or had her last meeting been the only opportunity she would have to see the woman?

Eventually, they reached the Homestead. Terry parked in the more public lot at the front of the building. Other police vehicles passed them to cover other parts of the building. Erin watched Terry walk in with K9 at his side and wondered what he would find. Was Freda waiting to turn herself in? Or had she taken her own life? Would she try to run?

It was hard to picture Terry's progress, since Erin had never walked in through the front doors herself. She could only imagine what the grand hall looked like, whether it was bustling with activity or quiet and still. Whether there was a receptionist that would greet Terry and take him around to Jones's office, or a security guard or other staff member who would escort him.

She pictured Jones's office as she had seen it. Neat and tidy. A big, heavy desk. Not something made of particle board and assembled there. A real solid, antique desk. Bookshelves, a computer on the desk, sparsely decorated considering that she had worked there for decades. There wouldn't be any sign of the poison in her office. Not if she had seen to it that Fontainebleau was fed fish contaminated by his own plants. She didn't have to have a chemistry degree like Matthew to compound raw elemental mercury into something that could be sprinkled on Fontainebleau's food or dissolved in his drink. They wouldn't be looking for any evidence of chemistry projects in her office.

It was an interminably long time. Jones did not come sprinting out of the building or race by in a little compact car with the police in hot pursuit. Eventually, Terry walked out, talking on his phone, with K9 keeping pace at his side. He hung up the call before approaching the truck. He swung himself up into the driver's seat to talk to Erin.

"Your Mrs. Jones has flown the coop. No sign of her."

"She's not *my* Mrs.—"

"I know. But she's not there. Looks like she cleaned everything up, packed her bags, and left. No one knows where she was headed or if she has any relatives that she might have gone to. She worked with Fontainebleau for a long time. People didn't really go to her unless there was trouble, so she didn't have a lot of friends in the company."

A lonely life, only ever dealing with the people Fontainebleau may have harmed. But she'd had other duties as well. Administrative stuff that didn't involve paying people off.

"Where does she live? In town or in the city? On a farm?"

"Here on the Homestead. We've already checked out her rooms, and there's nothing there that gives any clue as to where she might have gone. I don't know how much she had to pack, but with what I have experienced in moving apartments or houses... she must have been planning this for some time. She didn't just pack an overnight bag and make a run for it. Everything personal has been cleared out. We'll have to ask around, see whether anyone saw a moving truck or rented trailer around here the last day or two."

"Well, she was poisoning Fontainebleau for weeks, so she had plenty of time to plan her... exit," Erin observed.

"Yes. She's a cool customer, watching Fontainebleau dying over the past few months. A sociopath."

Erin grimaced and shook her head. "I don't think so. I think she had feelings, empathy for the people that Fontainebleau had hurt. The lives that he had ruined. She said that she couldn't stand by and watch it anymore. It got to be too much for her."

"That's what she says. But she'd stood by for years, so what had changed? She might have been on the verge of losing her job, being fired or forced into retirement. This could just as easily have been about getting back at him, emptying a bank account or two, and setting up a new life somewhere else as about protecting his future victims."

"It was because of—" Erin cut herself off. She couldn't give away Adrienne's secret. Couldn't tell him about what had happened to Hope or that Adrienne had refused to come forward to the police afterward. He could call in social services, saying that Adrienne had harmed Hope by not seeking treatment for her. It wouldn't help Hope to be taken away from her family. That would just be another blow to all of them.

Terry waited, then shook his head, scowling. "You need to tell me, Erin. Holding things back isn't going to help anyone. If you know what's going on, you need to come out with it."

"No. It's just… in the letter. She said that it was something to do with a child. That she couldn't just sit back and watch when he had attacked a child."

Terry nodded slowly. "Yes. Someone around here must know what she's talking about. Something like that, they wouldn't be able to cover up."

Erin nodded. Hopefully, he was wrong and people would stay quiet, as they had been doing for years. They had been conditioned to keep quiet about what they saw and heard, about all of the rumors of Fontainebleau's behavior. She hoped that they would protect Hope, just as Jones had done. Erin wasn't going to be the one to reveal the incident to the police.

Terry studied her, and Erin knew he suspected she knew more than she was saying.

"Do you have any idea where she would go? Did she say anything to you about somewhere she would like to go, family members, anything like that?"

"No. Our conversation was pretty short. She didn't say anything personal like that."

"You just asked her for Matthew's information, and she gave it to you."

Erin shrugged and nodded. "Yes."

"I guess the two of them were in collusion… she knew he was sending you clues. And she had sent him the letter or was planning to. Maybe he had told her it was okay to give you his information if you went looking for him. It doesn't seem like he was making much effort to keep his identity a secret."

"No. I think that he wanted me to find him, in the end. Even if he couldn't tell me anything, he wanted me to know that he had done his best to reveal the truth."

"Only the truth that he wanted to reveal was about what Fontainebleau had been doing, not who had killed him," Terry pointed out. "He never sent you anything that pointed to Freda Jones until she gave him the letter to give to you."

"Maybe that had been the plan all along."

Terry shook his head slowly. "You think she always planned to confess? Not just when she thought we were closing in on her?"

"We never really had anything that pointed to her… other than her promise that she would make things right. And I never thought…" Erin trailed off.

"What promise?" Terry demanded.

Erin scrambled to repair her mistake. "Like she said in her letter. That she promised someone she would make things right. I thought that meant that she would go to the police about Fontainebleau, but maybe she meant that she would make sure it never happened again by getting rid of him."

"When did you know that she promised to make things right?" Terry countered.

"I… don't know. When I read the letter."

"You didn't think she was going to the police when she said that in the letter. You had her confession right in front of you. You knew that when she said she was going to make things right, she meant that she had killed him. *Unless* you found out about this promise before today."

Erin breathed slowly in and out, trying not to let anything in her face give away the truth to Terry.

"Who did she make this promise to? You know more than you're letting on, Erin. Who was the child that was attacked? Who did she promise that she would make things right?"

"I… can't say."

"You never signed a non-disclosure agreement. You can't with-hold evidence from the police."

"I'm not. It's just… hearsay. I heard something from someone who heard it from someone else… It isn't evidence."

"You still need to tell us what you know."

"I don't *know* anything. And what I was told, I promised not to share."

"Crimes need to be reported to the police. Especially crimes against children, who need to be protected. You have a duty to report that."

"No, I don't."

He looked for some argument to persuade her that she needed to tell him. But Erin kept her mouth shut. She wasn't a nurse or a teacher or someone else who was required by law to report any suspicions about child abuse. She was just a regular citizen. And a regular citizen wasn't required to report rumors to the police. What Adrienne said Jones had said was not evidence.

Terry scowled. He climbed out of the truck without another word and returned to the Homestead to continue his investigation. Erin would have a long evening sitting in the truck waiting for him. But she was the one who had insisted she had to ride along.

CHAPTER 40

"Special order came in," Bella informed Erin as they switched places, Erin entering the kitchen and Bella going out to the front to serve customers. There was a green special-order sheet on the counter.

Erin picked it up and looked at it before putting the additional cookie sheets in the ovens. Not a birthday cake order, but a request for two lemon meringue pies. She had not made any since the day Mr. Fontainebleau had died. Even though everyone knew she'd had nothing to do with poisoning him, she still wanted to avoid any whispers behind her back or jokes about it. But apparently, someone had decided they weren't willing to wait until she felt like making them again. She looked up at the top of the order slip to see who it was for.

Matthew Harris.

Was he serious?

It seemed like poor taste for him to ask for the dessert she had made for his employer's last meal. Like he was celebrating Fontainebleau's demise.

Of course—many people *were* silently celebrating his demise.

Despite all of the non-disclosure agreements that had been signed, people were talking. The public funeral that had originally been planned had been canceled, with the announcement that the family had decided just to have a private memorial. Erin assumed they didn't want to deal with the possibility of victims showing up at the funeral and throwing eggs or shouting about what Fontainebleau had done to their families. A public funeral would probably have been only sparsely attended, now that the word was out about what kind of person he had been. Public figures were distancing themselves from Fontainebleau like rats fleeing a sinking ship.

Erin hesitated, then pulled out her phone and dialed the number beside Matthew's name.

"Hello?" his voice was cautious, uncertain. He didn't know her number.

"Mr. Harris, it's Erin Price from Auntie Clem's Bakery."

"Oh," his tone warmed. "Hello, Miss Price. You got my order."

"Yes, I did. Are you serious, though? You really want lemon meringue pies? You don't think that's too… morbid?"

"Of course not. There's nothing wrong with your lemon meringue pies, and I wouldn't want anyone to think there is. I *want* to be seen eating a pie from Auntie Clem's Bakery, to shake people off of this idea that it's something to whisper about once and for all."

"Well… that's very kind of you. I certainly wasn't expecting you to act as my PR agent."

He chuckled. "Your assistant wasn't sure when they would be ready. If you can let me know, I will be happy to come pick them up."

"If you're not in a rush, how would tomorrow afternoon be?"

"That would be just fine. Do you want to call me when they are ready, or should I just pop by?"

"I'll have them ready by mid-afternoon. Any time after two." Erin could work that into her schedule and it would give the pies enough time to chill before he picked them up. "And I'm assuming you'll be taking them straight home to the fridge? They can't be left in the vehicle while you shop, or they'll melt in this heat."

"I will take them straight home," he promised.

"Okay… I'll see you tomorrow."

∾

Erin heard the crunch of gravel behind the house and got up from the couch to look into the kitchen and out the back window to confirm that Vic and Willie had returned. She knew that they had been to the city to see some kind of specialist, but she hadn't pried to find out which one of them needed to see a medical professional or what for. She just hoped it wasn't anything serious.

Their body language was stiff and they didn't look at each other, like they had been arguing on the way home.

Erin put the kettle on. She didn't know whether Vic would come to talk to her or not, but she was in need of a nice calming tea herself. She didn't like to see them fighting. She looked studiously away from the window, not watching them return to the loft. She waited until she had heard the loft door shut before turning to look out the window again. Vic was making her way to the back door.

Erin turned back to the tea kettle and prepared the tea things. Maybe a few defrosted cookies to go with it… a little sugar went a long way to easing hurt feelings.

Vic tapped on the back door and entered. "Whew, these dogs are barking," she told Erin. "We must have walked twenty miles today." She sat down at the kitchen table and pried off her shoes. "Sorry for being so rude, but I really can't wear these another instant!"

Erin chuckled and continued to get their tea ready. The kettle began to sing. In a few minutes, she took everything over to the table and sat down. Vic immediately reached for a cookie.

"You always know just what to do," she complimented. "Tea and cookies are perfect."

"Good. Sounds like you had a long day."

"Long doesn't even begin to cover it. And Mr. Cranky-pants over there," she indicated the loft apartment with her eyes, "has not been the best of company."

"Well, you can relax now." Erin was determined not to ask where they had been and what the results of their consultation with the specialist had been.

"It's all your fault, you know," Vic told her. "Asking about Willie and whether his work could be causing health problems. Heavy metal poisoning and all that."

"Oh." Erin put her hand over her heart. "I'm sorry! I didn't mean to cause problems."

"Well, somebody needed to say it. What sense would it make just to let him keep poisoning himself?"

"I hope… well, did everything go okay? Is he…?"

"The doctor was pretty shocked by his condition. Said that people hadn't been working in conditions like that for a hundred years, and what made him think that exposing himself to those kinds of toxins was a good idea?" Vic rolled her eyes. "She didn't mince words. Which is good, because you and I both know that nothing is going to get into that hard head of Willie's if she held back."

"What does that mean for him?"

"He needs to detox immediately. And I'm not talking about wheatgrass shots for a week. I mean real medical intervention. They did his first chelation therapy today, and his calendar is booked up for some time to come. No alcohol, to give his liver the best chance possible to do its job. A special diet to give him all of the extra vitamins and minerals he needs to deal with the chelation and support liver and kidney function. She said he'll probably feel like he's got the flu for a few weeks and be restless and irritable. He'll want to stop. But he has to keep going and complete the protocol if he wants to clear all of the heavy metals and other toxins that he's been exposed to since he started mining and doing his own processing, however many years that's been. It's apparently a miracle that he's even functional right now."

Erin shook her head in amazement. "Wow. I'm glad they caught it now. Do you think you'll be able to keep him on the program?"

"I can't force him. I'll do my best, but it's gotta come from him.

And he's going to have to upgrade to modern processing methods and protective gear and all of the proper precautions. To keep from poisoning himself more."

"Poor Willie. I feel bad about it… but I'm glad he saw someone and is doing something about it. We don't want him just dropping dead one day!"

"That's what I told him," Vic agreed, nodding. "He says that he'll live his life how he wants to and doesn't buy into all of this stuff, but… I can tell it scared him. She showed him all of his levels, and everything is in the red 'danger' zone. If he wants to live to be an old man, he's got to change."

Erin looked toward the loft apartment. "Is he pretty mad at me?"

"At you? No. At life. At the doctors. At everything. Maybe even me, because I pushed him so hard to get this testing done. But not at you. You saved his life."

"He's saved mine more than once." Erin's eyes burned with tears as she thought about how important Willie had been in her life, how gentle he was toward her, and how he always looked out for her and Vic. "I'm glad to return the favor."

Vic took another cookie and munched on it. There was a yip at the back door, and she got up and padded across the kitchen barefoot to open it and let Nilla in. Nilla ran around for a while, seeing where everyone was, including the animals, before finally lying down by the kitchen table to watch Vic and Erin.

"Things are going to change around here," Vic said. "Things are due for a change."

rin had Matthew's two lemon meringue pies ready for him at the front of the store. He had refused to pick them up in the back, insisting again that he wanted people to see him with the lemon meringue pies to reassure everyone that they were safe. He stood in line while Erin served other customers and, when he got to the counter, she handed him the two boxes.

"Don't go over any bumps. You don't want the meringue getting stuck to the inside of the box."

"I'll be careful," he assured her.

Erin moved to the till to ring up the total. When she reached out to take his money, he put an envelope in her hand. Erin looked down at it, then at his face.

"One last delivery," Matthew told her.

"That's what you said about the last one."

"Well… it was. This one isn't about Fontainebleau. It's just… to say thank you."

Erin opened the envelope, which contained a photograph. Funny how few actual photographs she saw anymore. Everything was electronic, on people's computers, phones, or fancy digital photo displays. In the photo were Matthew, his son, his daughter, and the new baby. They were all smiling. Matthew looked happy and peaceful in the picture.

"Thank you," Matthew said.

"I didn't really do anything. It was a police case."

He nodded and handed her the money for the pies. "Put the change in the tips jar. And I guess I'll see you around town."

Erin nodded. "Take care, Matthew."

"You too."

He left with his pies. Erin tucked the photograph into her apron pocket. The bakery was quiet. Bella had left to deal with a personal issue, but promised to be back in time for the after-school rush and to help close. Erin busied herself with straightening up, restocking a couple of things in the display case, and wiping down the counters in the kitchen.

She heard the bells at the front door and returned to the counter to deal with her next customer. Bella had come through the front door instead of the back. Not only that, but Adrienne was behind her. She had Sarah in her arms, but the rest of the children were not in evidence.

"She did it!" Bella announced. "Before Mrs. Jones left, she saw that everyone who was owed received the money they had been promised, deposited directly into their bank accounts."

Erin studied Adrienne, who looked rather shy. She had always faced Erin with some level of defensiveness before. She tended to come off as angry and confrontational, but Erin knew that a lot of it was vulnerability. Like an animal that puffed out its fur to make itself look bigger. Pretending to be confident and tough when she felt anything but. This time, though, the barriers were down.

"That means I have enough money to buy a property," Adrienne told her with teary eyes. "And to fix the car and look into building a house. A house instead of a tent!"

"That's wonderful," Erin told her. "You won't have to keep moving. You can settle down and have a stable life. The kids can go to school. That's so nice. It must be a big relief."

"I'm still going to homeschool the kids," Adrienne told her, hugging the baby closer, possessively. "But no one will be able to kick us out. We'll be able to live on our own property, and no one can complain that we're trespassing or squatting."

Erin nodded. "I'm really glad that it worked out for you. And… how is Hope doing?"

She wasn't there clinging to her mother, which was a good sign.

Adrienne looked toward the door. "She's watching the other kids in the park. I didn't want them all going to the bank with me." She rolled her eyes. "All of that paperwork and restless children!" She hesitated for a moment. "Maybe I'll have her see someone," she said. "I don't know yet. I know that's what everyone thinks I should do, but I don't know if it is right for her. We'll see."

"Terry might be able to recommend someone. He had to see a therapist after his head injury. He didn't like having to do it, but he said the doctor was pretty good."

Adrienne looked off into the distance, nodding to herself. "Maybe," she agreed. She might be imagining the home she would build for her and her kids; a safe place free of the evil man. Maybe just coming to terms with it all and finally feeling at peace. She and her kids would finally have a home of their own. The rest could be worked out.

"So…" Erin frowned. "It wasn't Freda who was trying to scare you off. She wasn't trying to get you to leave because she was afraid you were going to talk about what Fontainebleau had done or that she had promised you she would make things right."

Adrienne shook her head. "I wondered… obviously someone didn't want me and my kids around, and I could have made trouble for her."

"Then who was it? I guess we'll never know."

"Actually… I just ran into Marcelle in the bank, and…" Adrienne looked back in the direction of the bank.

"Marcelle? Fontainebleau's ex-wife?"

"Yeah. I guess she's lost a lot of money."

Erin nodded. "When Fontainebleau was sick and started to make bad decisions and run the company into the ground."

"And then all of the money Freda paid out… what everyone

was owed. I don't know how much it was, but Marcelle was as mad as a spitting cat."

Bella shook her head. "She lit into Adrienne like she'd stolen all that money from her personally. Screaming about how she was supposed to leave town so that the people who really deserved the money would get it."

Erin rolled her eyes. "She's probably still got more than you've ever had in your life," she told Adrienne.

Adrienne nodded. "Ain't that the truth." She sighed. "But I don't need it all. Just one little corner under the trees, where the kids can run free and we can have our own roof over our heads. That would be heavenly."

"Will be," Bella amended.

Adrienne nodded, that shy smile spreading across her face again.

"Will be."

CHAPTER 42

The bells rang, and Erin looked up from the price label she had been writing for goods in the display case. Usually, she had Vic do them because she had much more attractive printing than Erin. Erin's numbers or letters never seemed to stay a consistent size, no matter how much she practiced. But Vic and Willie were off on a retreat, and Erin needed a few more labels written.

She didn't know the man who had walked into the store. He looked a little rough and down on his luck. Or maybe he'd just been traveling and was in need of refreshment. Erin gave him a pleasant smile, hoping to lift his spirits.

"Hi. Welcome to Auntie Clem's."

He nodded at her and looked around. Besides the bakery display case, there wasn't much to see, so his eyes soon returned to her.

"I was told that Adrienne's friend worked here. Would that be you?"

"I know Adrienne," Erin admitted. "But they were probably referring to Bella. She's not here at the moment."

"Well, if you know Adrienne, then maybe you can tell me where I can find her."

Erin was cautious. She didn't know who this guy was or why he would be trying to find Adrienne. Adrienne was a private person and would not want Erin giving out her personal details without permission.

"I could maybe get her a message. Would that help?"

"You have her phone number?"

"I have Bella's phone number. Bella will be able to get ahold of her."

"I don't want to be sent around in circles," he growled. "Do you know where Adrienne is or how to get her?"

"No. Sorry, I don't."

"You know where she lives? Someone said she was outside the town limits. Out in the sticks."

"Yes. I don't know exactly where. I haven't been out there myself. Sorry."

He scowled and shook his head. "If you can get a message to her, tell her that Simon is looking for her." He gave her a hard look. "Her husband."

Did you enjoy this book? Reviews and recommendations are vital to making a book successful.

Please leave a review at your favorite book store or review site and share it with your friends.

Don't miss the following bonus material:
Sign up for mailing list to get a free ebook
Read a sneak preview chapter
Other books by P.D. Workman
Learn more about the author

DON'T MISS A THING! GET THE LATEST NEWS AND A FREE EBOOK

PDWORKMAN.COM/SIGNUP

PREVIEW OF WHAT THE CAT KNEW

More Auntie Clem's Bakery are in the oven.

In the meantime, have you read about Reg Rawlins, Erin's foster sister, and her adventures as a Psychic Investigator?

CHAPTER 1

Reg Rawlins climbed out of the car and stretched, her muscles cramped after being in the car all day. According to the dashboard readout, it was a few degrees warmer than it had been in Tennessee. Added to that, it was humid and the air felt muggy. She could smell the ocean. She'd heard that all points in Florida were within sixty miles of the ocean as the crow flies. She was looking forward to spending some time swimming and looking for seashells. She'd always wanted to live near a real beach. A warm, sandy beach.

"Witch!" accused a homeless man sitting on the sidewalk with a cardboard sign. He had long, scraggly hair and a beard, streaked with gray, and he was missing several teeth. His clothes were ragged, and even though he was a few feet away, Reg could smell his unwashed body.

She gave him a scowl, but didn't turn away. His reaction interested her. She was dressed for the part she intended to play—headscarf, heavy jewelry and hoop earrings, a long, flowing peasant dress —so it was not unexpected that he would notice her and comment on her getup. But he had gone with *witch* rather than a fortune-teller or medium, which she thought was an odd choice. She wasn't wearing a pointed hat or black robe.

"What makes you think I'm a witch?" she demanded.

"All redheads are witches!" he informed her.

"Ah." Reg's red hair was all done in cornrow braids, which hung free around her face rather than being wound up under her headscarf. She liked the effect. And she liked the way the braids felt when she turned her head and they all swished back and forth. She ignored the homeless man and looked up and down the boardwalk.

She liked the atmosphere of Florida. Laid back and relaxed, not like in Tennessee where she had visited Erin. There had certainly been some uptight ladies there. She didn't regret leaving, though she was sad things hadn't worked out with Erin. Erin had been a lot more fun when they were kids. She'd grown up too much and become a stuffy old woman instead of the lost child she'd been when they had lived with the Harrises and then again when they had both aged out of foster care and had run a few cons together. Now she was grown up and mature and responsible, no longer interested in Reg's ideas.

"You don't know what you're missing, Erin," Reg murmured, looking around at the blue sky and the green vegetation, the tang of salt hanging in the air. Swimming in Florida was going to be nothing like a dip in the ocean in Maine. Miles of sandy beaches, warm water, and not a care in the world.

She gathered up her braids with both hands and pulled them back behind her shoulders, letting them fall again.

"There somewhere good to eat around here?" she asked the bum.

People looked at her oddly as they passed, and Reg didn't know if it was because of her outfit or the fact that she was talking to a non-person.

"Only if you like seafood!" the man cackled.

Luckily, Reg did.

"You should go to The Crystal Bowl," he told her. "That's where the witches gather."

Reg pursed her lips, considering him. "The Crystal Ball?"

"The Crystal *Bowl*. Get it?"

"Where is The Crystal Bowl?"

He gestured down the boardwalk. "Yonder about two blocks. Big sign. Can't miss it."

Reg had been told that Florida, and Black Sands in particular, was *the place* for psychics and mediums but she hadn't expected there to actually be enough of a community to warrant a restaurant of their own. She was glad she'd picked Florida over Massachusetts; she'd had enough of New England to last her a lifetime.

The Crystal Bowl had satisfyingly dramatic decor and furnishings. Blacks, reds, and golds combined into a rich tapestry of mysticism, lit by flickering candles which were actually tiny electric lights. East met West in a sort of a cross between an opium den and a carnival fortune-teller set. They worked together in harmony rather than clashing.

The patrons of the restaurant, however, were disappointingly normal. Shorts with t-shirts or light blouses, sunglasses propped on foreheads, everybody looking at their phones or calling across the room to greet each other. No sense of mystical decorum.

The sign said 'please wait to be seated,' but Reg walked across to the bar counter and selected a stool.

The bartender was spare, his skin too pale for a Floridian. He obviously spent too much time in the restaurant out of the sun. Either that or he was a vampire.

"Afternoon," he greeted, adjusting the spacing between the various bottles on the counter and turning their labels out.

"Hi."

"Don't think I've seen you here before."

"No, just flew in on my broomstick."

He eyed her. "Wrong costume."

Reg grinned. "Good. The old bum down the street said that I was a witch, and I was afraid I'd gotten it wrong."

"It's the red hair."

"So I hear. Mediums can't have red hair?"

"Mediums can have whatever they want. So what will it be?" He gestured to the neat rows of bottles behind the bar and the chalkboard on the wall behind them.

Reg looked over the options. Should she establish herself as someone with exacting and eclectic tastes? A connoisseur? Someone who was obviously unique and memorable?

But she wanted the bar to be somewhere she could let her hair down, not where she had to always be playing a part.

"Just a draft," she sighed. "Whatever is on tap."

He nodded and grabbed a beer stein. He filled it and placed it neatly on a coaster in front of her, pushing a bowl of pretzels closer to her. Something nice and salty to encourage thirst.

"So, Miss Medium, your name is…?"

"Reg Rawlins." She figured she was okay using the name, even though that was what she had used in Bald Eagle Falls. She didn't think any charges would follow her all the way to Florida. It wasn't like she was going to be filing taxes under the name.

He gave a nod. "Bill Johnson."

Reg took a pull on her beer. It had been a long drive and she was glad to be able to relax and recharge her batteries. Thinking of figurative batteries, she decided she'd better check her actual battery. Reg pulled out her phone and checked the charge. Not too bad. It would last her a couple more hours, and maybe by that time, she would have settled somewhere. She launched her browser and tapped in a search for lodgings. There were plenty of hits for short-term rentals. Lots of vacationers. Finding somewhere permanent might take a bit longer, but at least she'd have a place to hang her hat. Or her headscarf. And plug in her phone.

"You need a place to stay?" Bill asked, obviously recognizing the website.

"Looks like there are lots of options."

"Sarah Bishop is looking for a tenant. She's easy to get along with. You two would probably hit it off."

"Oh?"

Bill looked around the room. "She's not here yet. She often

shows up for supper. If she doesn't, I can give her a call and let her know you're interested."

Reg raised an eyebrow. "You don't know me from Adam. What makes you think I would hit it off with Sarah Bishop or that you can recommend me to her?"

"Let's just say… I'm good at reading people. And I would know you from Adam, given that Adam was of the male persuasion."

Reg considered pointing out that there were plenty of men who could pass as women or had transitioned from one to the other, but decided that antagonizing him wouldn't be the wisest thing for her to do. So she took a sip of her beer and didn't challenge him.

"Okay. Well, I'd appreciate that. Being able to move in somewhere long-term right away would be a real plus. Thanks."

"No problem." He moved away to help another patron.

Reg continued to browse through the lodging listings to get a sense of what costs to expect for rent and what her options were if she didn't like Sarah Bishop's place. It could be a dump. Sarah Bishop could be Bill's sister or ex and he just wanted her off of his back. He had been pretty quick to offer his help and judge Reg worthy as a tenant for his friend.

Someone took the stool next to Reg's, and she looked up to see who it was. A strikingly handsome man. Thirty-something, short hair slicked back from his face to show off a widow's peak, a stubbly beard that at first glance made it look like he had forgotten to shave for a couple of days, but on a more careful examination was painstakingly trimmed. His eyes were dark but glowed almost red in the dim lighting of the restaurant, reflecting the red furnishings and wall coverings. Add a cape, and he'd be perfect to cast as a vampire.

He gave her an enigmatic look. Almost smiling, but not quite. A smirk. She thought he was going to greet her as Bill had, recognizing her as a stranger and asking who she was. But he merely inclined his head slightly and waited for his drink, which Bill brought over without being asked. Obviously his 'usual.'

"Reg Rawlins, Uriel Hawthorne," Bill said, making a gesture from one to the other by way of introduction.

Great choice of name. Reg was impressed. Still, Uriel said nothing, just threw back his shot and watched her.

"Nice to meet you," Reg said, thrusting her hand out to shake his, forcing him to acknowledge her presence.

He left her hanging for a moment, not moving to take her hand, and then finally responded, taking her hand in his in a soft, caressing gesture that made her immediately want to pull back. But she set her teeth and gave him a warm smile. She gave him one more squeeze before letting go and pulling back again.

"A pleasure to meet you," Uriel returned. "Are you thinking of joining our little community?"

"Well, we'll see how it goes," Reg said with a shrug. "I'm new in town and I've never been part of… this kind of community before. I've always just been on my own."

"There is something to be said for that."

Reg raised her eyebrows in query.

"Setting your own rules, doing your own thing," Uriel said. "No one with preconceptions as to how things should be done."

"Right." Reg nodded. Rules, in her opinion, were made to be broken. She wasn't about to buy into a social construct that tried to control her activities.

"Ah, here's Sarah," Bill said, hovering near Reg.

It took her a moment to remember who Sarah was and why she should care. Sarah was the landlord looking for a tenant.

Reg turned, following Bill's gaze. She was looking for a woman of around her age, since Bill had said that he thought she and Sarah would hit it off. But she didn't see anyone who fit her preconception.

Bill gave a little wave, and a woman nodded to him and corrected her course to join him at the bar.

She was an older woman, at least in her sixties, with a round face, bottle blond hair that curved around her face, and wire frame glasses. She looked like a friendly grandmother, lips pink with freshly-applied lipstick, a flowered shirt, pink slacks, and flat white sandals. She smiled at Bill.

"Good evening, Bill. How are you today?"

He nodded and didn't bother to answer the greeting. "Sarah, meet Reg Rawlins. She has just arrived in town and is looking for accommodations."

"Oh!" Sarah's face lit up. "Well, my dear, isn't that wonderful! I just happen to have a cottage that I am trying to rent out! Would you join me for dinner?" She motioned to the tables in the dining area. "I'm afraid I can't manage bar stools these days."

"Sure," Reg agreed, sliding down from hers and taking her drink with her. "That would be nice."

She didn't bother saying goodbye to Uriel, irritated with his distant, disinterested manner. Sarah led her to a table which was probably her regular, as there didn't seem to be any problem with her seating herself instead of waiting to be seated. She smiled and chatted with some of the other patrons as she made her way to her seat.

"Sit down, sit down," she encouraged Reg, as if Reg had somehow been holding her back. "Reg? Is that short for something? Where did you come from?"

"Regina. I've lived all over."

"Well, that's a pretty name. Did you pick it, or was it already yours?"

Reg laughed at the question. "I was saddled with Regina, but I picked Reg."

"Very nice. I like it. And what do you do?" She made a little gesture to indicate Reg's costume. "You read palms? Tarot?"

"A little of everything. Mostly, I talk to the dead."

"Oh." Sarah nodded wisely. "That's a good gig. Have you been doing it for long?"

Reg studied the woman, not sure how honest to be. She wasn't sure whether she should be open about being a medium or a con. Both paths seemed equally treacherous.

"I've always had... certain tendencies... gifts, if you like..." she said obliquely. "I'm just testing the waters now… seeing whether this is something I should pursue…"

Sarah nodded. A waitress came over and handed them menus, introducing herself and showing off a couple of rather long canine teeth when she smiled. Sarah took no note, and barely gave the menu a glance. She'd obviously been there enough times to know what she wanted.

"What's good?" Reg asked, glancing over the offerings.

"The seafood is fresh. Other than that… burger and fries… I wouldn't try anything too adventurous."

"Good to know."

After placing her order, Reg leaned back in her seat, looking Sarah over.

"How about you? Did you retire to Florida, or have you always lived here?"

"I've lived lots of places, dear. Florida is good for my old bones. As for retiring… maybe someday, but not yet."

"What is it you do?"

Sarah raised her brows, as if surprised that Reg didn't know. Was she supposed to have guessed? Did Sarah think that Bill had told her?

"Well, I'm a witch," Sarah said, as if it should have been obvious.

"Oh." Reg sat like a lump, with no idea what to say or how to respond. Sarah had turned the tables on her. Reg was used to provoking a reaction from other people. She liked to dress up and to say extravagant things to see how people reacted to her different personas. This time she was in the hot seat. "Oh. I guess I should have guessed." Reg threw her hands up in what was both a shrug and indicating their surroundings. "After all, we are in the Magic Cauldron."

Sarah blinked. "The Crystal Bowl."

"Whatever. This is a witch hangout, right? So of course that's what you are."

"I thought you knew. You didn't just wander in here of your own accord, did you?"

"There was an old bum down the boardwalk… he called me a witch, and he pointed me this way. So, yes… I knew… It's all just a bit much." Reg looked around the restaurant. "I mean, *everyone* here can't be a witch."

"Of course not," Sarah agreed. "We have people of all different spiritual and paranormal persuasions. Witches, warlocks, wizards, mediums," she gave Reg a nod, "fortune-tellers, healers… people who are gifted and people who are seekers."

"Okay, then." Reg looked around at the patrons and shook her head, having a hard time believing that they were all running the same con. "And there isn't too much competition for the same… customers?"

"Some people think Black Sands has gotten too commercial, and some people complain it has gotten too crowded. But for the most part… people are willing to live and let live. We are peaceful people."

"Uh-huh."

Sarah launched into a lyrical description of the town and its more interesting citizens. Reg tried not to sit with her mouth open as she listened. The waitress eventually came over with their meals. Reg hadn't realized how hungry she was getting, but when the platter was placed in front of her, she suddenly realized she was famished.

"This looks lovely," she told the waitress, not expecting to be getting a beautifully plated fish at the offbeat witches' diner. She dug in immediately, taking several delicious bites before looking at Sarah to ask her if she was enjoying her food.

Sarah's eyes were closed and her hands hovered over her plate as if she were warming them in the steam rising from the food. Reg turned to look at the waitress, but she was already gone. Reg looked uncomfortably at Sarah, wondering if she should follow suit.

Sarah's eyes opened, catching Reg staring at her.

"Uh…" Reg fumbled. "Amen?"

Sarah nodded slightly. Then she started to eat.

"It really is good," Reg said. "Really nice."

"I wouldn't eat here all the time if it wasn't," Sarah agreed. She patted her stomach. "I wouldn't have to worry so much about my waistline if I was cooking for myself!"

She was plump, but in a grandmotherly sort of way. Reg couldn't imagine her skinny; it just wouldn't have fit. Adele, Erin's witch friend back in Tennessee was tall and slender, and that worked for her, but it just wouldn't work for Sarah.

"So why don't you tell me about this cottage of yours?" she asked. "Bill seemed to think that we'd be able to come to terms."

"He's very empathic," Sarah said. "He reads people."

"Ah. Of course." It made sense for a bartender. Reg had known her share of good and bad barkeeps.

"It's just a little two-bedroom," Sarah said, answering Reg's question. "But it's just you…?"

"Yes. No dependents."

"So you could use one room as your bedroom and the other as an office, and still have space for entertaining in the living room."

"Right," Reg agreed. She hadn't thought about seeing clients in her home. She wasn't sure she wanted anyone to know where she lived. If they didn't like what she had to say, they wouldn't know where she lived to confront her. She had thought she would go to them, do readings in their own spaces. She could read a client a lot better if surrounded by their own things. People gave a lot away by the way they lived.

"It's separate from the main house, so we wouldn't be on top of each other. We can each keep our own hours. That can be a problem with night people and day people mixing. The kitchen is small, really just a prep area. You could come use the big kitchen if you needed to do any major baking or entertaining. I really don't use it that much."

"I don't expect I would either. I don't do a lot of my own cooking."

"You see? You'd be perfect. You wouldn't be complaining to me that there's no oven. It really does have everything you really need."

"Well, maybe we could go see it after dinner, and talk business."

"You're going to like it just fine. I can tell."

As Reg wasn't that picky, Sarah was probably right. If Reg didn't like it after a month or two, she'd have a good idea by that point of where to look for somewhere better. It wasn't a long-term commitment.

Which was good, because Reg Rawlins didn't like long commitments.

CHAPTER 2

Cold, clammy fingers traced across Reg's face, awakening her in the wee hours of the morning.

She sat bolt upright, her heart racing. She looked quickly around her, trying to remember where she was and who was there with her. A chaotic childhood had conditioned her to be instantly awake and ready to fight. Strike fast to protect herself and escape to somewhere safe. But there was no one else in the room. Maybe the roof leaked and a drop of cold water had traced its way across her cheek.

She touched it, but it was dry, with only the memory of those icy fingers lingering behind.

Reg listened for a long time, hearing the lap of the waves in the distance. It was a restful, peaceful noise, and gradually the slamming of her heart slowed to its normal rate, though it was still pounding too hard to get back to sleep.

"There's no one here," Reg said aloud, very quietly. "You're perfectly safe, Reg. No one is going to hurt you."

It was comforting to hear those words.

When she was a kid, therapists had told her social worker and foster parents she had PTSD, and that was the reason for much of her unwanted behavior. It was nonsense, of course. Reg had never been in a war or terrorist attack. She'd never been kidnapped. Sure, she'd grown up rough, but a lot of kids had. And Reg was good at adapting. You couldn't call a few nightmares PTSD just because it was the fashion.

She listened to the waves for a long time. It was growing light as she drifted off to sleep again, still not sure what had awakened her in the night.

~

When she got up in the morning, it was with the clear plan to get a cat. She needed a cat. It would be a good prop. Witches had cats or other familiars. People instinctively felt that people who owned pets were kinder and more trustworthy than those who didn't. And it would give her a little company, without having to resort to having another person around the house. Reg liked company, but she liked having her own space.

A cat was the perfect idea.

Reg giggled to herself at the pun. A purrfect idea.

She checked addresses on her phone, thinking about what else she would need to buy in order to settle into her new living space. The fact that it came furnished was a bonus. She packed and traveled light and was used to operating on a shoestring. A fully-furnished cottage was a level of luxury she wasn't used to.

She picked up groceries and the basics she would need to care for a cat before going to the pound, patting herself on the back for thinking ahead and realizing that she wouldn't be able to do the other shopping once she had the cat in the car. She'd have to go straight home, and she wouldn't want to just abandon the poor critter there to go run errands.

At the animal shelter, self-styled as a pet sanctuary, before she was even allowed to look at the animals, Reg had to fill in a bunch of paperwork indicating her willingness to take care of a pet for the rest of its natural life and to follow all of the rules that the shelter set forth, such as not declawing a cat.

The place was noisy and smelly. Every effort had been made to make it a nice place, comfortable and humane for the animals, but it still stank. Reg thought about Erin. She probably would have run out of there puking, she was so sensitive to bad smells. Reg wasn't sure how she even managed to keep pets of her own, what with having to change litter and clean up after any accidents. They hadn't been allowed pets when they had lived with the Harrises, but Reg had seen enough examples of Erin reacting to human smells and accidents that she had no doubt she'd have difficulty cleaning up after animals.

There were old cats and tiny kittens and everything in between. Orange cats and tabbies and calicos. Short hair and long. Unlike the dogs, most of the cats didn't interact with the people walking by their cages, but simply slept, curled up in the corners of the cages. Occasionally, one of them would open its eyes or lift its head for a moment, but mostly they just continued to sleep.

She had thought she would be tempted by the playful younger kitties, but she thought of them keeping her up all night and wasn't sure that was what she wanted.

Maybe getting a cat had just been an impulse. Buying a pet was one of those things you were never supposed to do on impulse.

There were good reasons for getting a cat, but there were reasons not to as well. It might be noisy and wake her up nights. Have hairballs. Scatter litter and shed all over the house. It might jump up on the counter and get into things. Get out of the house and run out into the street.

It was probably a bad idea.

Reg looked into the next cage. The black and white cat raised his head, then climbed out of the nest of blankets in the corner, stretched, and walked up to the front of the enclosure.

"Hey, cat," Reg murmured.

He sat up tall and gazed at her, serious and still. Reg poked her finger through the bars at him, hearing a voice in the back of her head warning her never to poke her finger into an animal's cage. Even a hamster would bite you if you stuck your fingers through the bars. But just like she had ignored the foster mothers who had warned her not to do dangerous things, Reg ignored the voice in her head.

The cat's nose twitched as he caught her scent. For a minute, he just sat there. Then he leaned forward and took a step closer, touching his nose to her finger, and then rubbing his cheek against it. She felt his teeth brush over her finger as he rubbed. She scratched under his chin.

"Hey, you like that? Does that feel good?"

He rubbed against her and started purring a deep, satisfied rumble.

One of the shelter workers walked up.

"Wow, you connected with the tux!"

Reg looked at her. The girl was a teenager, maybe sixteen or seventeen, blond, with round cheeks. "The tux?"

"See, he's black with a white chest. Like he's wearing a black tuxedo and white shirt. So we call him a tuxedo cat."

"Oh, that's cool."

"And he has two different colors of eyes, too. I love that."

Reg looked at him and realized he had one green eye and one blue. "I guess that means he's special."

"I think he is." The girl poked her finger through the bars to try to scratch the tuxedo cat as well, but he only rubbed against Reg's finger. "He's been pretty depressed since he was brought in. His owner died and he hasn't really clicked with anyone. We've tried to play with him and to get him interested in things, but he's been so sad, pretty much all he'll do is sleep. He barely even eats."

In direct contradiction to her words, the cat stopped rubbing against Reg's finger and went over to his food bowl. He sniffed at the food, then began to eat, crunching the kibble.

Reg laughed.

"Well, he wouldn't!" the girl protested. "It must be you. Maybe you remind him of his owner."

Reg watched the cat. "What do you know about her?"

"Her? He's a he. A boy."

"No, I mean his owner. What do you know about her?"

"Oh. Well, he's also a he. A man. Don't really know much about him, just that Tux must have really been attached to him."

If she were going to get a cat, then it was obviously going to have to be that one. None of the other cats had shown Reg any interest at all, and she hadn't been particularly attracted to them. She clicked her tongue, thinking about it, and the noise made the cat turn his head to look at her again. He left his food bowl and again walked to the front of the cage, purring.

"I guess… this is the one," Reg said.

At least he was a short-hair, so he wouldn't get too much fur scattered around the cottage. And he seemed very quiet and sedate, not like a kitten that was going to jump on her face in the middle of the night and keep her awake.

"Oh, good!" the girl exclaimed. "I'll go get Marion, and she can help you with the adoption."

"Okay. Sure."

Reg waited there, scratching and quietly communing with her cat until the older supervisor approached to talk to her about the process.

If Reg had been expecting to just walk in and get a cat and walk out ten minutes later, she was sadly mistaken. Even the intake had taken longer than ten minutes. Apparently she needed counseling, needed to be walked through how to care for a cat, all of the things that could go wrong, budgeting for food and vets, what to do for behavioral issues, and on and on.

Reg had a headache by the time they were done and was ready to just pack it in and go home without a cat. But that would make the hours that she had been there wasted time, and she wasn't going to waste her first full day in Florida. Half of her groceries were already sitting spoiling in the car, and she wasn't going to walk out of there empty-handed.

Marion finally decided that Reg was ready to go and took the tuxedo cat out of his cage and settled him into a cardboard box, transferring the furry blanket he had been sleeping on into the box as well.

"That will help him transition, having something that already smells like home with him. Now you be sure to call if you have any questions about his care. Normally I would recommend that a first-time pet owner start out with a smaller animal, like a hamster, but… that tux needs a home badly, and he seems to like you."

Reg watched Marion close the box securely, and then took it from her. She didn't want to stand there discussing it any further. She wanted her cat home.

~

What the Cat Knew, Book #1 of the Reg Rawlins, Psychic Investigator series by P.D. Workman can be purchased at pdworkman.com

ABOUT THE AUTHOR

P.D. Workman is a USA Today Bestselling author, winner of several awards from Library Services for Youth in Custody and the InD'tale Magazine's Crowned Heart award, and has published over 100 mystery/suspense/thriller and young adult books, including stand alones and these series: Auntie Clem's Bakery cozy mysteries, Reg Rawlins Psychic Investigator paranormal mysteries, Zachary Goldman Mysteries (PI), Kenzie Kirsch Medical Thrillers, Parks Pat Mysteries (police procedural), and YA series: Tamara's Teardrops, Between the Cracks, and Breaking the Pattern.

Workman loves writing about the underdog, who the reader may love or hate. She has been praised for her realistic details, deep characterization, and sensitive handling of the serious social issues that appear in all of her stories, from light cozy mysteries through to darker, grittier young adult and mystery/suspense books.

> P. D. Workman, does not shy from probing the deep psychological scars of childhood trauma, mental illness, and addiction. Also characteristic of this author, these extremely sensitive issues are explored with extensive empathy, described with incredible clarity, and portrayed with profound insight.
>
> — —KIM, GOODREADS REVIEWER

Some of Workman's titles have been translated into Spanish, French, Portuguese, German, and Italian.

Workman began writing at an early age and is a prolific reader as well as writer. She is also passionate about teaching and learning, expresses her creativity through art and cooking, and loves exploring the Calgary parks and green spaces where the Parks Pat Mysteries are set. She was a legal assistant for many years and has done extensive charitable work.

Workman was born and raised in Alberta, Canada, and is married with one adult son.

Please visit P.D. Workman at pdworkman.com to see what else she is working on, to join her mailing list, and to link to her social networks.

If you enjoyed this book, please take the time to recommend it to other purchasers with a review or star rating and share it with your friends!

tiktok.com/@pdworkmanauthor

facebook.com/pdworkmanauthor

twitter.com/pdworkmanauthor

instagram.com/pdworkmanauthor

amazon.com/author/pdworkman

bookbub.com/authors/p-d-workman

goodreads.com/pdworkman

linkedin.com/in/pdworkman

pinterest.com/pdworkmanauthor

youtube.com/pdworkman

Find P.D. Workman's books at

PDWORKMAN.COM

Scan the QR code below